Anonymous

The Present State of the Empire of Morocco.

Its Animals, Products, Climate, Soil, Cities, Ports, Provinces, Coins, Weights, and

Measures . With the Language, Religion, Laws, Manners, Customs, and Character,

of the Moors

Anonymous

The Present State of the Empire of Morocco.
Its Animals, Products, Climate, Soil, Cities, Ports, Provinces, Coins, Weights, and Measures . With the Language, Religion, Laws, Manners, Customs, and Character, of the Moors

ISBN/EAN: 9783742804129

Manufactured in Europe, USA, Canada, Australia, Japa

Cover: Foto ©Andreas Hilbeck / pixelio.de

Manufactured and distributed by brebook publishing software
(www.brebook.com)

Anonymous

The Present State of the Empire of Morocco.

THE

PRESENT STATE

OF THE

EMPIRE OF MOROCCO.

ITS

ANIMALS, PRODUCTS, CLIMATE, SOIL,
CITIES, PORTS, PROVINCES, COINS,
WEIGHTS, AND MEASURES. WITH THE
LANGUAGE, RELIGION, LAWS, MAN-
NERS, CUSTOMS, AND CHARACTER.

OF THE

MOORS;

THE HISTORY OF THE
DYNASTIES SINCE EDRIS;

THE NAVAL FORCE AND COMMERCE OF MO-
ROCCO; AND THE CHARACTER, CONDUCT, AND
VIEWS, POLITICAL AND COMMERCIAL,

OF THE

REIGNING EMPEROR.

TRANSLATED FROM THE FRENCH OF
M. CHENIER.

VOL. I.

PREFACE

BY THE

TRANSLATOR.

OF all the people, with whom Europeans have any continued intercourse, those who inhabit the coasts of Barbary seem to be the least known. This is the more extraordinary because that their manners, customs, government, and the ignorance in which they remain, when we recollect their proximity to Europe, are very remarkable. To give

authen-

authenticity to a performance which would describe this peculiar people, it is neceſſary that the writer ſhould have been himſelf a witneſs of the facts he relates.

M. Chenier, author of the following work, was appointed Conſul, by the court of France, in 1767, and reſided in Morocco many years. Several Engliſh gentlemen, and merchants, now in London, were acquainted with him at Mogodor, and bear teſtimony to the veracity of his character, and of his narration. Various authors, who, by accident, have made ſome ſhort reſidence in Morocco, have written concerning the manners of the Moors; but their accounts are uſually little more than journals. They all, however, prove, by the incidents they relate, that M. Chenier cannot be accuſed of being diſpoſed to exaggerate. They all mention events that confirm, and often exceed, the moſt uncommon of thoſe recorded by our author.

author. The work of M. Chenier is the fulleſt and moſt complete, as well as the moſt authentic, of any hitherto preſented to the public ; conſequently there is little danger that the public ſhould think ſuch a work ſuperfluous.

The following tranſlation, however, is only a part of the *Recherches hiſtoriques ſur les Maures*, by M. Chenier : but it is preſumed it is that part which alone was wanting. His two firſt volumes relate to the ancient hiſtory of Mauritania, the Arabs under the Caliphs, and the conqueſt of Spain by the Mahometans. On this ſubject there are already many hiſtories, which include information equally full, at leaſt, with that contained in the former part of the work of M. Chenier. To have tranſlated theſe volumes would have been to have made the public pay thrice the ſum for knowledge, two thirds of which they already poſſeſſed.

That

To contribute to order, and increase perspicuity, the tranflation differs from the original, by being divided into books and chapters. For a fimilar reafon, a very copious index is added.

The tranflator held it his duty to examine the accounts given of Morocco, by other authors, in order to eftimate the real value of the work he meant to publifh. While performing this tafk, he met with many curious anecdotes, that tended farther to difplay the character of the people, and confirm the facts related by M. Chenier. Thefe he has collected, arranged, and inferted, in a feparate chapter, at the conclufion of the firft volume, to which place they moft properly belong. That the reader may determine for himfelf how far they have a claim to his belief, it is requifite he fhould be informed who the perfons were by whom they are recorded. The authors are not numerous,

neither

neither are their works scarce. The first, in point of date, is M. de St. Olon *, ambaffador from the court of France to Muley Ifhmael. The next is Bufnot +, a father of the order of the Holy Trinity, who went, accompanied by fome of the monks, to Morocco, for the redemption of French captives. The third, Mr. Windus ‡, who accompanied the Englifh ambaffador, the honourable Charles Stewart, in the year 1721. To render his embaffy more effectual, Stewart was commodore of a fquadron of fhips, and his negociation was fpoken of in terms of the higheft approbation. The fourth was Jean de la Faye §, and the fathers of his order, who, like Bufnot, were fent to effect

---

* Relation de l' Empire de Maroc, par M. de St. Olon. A Paris, 1695.

+ Hiftoire du regne de Mouley Ifhmael, A Rouen, 1714.

‡ A Journey to Mequinez. London, 1725.

§ Relation, en forme de Journal, du voyage pour la redemption des captifs. A Paris, 1726.

the redemtion of French captives: and the fifth Captain Braithwaite, who accompanied Mr. Ruffell, the Englifh ambaffador, to Morocco*. To infift upon the refpectability of fuch authorities were unneceffary; it is fufficient for the tranflator to fay that all the facts, related in the additional chapter above mentioned, are to be found in thefe authors.

* Hiftory of the revolutions in the Empire of Morocco; London, 1729.

THE

PRESENT STATE

OF THE

EMPIRE OF MOROCCO.

BOOK I.

Geographical Extent of the Empire of Morocco—Provinces—Cities—Rivers—Ports and Harbours—Climate — Soil — Fruits — Products — Mines—Ancient Commerce and fources of Wealth—Inhabitants — Tribes — Drefs — Renegados— Jews—Animals.

CHAP. I.

Geographical Situation and Extent of the Empire of Morocco.

THE Empire of Morocco extends from the twenty-eighth to the thirty-fixth degree of north latitude; its length, from north to fouth, I imagine to be nearly two hundred leagues; its breadth in the northern part is about five degrees, fix or feven in the middle, and about a hundred and thirty leagues where it is broadeft. It is bounded to the north by the Straits of Gibraltar and the Mediterranean, to the eaft by the kingdom of Tremecen and Vled d'Elgerid, to the fouth by the Defert, and to the weft by the Atlantic Ocean.

The territories of Morocco are formed by the union of feveral fmall kingdoms, anciently limited to a fingle province, and perpetually at variance among themfelves, till at length they were fubdued and united under one fovereign by the Sharifs. The fouthern part of the Empire contains the kingdoms of Suz, Tarudant, Morocco, Tafilet, and Sugulmeffa, and the northern thofe of Fez, Mequinez, and Tremecen; the latter, which was formerly fubject to Morocco, having been conquered by the Turks of Algiers, is now a part of the territories of that Regency.

The kingdom of Morocco comprehends at prefent the provinces of Morocco, Efcura, Ramna, Duquella, Abda, Sherma, Hea, Suo, Dra, and Gefula; that of Fez contains thofe of Temfena, Shavoya, Ted-

la,

la, Beni-Haffen, Fez, Rif, Garet, Shaus, and Algarb. Several authors, who have copied from each other, have given other names to some of these provinces, but I have taken the natives for my guide, who must certainly be beft acquainted with the names of the feveral diftricts : to this may be added that the limits of thefe provinces have frequently varied, according as they have been occupied by different tribes ; this variation of extent may have caufed a variation of name.

Befide the provinces which compofe the Empire of Morocco, the Sharifs claim the fovereignty of the Vled de Nun, and the defert of Zahara (an Arabic word fignifying defert) but their authority over thefe provinces is very precarious, as it depends on the pleafure of their fubjects and temporary circumftances. The people who inhabit thefe deferts, far removed from the center of defpotic authority, live in tribes or fmall republics, and chufe their own chiefs. They retain for the Emperor of Morocco that refpect and veneration which his power, and the idea they have of

his

his supremacy, as head of the church, inspire; but they pay or refuse tribute as they
think fit, since it is not possible for him to
obtain it by force in a parched and burning
country, where the people have no fixed
habitation, and where an army would neither be able to act nor to subsist. This
part of the coast has been called Vled de
Nun, from Cape Non, which was disco-
vered by the Portugueze in the beginning
of the fifteenth century, and to which
they gave this name, because those who
doubled it first never returned.

The whole Empire of Morocco is surrounded to the east, north, and south, by
a chain of vallies and mountains, which
are distinguished according to the number
and names of the tribes by whom they are
inhabited : from Laracha to near Saffi,
the western part of it forms a sort of plain,
which, in many places, is fifteen or twenty leagues in breadth, from east to west.

CHAP.

C H A P. II.

Provinces of the Empire of Morocco.

IT is impossible to be very accurate in the geography of this country. The prejudices of the Moors, who are not accustomed to the sight of Europeans, will not permit us to visit the inland provinces: such researches would only serve to awaken their jealousy. They, in fact, scarcely know themselves the extent of their provinces, which varies according to the will or interest of the prince, the favour the governors are in at court, and other temporary circumstances.

In describing this Empire I shall first treat of the maritime provinces which I have travelled through, almost from one end to the other, as these, from their situation, are more interesting than those of the interior country, of which I shall speak hereafter.

The most northern province is that of

Garet,

Garet, on the western banks of the Mulluvia, which divides the Empire of Morocco from the province of Tremecen.
This province, about twenty or twenty-
five leagues in length, is bounded to the
north by the Mediterranean, Mount Atlas
to the south, and the province of Rif to
the west.

The province of Rif, which is one of
the largest, is situated amidst that chain of
mountains which forms a part of the lesser
Atlas. This province, the soil of which
is stoney, is bounded by that of Garet, to
the east, the Mediterranean to the north,
on the coast of which is the ancient city of
Gomera, as also Melilla and Veles de Pegnon, belonging to Spain ; by the province
of Garb to the west, and to the south by
those of Shaus, or Chaus, and Fez.

The province of Garb begins in the territory of Tetuan, and extends near a degree
in length from east to west, reaching quite
to Cape Spartel ; its length, from north
to south, is about thirty-six leagues ; it is
bounded to the north by the Straits of
Gibraltar,

Gibraltar, to the south by the river Mamora, to the west by the Ocean, and to the east by the kingdom of Fez. The northern part of this province is not very fruitful, as it is interfected with vallies, the lands are liable to be injured by the heavy rains, and the harveft is very uncertain; the reft of the province is extremely beautiful; it is watered by feveral rivers, and embellifhed by fome forefts. Leo Africanus, and all thofe who have copied him, call this province Afgar, which, I am inclined to believe, is an error either in tranfcribing or printing, and that the name intended was El-Garb, which fignifies the weft.

Next to the province of Garb, or El-Garb, lies that of Beni-Haffen, called by Leo Africanus, and thofe who have followed him, Habat, which was poffibly the ancient name; the prefent may have been received from fome new tribe which took poffeffion of it. This province is bounded to the north by the river Mamora, and extends to the fouth to that of Sarrat; four leagues from Rabat, to the eaft, are the provinces of

Fez

Fez and Tedla, and to the weft the ocean. This province is very extenfive, rich, and commercial, and produces wool of a very excellent quality.

The province of Temfena is contiguous to that of Beni-Haffen, and extends from the river Sarrat to that of Morbeya. It is bounded to the eaft by the provinces of Tedla and Shavoya, or Chavoya, that of Beni-Haffen to the north, Duquella to the fouth, and the Atlantic Ocean to the eaft. This province is rich and fertile, and abounds in excellent provifions of various kinds. Its name feems intended to fignify its falubrity and the purity of the climate. *Temfena* appears to be derived from the two Arabic words *Tamam Sana*, only a year; as if they fhould fay, that to refide here only a year would be fufficient to infure the fickly the return of their health, and fuch, in fact, is the firm belief of the natives. Corn is very plentiful in this province, it is of a very excellent kind, and the ears frequently bear feventy grains, or more. In the forefts is found a kind of cedar, called Ha-zar,

zar, of a refinous fmell; it is a hard and incorruptible wood, and the Moors employ it in building their houfes. Leo Africanus, mifled by the fimilarity of names, calls this province Tremecen, the name of a kingdom which does not belong to Morocco. Marmol, in copying him, has fallen into the fame error.

Paffing the river Morbeya, the fouthern limit of Temfena, we arrive at the province of Duquella, which extends to the walls of Saffi. This province is bounded on the north by that of Temfena; to the eaft by thofe of Efcura, Ramna, and Morocco; to the fouth by the province of Abda; and to the weft by the ocean. It is very populous, rich, and commercial, abounds in corn, and produces a great deal of wool, part of which is fold unwrought, and the reft employed in the manufactures, with which it fupplies the fouthern provinces. This province formerly extended to the river Taufif, but that of Abda has been taken out of it, in order to divide it between two brothers who difputed the government. The inhabitants

habitants of Duquella are, in general, of a large fize and robuft ; they are a trading people, and, as the fpirit of intereft has a great influence on the characters of men, they are more affable and engaging than thofe of the other fouthern provinces.

The province of Abda, which made a part of that of Duquella, begins at the city of Saffi, and extends to the river of Tanfif; it is of a triangular form. The inhabitants of this province are particularly addicted to the profeffion of arms, and many of them are in the fervice of the Court.

Next to the province of Abda is that of Hea, which is bounded to the north by the river Tanfif, to the eaft by the province of Sherma, or Cherma, to the weft by the ocean, and to the fouth by the province of Sus. The inhabitants of Hea are a trading people, but reftlefs, and little civilized ; they are perpetually diftracted by inteftine broils. The province of Sherma, which is between this and that of Morocco, has been difmembered from that of Hea.

The

The province of Sus is next to that of Hea. It is bounded to the east by the province of Dra and a part of Gesula, to the west by the sea, and to the south by the Vled de Nun. This was formerly a very trading province, from its connections with the southern districts; but the present Emperor of Morocco having destroyed the city of Sainte Croix (Santa Cruz), it has no longer the same resources; it may, however, indemnify itself for this loss by trading with the European settlements in Senegal.

These are the maritime provinces of the Empire of Morocco: as to those within land and on the eastern side of the country, as they cannot be frequented by Europeans, it is impossible to speak of them with the same precision. I shall now, however, return from the south to the north, and describe these according to the best accounts I have been able to procure.

To the east of the province of Sus, and to the north of Vled de Nun, are the provinces of Dra and Gesula, both in the

neigh-

neighbourhood of Mount Atlas, which, in this fouthern part of the country, extends almoft to the fea.

Proceeding northward we enter the province of Morocco, which is of confiderable extent. Between this province and that of Hea is fituated the province of Sherma, which has been difmembered from the latter. This fmall province and thofe of Abda and Duquella are to the weft of that of Morocco, which is bounded to the north by the province of Efcura, or Afcora, as it is called by Leo Africanus, and by Mount Atlas to the eaft,

Next to the province of Morocco is the province of Efcura, which, with that of Ramna, formerly compofed only one government ; it has been divided to keep the people of thefe countries, fo near to the mountains, more eafily in fubjection. Ramna and Efcura have the province of Morocco to the fouth, that of Duquella to the weft, the river Morbeya to the north, and Mount Atlas to the eaft.

Proceed-

Proceeding northward from the province of Efcura we enter that of Tedla, which extends along the eaftern fide of Mount Atlas, and has to the weft the province of Shavoya; the latter, inhabited by mountaineers addicted to robbery and violence, is bounded to the weft by the province of Temfena, and to the north by that of Beni-Haffen, with which it is frequently engaged in difputes.

The province of Fez is fituated to the north of Tedla and Shavoya, and has to the weft the provinces of Beni-Haffen and Garb, and Mount Atlas to the eaft, ftretching to the north as far as the provinces of Shaus, Rif, and Garet. The dependencies of the province of Fez are very extenfive, and include feveral mountains abounding in inhabitants, and well cultivated.

Mount Atlas is the eaftern boundary of all the weftern provinces of Morocco. This mountain is formed by an endlefs chain of lofty eminences, divided into different countries, inhabited by a multitude of tribes, whofe ferocity permits no ftranger

to approach. I have not been able to obtain a fufficient knowledge of thefe mountains to defcribe them accurately : what
Leo Africanus has faid of them is very
vague; and his account is the lefs to be
regarded, at prefent, as it is now about
three centuries fince he wrote, and the
face of the country has been in that time
totally changed. Nothing, perhaps, would
be more interefting to the curiofity of the
philofopher, or conduce more to the improvement of our knowledge in natural
hiftory, than a journey over Mount Atlas.
The climate, though extremely cold in winter, is very healthy and pleafant ; the vallies are well cultivated, abound in fruits,
and are diverfified by forefts and plentiful
fprings, the ftreams of which, uniting at a
little diftance, form great rivers, and lofe
themfelves in the ocean. According to
the reports of the Moors, there are many
quarries of marble, granite, and other valuable ftone, in thefe mountains : it is
probable, there are alfo mines, but the inhabitants have no idea of thefe riches ;
they confider their liberty, which their
fitua-

fituation enables them to defend, as the most ineftimable of all treafures.

To the eaft of Mount Atlas in a fandy plain, part of the ancient Numidia, is the kingdom of Tafilet, which was conquered by Jofeph Abu Tefeffin, one of the firft kings of Morocco ; this kingdom was then called Sugulmeffa. It is bounded to the north by the neighbouring mountains of Tremecen and Fez, and extends to the fouth to the province of Gefula, having Vled d'Elgerid, or Biledulgerid, to the eaft, and Atlas to the weft. The city of Sugulmeffa, which was formerly the capital of the kingdom of that name, is at prefent in that of Tafilet. There is no way from Morocco to this province but by croffing one of the extremities of Mount Atlas, that is, either by the fide of the province of Sus, or by that of Fez ; the latter road, as it is lefs fultry, is moft frequented.

CHAP.

C H A P.   III.

Of the Cities, Rivers, and Harbours, of the Empire of Morocco.

I SHALL not here confine myself to a mere description of the towns and ports of Morocco; to render my observations more useful, I shall subjoin some remarks relative to the navigation of the coast, the convenience of the rivers, ports, and roads, and the trade which may be carried on with the country.

Nature has defended the western coast of Morocco with an almost infurmountable barrier, in the numerous rocks level with the surface of the water which line the shore: a descent would be the more difficult to accomplish as the invaders could not be sure of a retreat, on account of the changes incessantly occasioned by the agitation of the sea and the variations of the tides.

The

The towns in this Empire are neither large, numerous, nor populous: The defpots, jealous of their authority, and fearful of being deprived of the power they abufe, confider cities and ftrong places as more favourable to rebellions, and the liberty of the fubject, than camps; their towns, therefore, are weakly fortified, and little capable of defence on the land fide.

The empire of Morocco is feparated on the north from the kingdom of Algiers, by the river Mulluvia, which falls into the Mediterranean. The Emperor is in poffeffion of no place on this northern coaft, which coaft is known by the name of *Rif*, the few he had having been taken by the Spaniards, who ftill poffefs them; fuch are, Alhufema, Melilla, and Veles de Pegnon, or Gomera.

Melilla, or Melela, is an ancient city, which was probably founded by the Carthaginians. Its name proves that honey was plentiful in its environs. The Goths, who had poffeffed themfelves of it, abandoned it when the Arabs invaded the coun-

  try.

try. It was forsaken in like manner by the Moors, and seized on by the Spaniards about the beginning of the fifteenth century. Sidy Mahomet ineffectually laid siege to this place in 1774.

Veles de Pegnon, or Gomera, is a castle built on a rock, whence its name is taken. Below this fortress there was anciently a city, called Bedis, supposed to have been founded by the Carthaginians: the Arabs have called it Belis and Velis, whence the name Veles. These two places, surrounded by mountains and forests, were supported by the building of ships, for fishing and piracy, before they were taken by the Spaniards. This part of the coast of Rif is of no utility to navigation. Traversing it from east to west we find the river of Boosfega, near Tetuan, where the Morocco gallies anchor and winter, protected by a bad fort.

A league and a half from the road up the country is the city of Tetuan, in the province of Garb, inhabited by Moors and Jews, who, most of them, speak Spanish;

they

they are commercial, gentle in their manners, and polite. The environs of this
city are planted with vineyards and gardens, kept in good order; and the fruits
here are better and more carefully nur-
tured than in the other parts of the
empire.. Leo Africanus attributes the
foundation of this city to the people of
Africa. Tetuan was embellished, and its
population increafed, when the Moors
were driven out of Spain : the Europeans
of the prefent century have traded here;
and this was the place of refidence for
feveral confuls till the year 1770, when
the reigning Emperor would no longer
permit them to remain, nor again to efta-
blifh themfelves, in this city. This place
has preferved a communication with Gibraltar, whence the fhips come to victual
when the wind is in the weft, and does
not permit them to make Tangiers. The
fhore of Tetuan is only fafe when the wind
is in the weft, at which time fhips ride fecure; but when it veers to the eaft, they
muft remain there no longer.

After Tetuan I muft fpeak of Ceuta,
C 2

which

which belongs to the Spaniards, and which serves as a harbour for small vessels : from thence to Tangiers, the coast, inhabited by Moors and rugged with projecting cliffs, is of no utility to navigation ; there are indeed a few coves where small boats, in case of necessity, may find shelter. Judging by probabilities, this place must have been built by the Carthaginians, and afterward appertained to the Romans, by whom it was colonized. It next became the metropolis of the places which the Goths held in *Hispania Transfretana*, was after that abandoned to the Arabs and the Moors by Count Julian, was taken by the Portugueze in 1415, and is at present under the dominion of Spain.

Tangiers, in the province of Garb, lies about ten leagues from the road of Tetuan, at the western mouth of the Strait. This place, which belonged first to the Romans, and afterward to the Goths, was likewise given up to the Mahometans by Count Julian. It was taken in 1471 by the Portuguese, and given to Charles II., King of England, in 1662, as a marriage portion with

the

the Princess Catharine of Portugal. The English abandoned it in 1684, after having destroyed the mole and the fortifications. Almost in ruins, at present, it still retains some batteries, in tolerable condition, facing the bay; but these could with difficulty resist any powerful attack. At the bottom of the bay, towards the east, opposite the ruins of old Tangiers, is the mouth of the river, where the Emperor formerly laid up his gallies during winter; but the sand banks and bars, at present, render the river useless.

The situation of the bay of Tangiers is, and always will be, favourable to Moorish piracy, who, from this the narrowest part of the Strait, may easily surprise merchant ships, that are incapable of defence.

Tangiers cannot become a commercial town, having but few productions in its environs; the Spaniards thence obtained some fowls and vegetables, formerly, and the English, at present, supplies for their garrison at Gibraltar.

The

The bay of Tangiers is not very safe when the wind is in the west, having been encumbered by the ruins of the mole and fortification; the cables are liable to be torn, and the ships to be driven on shore. The best anchorage, for frigates and the larger vessels, is at the eastern point, whence they may easily set sail whichever way the wind sets; the bay, however, is only dangerous during the winter.

To the west of Tangiers is Cape Spartel, which must be doubled to make Arzilla, that lies only five leagues from Tangiers. Arzilla is built at the mouth of a river, and inhabited by Moors and Jews, who carry on no trade; it was formerly a Roman colony, afterward fell under the government of the Goths, and was next taken by the Mahometans. Alphonso of Portugal, surnamed the African, mastered it in 1471 : and it was abandoned by the Portuguese toward the end of the sixteenth century.

Coasting along to the south we find, at the distance of twelve leagues, the city of
Laracha,

Laracha, built on the river Luecos, which is the Lixos of the Greeks. The name of this city comes from the Arabic El-Arrais, which signifies a place abounding in gardens: perhaps its founders were desirous to preserve the memory of the garden of the Hesperides, which is supposed to have been here situated. The environs of this place, intersected by woods and some marshes, are exceedingly pleasant; and it would be very proper for trade, the river having a sufficient depth of water, and the neighbourhood being capable of furnishing products for Europe.

Laracha was fortified by Muley Naffer at the end of the sixteenth century, was afterwards given up to Spain in 1610, and retaken in 1689 by Muley Ishmael. There is a fort still standing on the land side, which is regular, was built by the Spaniards, and is in good preservation: the castle, beside the road, has been put in good repair some years since, and reinforced by several batteries at the water's edge.

The French bombarded this place in

C 4

1765,

1765, and entered the river to set fire to two Corfairs; but the enterprife, though executed with courage, having been impeded by obftacles not fufficiently forefeen, had not by any means the fuccefs expected.

The Europeans have carried on fome commerce at Laracha, under the reign of the prefent Emperor, Sidy Mahomet; but, by one of thofe alterations the caufes of which we are ignorant, he obliged all the merchants to retire in 1780.

The paffage of the river of Laracha is of fufficient depth; the large veffels of the Emperor ufually winter there, where there are magazines for the refitting of veffels, but no docks for building, the wood proper for which is too diftant, and the foil, which is merely fand, not being fufficiently firm for the erecting of ftocks. The road of Laracha is infecure in winter when the winds frefhen from the weft and fouth weft, but there is no danger between the beginning of April and the end of September.

From

From Laracha to Mamora, containing about twenty leagues by land, the face of the country is variegated by divers lakes, forests, and vallies, which formerly were tolerably populous. Among these vallies, as we approach Mamora, we meet with lakes of soft water, which are nearly eight leagues in extent, abounding in ducks and water fowl, and where eels are taken in great numbers. The boats made use of by the fishermen are a kind of skiffs made of reeds and rushes, about six feet long and two broad, and will scarcely hold a man. The fisherman guides them with a pole, and pierces the eels, when he sees them in the water, with a sort of dart. On the banks of these lakes are to be seen several sanctuaries of the Maraboots, who are held in great veneration for their supposed holiness, and a number of camps of the Moors, who cultivate the neighbouring lands, which are but moderately productive. This valley is extremely pleasant in winter and spring, but in summer it is parched and disagreeable. At the southern extremity is a sanctuary on an eminence, appertaining to which are habitaitons

and

and gardens. Hence we perceive the windings of the river Seboo, which takes its course from Fez, and uniting with the Beth falls into the ocean. This river, which is crossed in boats much out of repair, is at about the distance of a league from the sanctuary, and is the boundary between the province of Garb and that of Beni-Haffen.

The fort of Mamora, which is to the south of the Seboo, is the first inhabited place in the province of Beni-Haffen. It was begun by the Portuguese in 1515, and destroyed the same year by the Moors. It was rebuilt in 1604 by the Spaniards, from whom it was taken by Muley Ifhmael in 1681. This fortress, which was originally built at the mouth of the river Seboo, is now two miles distant from it, in consequence of the drifted sand-banks and bars, which have rendered the entrance of this river so difficult and dangerous as to be no longer of any use to commerce or navigation. There are at this fort about five-and-thirty or forty families, who gain a wretched livelihood by the profits of their

ferry,

ferry, and fishing for shads, of which they take such numbers as to be able to supply all the neighbouring country between November and the end of March.

From Mamora it is five leagues to Sallee. This town is situated in the province of Beni-Hassen, at the mouth of the river of Sallee, which is formed by the union of the two smaller rivers, the Buregreb and the Gueroo. The river of Sallee was formerly a port capable of receiving large ships ; but the sand has now so choaked up the entrance, that ships of two hundred tons cannot enter it till their guns and ballast are taken out. This town was taken in 1261 by Don Alphonso X., King of Castile ; but he was not able to keep it, the King of Fez retaking it immediately after.

Sallee is a walled town, and has a battery of twenty-four pieces of cannon, which commands the road, and a redoubt which defends the entrance of the river. To the north we perceive the walls and ruins of a small inhabited town, which Muley

Muley Ishmael caused to be built for the families of his black soldiers.

On the south side of the river of Sallee is the town of Rabat. These two places are so near each other, that they ought not to be separated. As they are united by the same interests, they for some time formed a kind of union, and were governed by the same magistrates; and it is only within these thirty years that the reigning Emperor has abolished this form of government. There has been formerly, and at intervals, a number of European factories at Rabat; but the difficulty of navigating the river, the obstacles arising from the arbitrary power of the Sovereign, and the disposition and prejudices of the Moors, have disgusted the Europeans. Rabat is, however, the most proper place for trade of any upon this coast, both for its vicinity to Europe and the quantity of wool, leather, and wax, it is capable of furnishing. From its central situation, in the empire, it is also better adapted for conveying the commodities imported to every part of the country; but

a despotic

a defpotic government acknowledges no
principle but the convenience of the moment ; it commands, judges, and executes
without confidering either caufe or confequence.

At Rabat, near the mouth of the river,
are to be feen the ruins of a caftle, built by
Jacob Almonfor, or Al-Manfor, in the
twelfth century, but entirely demolifhed by
the reigning Emperor, who has only preferved fome magazines remarkable for their
ftrength and folidity. In this caftle, which
I have feen before it was deftroyed, was
the palace of Jacob Almonfor, where every
thing, either neceffary or convenient, was
to be found in miniature. Under the palace
were fubterranean magazines for ammunition, vaulted fo that they were bomb
proof. There was, alfo, fronting the road,
a fmall fort and a battery that defended
the entrance of the river, but which have
been laid in ruins by time. Thefe batteries were rebuilt in 1774 on a more extenfive plan ; but the workman who con-
ftructed them (an Englifh renegado and an
excellent mafon) has made the embrafures

fo

fo near each other that it will be difficult to ufe them with any effect. Other batteries have alfo been erected, lower down, to prevent a landing. At a fmall diftance from the caftle, toward the fouth, on an eminence, is a little fquare fort, built by Muley Archid, or Arfhid. This fort, which at prefent ftands alone, formerly was joined to the caftle by a wall, which ferved as a covered way, but which has been demolifhed by the reigning Emperor.

Jacob Almonfor, being defirous to fix his refidence at Rabat, and make it at the fame time a place of ftrength, and the magazine of his arms, that he might from thence more eafily pafs into Spain, of which he was Sovereign, built the walls, which ftill remain. They are near two miles round, and fortified by fquare towers. They enclofe the caftle, the town of Rabat *, and

a large

---

* The city was built on the eaftern declivity, befide the palace of Muley Arfhid. The houfes, according to Moorifh tradition, had been built by Spanifh flaves, with little folidity, purpofely that they might fall upon the Moors, which actually happened; the flaves were punifhed with death at

the

a large space of ground, where that prince
built beautiful palaces, and laid out delightful gardens, watered by plentiful
streams which he brought from the neighbouring spring*. These walls, as well as
the palace and the town, were built by
Spanish slaves, whom he took prisoners in
his first campaign.

This Monarch built within the same inclosure a very large mosque, the ruins of
which still remain. The roof was supported by three hundred and sixty columns
of rough marble. Beside the eastern front
were apartments for those who had any
employment in the mosque, and porticoes,
which were still standing, in 1773. On
the opposite side was a handsome square
tower, strongly built with cut stone. It is
near two hundred feet high, and called the

the iron gate of the grand inclosure, where there are five
gates, that of the sea, that of Morocco, that of the mount,
the iron gate, and the gate of Shella, or Chella.

* These waters come from a valley called Tamra, to
the south of Rabat, where there is a bubbling spring not
far from that which supplies Rabat with water.

tower

tower of Haſſen. This tower has the ſame form, the ſame ornaments, the ſame ſtaircaſe, and the ſame proportions as thoſe of Seville and Morocco; and, according to all tradition, is the work of the ſame architect. From this tower we have an extenſive view over the ſea, and ſhips may be diſcovered at a prodigious diſtance. This monument is in perfect preſervation, notwithſtanding the natural propenſity of the Moors to deſtroy every thing. The ſtaircaſe only has been a little damaged, as has the eaſt-ſouth-eaſt corner, which has been beaten down by lightning. At a ſmall diſtance from this tower, on the north ſide, are ſtill to be ſeen the ruins of a wall, on which formerly ſtood a caſtle.

After that ſeries of revolutions which ſo long convulſed the empire of Morocco, the Mooriſh inhabitants poſſeſſed themſelves of the ground of this vaſt incloſure, and planted gardens and vineyards, which rendered it extremely agreeable: but the reigning Emperor, notwithſtanding the land had been private property for three hundred years, and tranſmitted to the

the poffeffors by their anceftors for many generations, reclaimed it in 1774 as the right of the crown, feized every thing he found on it, and built a town for thofe foldiers who have ftill preferved the name of Negroes; but, thefe troops having been difbanded, the town has been deferted, and nothing now remains of it but a heap of ruins. This Monarch, in 1785, began to erect a palace here, in which he propofes to refide, if no new caprice fhould induce him to alter his intentions.

There are fome docks for building fhips at Sallee and Rabat; but the difficulty of navigating the channel, and the probability that the fand will continue to accumulate, give ground to predict that, very foon, only veffels with oars will be able to enter the river.

The road of Sallee is only to be frequented in the fine feafon, from the beginning of April to the end of September; when the wind blows from the fouth fouth weft, which feldom happens but in winter, this road is no longer fafe;

ships are exposed to be driven out to sea, and the shifting of the sands of the bar render any communication with the town extremely difficult. The best anchorage to be found is on the south side of the river next Rabat, and the ship should be moored between the tower of the mosque and that called Haslen, having the latter to the north. Great attention should be paid to the cables, as a great number of anchors have here been lost.

On the eastern side of Rabat we meet with a small ruinous town called Shella, which contains many Moorish tombs, held in great veneration. The town itself is considered as a sacred asylum, and is only permitted to be entered by Mahometans. It seems probable this was the metropolis of the Carthaginian colonies on the western coast of Africa.

Eight leagues from Rabat, toward the south, in the province of Temsena, we find a wretched castle, named Mensooria: it was built in the twelfth century, by Jacob Almonsor, to afford an asylum to

travellers

travellers during the night, the inhabitants of the country round it being a mischievous and thievish people.

Proceeding along the same coast, eight leagues from Mensooria, we arrive at the road of Fedala. The name of island is improperly given to a little point of land which projects into the sea, and forms a bay scarcely sufficient to shelter a few small vessels. The reigning Emperor, in 1773, having permitted a great quantity of corn to be brought out of the mata-mores * contiguous to this road, endeavoured to take advantage of the opportunity to procure a city to be built, by obliging the merchants, who wished to have any of the corn, to build some houses ; in consequence of which the town of Fedala was begun in a very advantageous situation, but no sooner was the corn disposed of than it was abandoned. Such is the brief

* Matamores are holes dug in the earth, in which corn is long preserved, as will be more circumstantially related in the account I shall give of the manners and customs of the Moors.

history

hiſtory of Fedala, a town ruined before it was finiſhed; and ſuch is indeed the hiſtory of nearly the whole country.

As this road is defended by the coaſt, which, on the ſouthern ſide, perceptibly extends to the weſt, ſhips may anchor here in ſecurity in winter; but, in ſummer, when the winds blow ſtrong from the north north weſt, the ſwell of the ſea is very incommodious.

Four leagues to the ſouth of Fedala we meet with Anafa, at preſent called Dar Beyda, a town formerly in the poſſeſſion of the Portugueſe, but of which nothing now remains but ſome ruins, among which are a number of Mooriſh huts. It is ſituated near a pleaſant bay, and in an extenſive plain, which, if well cultivated, would be very fertile.

Fifteen leagues from Anafa, or Dar Beyda, by following the coaſt toward the ſouth, we arrive at the town of Azamore, in the province of Duquella, on the river Morbeya,

Morbeya*, and at some distance from its mouth. This town is not proper for maritime commerce, because the entrance of the river is dangerous. Azamore was unsuccessfully besieged by the Portuguese in 1508; it was taken, however, in 1513, by the Duke of Braganza, but abandoned about the end of the sixteenth century.

At a little distance from Azamore, facing a spacious bay, are the ruins of the ancient city of. Titus, which I imagine likewise to have been one of the cities founded by order of the Senate of Carthage. Near the same place are the ruins of Almedina, a town built by the Moors.

Beside the same bay, four leagues to the south of Azamore, is situated the city of Mazagan, which was built by the Portuguese in 1506, and named by them Castillo Real. Under the walls of this place,

* The true name of this river is Om-Arbaym; that is to say, forty springs, or forty mothers, and it is called Morbeya only by a corruption of the word.

on the north side, a dock has been made, which will admit small vessels; but large ships are obliged to anchor two leagues out at sea, on account of the cape of Azamore, which stretches to the west, and which it would be difficult to double if a south-west wind should drive them from their anchors. Mazagan was besieged without effect in 1562 by the Sharif of Morocco, and remained in the possession of the Portuguese till 1769, when the present Emperor laid siege to it just as it was determined to be abandoned by the court of Lisbon. The Moors of the province of Duquella, who carried on a clandestine trade with the Portuguese, greatly regret that it has changed its master.

The town of Mazagan is at present entirely ruined, and almost uninhabited. The Moors have taken away the timber of the houses, and left the walls standing. I saw, in 1781, a cistern, still remaining, though damaged by the bombs, which deserves the notice of travellers for the elegance of its construction: the descent is by stairs; the effusion of light is splendid, and

the

the vaulted roof is supported by twenty-four very regular columns. At a little distance to the south west of Mazagan is an old tower, called Borisha; whence the name of Bridja, which the Moors confound with that of Mazagan.

When this town belonged to the Portuguese, the southern Moors, who were not able to make the pilgrimage to Mecca, imagined the neglect of this devotion might be compensated by coming and discharging their muskets at the Christian town of Mazagan. One of these fanatics having been killed by a cannon shot from the place, his comrades buried him as a saint, and carried away the ball as a trophy of victory; they took care, however, for the future, to fire their pieces at a greater distance.

Twelve leagues from Mazagan, proceeding along the coast, we find the town of Valedia situated in a stony plain, extremely incommodious to the traveller. Here is a very spacious natural bason, surrounded by rocks, which would contain more than

a thou-

a thoufand fhips ; but the entrance, which
is narrow, and entirely open to the weft, is
equally difficult and dangerous. The coaft
of Valedia is lined with rocks near thirty
feet high, which anciently muft have been
wafhed by the fea, the Moors living in the
caverns the waters have hollowed out. At
the bottom of thefe rocks the fands, heaped
up during fucceffive ages, have formed an
extenfive and pleafant plain, where the
Moors cultivate pulfe and vegetables, which
they fell in the province of Duquella,
where the want of water renders all kind
of garden productions extremely fcarce.

The little town of Valedia is only a
circle of walls, containing but few habitations. Its name indicates that it was built
under the reign of Muley Valid, who died
in 1647. This town feems to be fituated
nearly on the fame fpot where Leo Africanus places Conte, which, he fays, was
built by the Africans twenty miles from
Saffi. Marmol has copied him exactly ;
but, by fome miftake in the name, con-
founds Conte with cape Cottes, at prefent
cape

cape Spartel, which is a hundred leagues more to the north. ·

Eight leagues from Valedia toward the south, after doubling cape Cantin, we arrive at the town of Saffi, the only one in the province of Abda. This place is very ancient, and was probably one of the cities built by the Carthaginians. The Portuguese made themselves masters of it in 1508, and abandoned it in 1641, after having resisted every effort of the Sharifs, who were not able to take it from them.

Saffi was long the centre of the commerce carried on with Europe. The French, who had several factories there before the peace, and who resided there, confiding in the laws of hospitality, brought thence great quantities of wool, wax, gum and leather ; but the present Emperor having made Mogodor a principal port, Saffi has no longer any trade. This town has a very fine road, where ships may anchor very safely, except in winter, when the winds blow from the south or south west.

weſt, for they are then ſure to be driven out to ſea.

The environs of Saffi are a dry and parched deſert, and the Moors of the town rude, fanatical, and unſociable. There are a number of tombs, or aſylums of ſaints at the entrance of this town, which have been made a pretext for obliging the Jews to enter it barefooted ; nor was any Chriſtian till lately permitted to ride in on horſeback. I was the firſt who freed the Europeans from this ridiculous reſtriction, to which they had long been ſubjected ; and it is only ſince 1767, when I reſided a whole year at Saffi, after the peace, that they have been allowed to go in or out of this town on horſeback *.

About five leagues to the ſouth of Saffi is the river of Tanſif, which is the boundary of the province of Abda. This river

---

* This ridiculous devotion firſt began toward the cloſe of the ſeventeenth century ; for the Portugueſe, who were maſters of that place, did not abandon it till the year 1641.

rifes in Mount Atlas, and, taking its courfe near Morocco, falls into the Atlantic ocean. At the mouth of this river, on the northern fide, amid fome fands and marfhes, are the ruins of a fmall town, called by the Moors Suera, from which the unwholefomenefs of the air, or the inundations of the Tanfif, has driven the inhabitants. On the other fide of the Tanfif, which is paffed by fording, or on rafts made of reeds tied to leathern bags filled with wind, we find a fquare caftle, built in the reign of Muley Ifhmael, to defend the paffage of the river during the time of the inteftine difturbances of the empire. This caftle at prefent only contains a few families, and the country round it is not cultivated.

From the Tanfif it is eighteen leagues to Mogodor, in the province of Hea. The intermediate country is interfperfed with vallies, which are tolerably pleafant, though ftony, and in which, from time to time, we meet with cultivation. This place, which the Moors call, indifferently, Suera, or Mogodor, receives its name from a faint,

held

held here in great veneration by the name of Sidi Mogodoor, whofe tomb is to be feen at a fmall diftance to the fouth of the town. Mogodor formerly had a wretched caftle, built by the Portuguefe, to preferve a communication with their fettlements to the fouth of this coaft. This caftle protected alfo the entrance of a harbour, formed by a channel between the main land and a fmall ifland. Such a fituation appearing favourable to make it a place of trade, the prefent Emperor refolved to found a city here, and the wealthier Moors began to build houfes to pleafe their Sovereign. Foreign merchants were invited to do the fame, and, to induce them, large abatements were offered in the cuftom duties. Thefe promifes, however, though folemnly made, were not fo fcrupuloufly obferved.

This city, which was begun in 1760, is now compleatly finifhed: it contains a great number of houfes, handfomely and folidly built. The ftreets are all ftraight lines, and there is no town in the empire

in

in which we fee fuch a regularity of plan*.
It is furrounded with walls, and batteries
are erected, not only on the fea fide but
toward the land, to defend it from any in-
curfion of the fouthern Moors. In cafe
of an attack, however, this city, which
has no water, and is half a league diftant
from the river, would foon be at the mercy
of the enemy.

The prefent Emperor has brought all
the European merchants to fettle at Mogodor ; and, diftant as it is from Europe, it
is the only port on the coaft which maintains a continued commercial intercourfe
with that quarter of the world. This
city ftands on marfhy ground, and fo
low that, at fpring-tides, it is almoft furrounded by the fea. The country about it

* A French engineer, named Cornut, from the country
near Avignon, who, feeking his fortune, croffed from Gibraltar to Morocco, laid the foundations of the town of
Mogodor. He was kindly received by the Emperor, who
defired to diftinguifh his reign by the foundation of a new
city ; but after ten years fervice this engineer returned to
France as poor as he went. The city was afterwards
finifhed by renegadoes and mafons brought from Europe.

is a melancholy defert of accumulated fand. The Europeans, however, enjoy here the advantage of a more eafy communication with the fouthern provinces, which, by exchanging their productions for the commodities of Europe, render the trade of this place very flourifhing.

The port of Mogodor is formed by a channel, between the main land and an ifland more than a mile in length. The entrance of this channel is to the north weft, and its outlet to the fouth. It is fufficiently large for fhips of a middling fize, but in general it has not fufficient depth; which difadvantage is increafed every day by the accumulation of the fand. The number of fhips which have been loft in this port in winter, by violent ftorms from the fouth weft, fufficiently prove how very dangerous it is in bad weather.

Following the coaft, to the fouth, about thirty-five leagues from Mogodor, we arrive at the town of Santa Cruz, in the province of Suz, called by the Arabs Aguadir,

Aguadir, or Cape Aguer. The fpacious bay of this place and the neighbouring fea abound greatly in fifh. A Portuguefe gentleman built a wooden houfe on this coaft for the purpofe of fifhing,. and found it a very profitable undertaking. The Moors called this place *El dar del Roomi*; that is, the houfe of the Roman. Don Emanuel, King of Portugal, perceiving the importance of this poft for the prefervation of the conquefts he had already made, and facilitating thofe he meditated, bought the ground about the beginning of the fixteenth century, and built there a fortrefs called Santa Cruz, which was taken from the Portuguefe in 1536. This town was long the centre of an extenfive commerce, and different European nations had feveral factories there till 1773, when the Emperor obliged them to remove to Mogodor, after demolifhing the fortifications of Santa Cruz. It has been imagined that this Prince, whofe character is fuch that no very certain judgement can be formed of the motives of his actions, was induced to this meafure for fear the Spaniards fhould befiege Santa Cruz, while he was occupied

pied

pied in the siege of Melilla, which he undertook in 1774.

The port of Santa Cruz is a large and
very secure bay, capable of containing a
great number of ships, and well defended
from the wind on every side. The communication between this place and the
southern provinces renders it more convenient for commerce than any other on the
coast.

Beyond Santa Cruz there is no frequented port. The country of Tarudant, which
is to the south of this place, and which is
a part of the province of Suz, is the southern boundary of the Empire of Morocco.

The country of Vled de Nun, which
is next to the province of Suz, is separated
from it by sandy deserts. The Emperor
of Morocco, indeed, as I have observed at
the beginning of this chapter, arrogates to
himself the sovereignty of Vled de Nun;
but his real authority is here extremely
feeble. This vast, but desert, province affords

fords not a single harbour or anchoring place along a coast of sixty leagues, that is, quite to cape Bajador. It is inhabited by different tribes of Arabs, whose camps are scattered over such parts of the interior country as are capable of cultivation. The side next the sea is a sandy shore, lined with rocks under water, over which the waves break violently. Ships are often driven on this coast by rapid currents formed between the Continent and the Canary islands, and Spanish, English, and French vessels, are frequently shipwrecked*. When such a misfortune happens the fate of the unhappy mariners is most deplorable; they are immediately seized and stripped by the Arabs, who, not-

* These accidents, which may depend on a concatenation of unlucky circumstances, have often been occasioned by the ignorance of the mariners, as we may be convinced from the deposition of those who have escaped after shipwreck. They might be prevented, by subjecting vessels destined for the coast of Africa to pass to the west of the Canaries, and especially by examining, with more severity, the orders of Captains, and supplying ships, intended to make long voyages, with three officers capable of command, the Captain included.

withstanding the laws observed among themselves in their robberies, take from each other their slaves and booty by open force. Their wretched prisoners are exposed to hunger, thirst, the caprices of their masters, and every humiliation of misery. To the shame of humanity, they are bought and sold, and frequently exchanged for camels, or other beasts, in the markets of the deserts. The Emperor of Morocco uses all his influence to procure these unfortunate sufferers to be delivered up to him; but the slowness of the negociations, and the obstacles met with at every step, render their issue very uncertain ; and should they even be surrendered to this Prince, his justice and generosity must again be long, and patiently solicited, before they are finally set at liberty *.

In these southern climates Mahometanism is mixed with more superstitions than even among the people of Morocco. The

* The seamen of a ship from Nantz, in the Guinea trade, which was shipwrecked on this coast about the end of the year 1775, were two years before they returned to France.

heat

heat inflaming the imagination multiplies the number of fanatics, who, under the name of saints, impose on the piety and credulity of the people. They have neither mosques nor any stated places for their prayers, but pray in their tents, or wherever they happen to be; and, when they want water, make their ablutions with sand, as is permitted them by their law. The spirit of pillage keeps the people of these countries in constant motion; they traverse the deserts quite to Nigritia, whence they even carry off the Negroes. They regulate their route, and judge of their approach to rivers by the flight of certain birds.

The province of Vled de Nun has a considerable trade. After having passed the deserts, that separate it from Morocco, we find many tracts of land capable of cultivation, and which produce gums and excellent wax. As these people are so far removed from the reach of tyranny as to live in a kind of independence, luxuries are more indulged among them; and they make use of many European commodi-

ties,

ties, especially linen. Several of these Arab tribes are more affable and honest than the other Moors. They trade to Mogodor, but with reserve and circumspection, that they may not expose their riches to the uncertainty of accident. It is probable they have a more immediate communication with the factories of Senegal, with which they may trade with less restraint; and it is only by their means that the western Moors have any intercourse with the people of Nigritia. If it were practicable to form settlements on the coast of cape Bajador, a very profitable commerce might be established with these Arabs; and mariners, who might have the misfortune to be shipwrecked on the coast, would be able to obtain more certain and speedy assistance; but such a plan is exposed to too many difficulties ever to be realized.

As a knowledge of the coast of Morocco is of more utility than descriptions of the inland towns, I have treated this subject more at length; but I shall now proceed to enumerate the cities of the interior pro-

provinces, which are not many in number, returning from the fouth to the north.

 CHAP.

CHAP. IV.

Inland Cities and Towns of the Empire of Morocco.

THE city of Tarudant, in the province of Suz, is situated almost at the extremity of the empire of Morocco. It was formerly the capital of a small kingdom, and is at present the residence of a governor, in whom great confidence is reposed, or some Sharif related to the Emperor. This province also contains the cities of Climi, Aguadir-Toma, and several other towns, which, as well as Tarudant, are built with stone. As the province of Suz has no harbours, the Moors carry its productions to Mogodor.

Morocco, which has become the metropolis of the empire, and given name to it, was formerly the capital of the kingdom of Morocco, which was bounded by the river Om-Arbaym, or Morbeya. This city is

twenty

twenty leagues from the fea, to the eaft-
fouth-eaft of Saffi, and a fmall diftance
from Mount Atlas. It is built nearly in
the fituatioh, where the ancients placed
the Bocanum Hemerum.

Abu Teffifin, firft King of the Moors,
of the race of the *Morabethoon*, or Maraboots, firft fixed his refidence at the city.
of Agmet, on the weftern declivity of
Mount Atlas, a little diftance from Morocco. Defiring to found a capital for his
dominions in a more eligible fituation, he
chofe the fpot where Morocco now ftands,
which is called by the Arabs Marrakefch,
and by the Spaniards Marrueccos. This city
was begun by that Prince in 1052, and continued by his fon and fucceffor Jofeph Ben
Abu Teffifin, who kept his court here. Its
walls are extremely thick, and formed of a
cement, compofed of lime and fand, which
is put in cafes, and beaten with rammers.
This mortar hardens in time, and turns to
ftone, efpecially when the compofition is
well made, and contains a fufficient quantity of lime *.

* The Spaniards ufe this mortar, and, like the Moors,
 call

The city of Morocco * is fituated in a pleafant plain, planted with palm trees, having Mount Atlas to the eaft, which has a fine and romantic effect. The numerous ftreams which meander through this fertile plain render it capable of the higheft cultivation. It was formerly divided into a prodigious number of enclofed gardens and beautiful plantations of olive trees, which have, in part, efcaped the barbarous devaftations of contending factions. More than fix thoufand fprings poured their waters from Mount Atlas to fructify and enrich this plain, which was filled with country-houfes and pleafure grounds; but thefe have been all laid in ruins by the revolutions which preceded and diftin-

call it Tapia : hence, perhaps, the French derive the word Taper; that is, to ftrike upon, or beat with the hand. This, probably, was the manner of building among the ancients. Livy informs us, the walls of Saguntum were built with mortar made of earth.

* According to Marmol and Martiniere, there was an ancient city called Morocco, mentioned in the Roman hiftory, which Marmol names Tamaroc. It was fituated on the river Morbeya, has been deftroyed, and now no traces of is remain.

guifhed

gulſhed the reign of Muley Iſhmael ; and
it was with difficulty, that, in 1768, tho
eourſe of twelve hundred ſtreams, which .
wind through this fertilo country was re-
newed. The city of Morocco itſelf, expoſed to the devaſtations of different conquerors, has preſerved nothing but its
form. The extent of the walls, which
ſtill exiſt entire, except in ſome few places,
ſuppoſes a city, which might contain
three hundred thouſand ſouls : at preſent
this capital is little better that a Deſert. The
ruins of houſes, heaped one upon another,
ſerve only to harbour thieves, who lurk
among them to rob the paſſenger. The
quarters, which have been rebuilt, are conſiderably diſtant from each other ; and the
houſes are low, dirty, and extremely inconvenient. It is difficult to conceive how an
imperial city can have become ſo miſerable
and ſo deſerted. I doubt whether it contains thirty thouſand inhabitants, even
when the court is there.

Morocco poſſeſſes ſeveral large moſques,
but they have no pretenſions to magnifi-
çence. One of theſe has a tower ſimilar

to thofe at Sallee and Seville, and which may be feen at a very great diftance. Within the walls are a number of large enclofed fpaces, almoft entirely detached, containing gardens of orange trees, and pavilions, in which the princes lodge. Thefe pavilions, covered with coloured tiles, are the more remarkable, as the gaiety and fplendor of their appearance form a ftriking contraft with the wretchednefs and poverty of the furrounding buildings.

Among the number of the public edifices at Morocco, we muft not forget to mention the Elcaifferia *, a place where ftuffs, and other valuable commodities, are expofed to fale. We find fimilar buildings in all the other cities of the empire; but in Barbary they are by no means eqnal to thofe of the fame kind in Turkey called Bezeflins.

At the extremity of the city of Morocco, and very near the palace, is the

* Elcaiffcria is only a corruption of the word Cæfarea.

quarter

quarter of the Jews, inclofed by walls near two miles round, where the Jews refide, under the guard of an Alcaid, to protect them from infult. This fame quarter was formerly the refidence of the Spanifh nobles, or others of that nation, who, from difcontent, or other motives, entered into the fervice of the Kings of Morocco; and there is ftill a part of the city, called the quarter of Andalufia. Not lefs than three thoufand Jewifh families formerly refided here, as may be eftimated by the ruins of houfes and fynagogues. Of this great number there at prefent fcarcely remain two hundred families, expofed to tyranny and poverty; oppreffion has obliged all the reft to take refuge among the mountains, where they live more at their eafe, notwithftanding the ferocity of the inhabitants of that part of the country.

The Emperor's palace, at the extremity of the city of Morocco, fronting Mount Atlas, is a very extenfive and folid building. The principal gates are gothic arches of cut ftone, embellifhed with ornaments in the Arabian tafte. Within the walls

are

4

are various courts and gardens, elegantly laid out by European gardeners. In each of these gardens is a pavilion, to which the Emperor frequently retires to take his repose, or amuse himself with his courtiers. These pavilions are square pyramidal edifices, about forty feet in length, and somewhat less in heighth: they are covered with varnished tiles, of various colours; the inside is a kind of spacious hall, that receives light and air from four large doors, in the four sides, which are opened, more or less, according to the position of the sun, or the coolness they may produce. These halls within are painted and gilt in the stile we call arabesque, and ornamented with cartouches, containing passages of the Koran, or other Arabic sentences. The furniture of these apartments is very simple; it consists only of a couch, some arm chairs, tables, and china, or other embellishments; tea equipage, clocks, arms hung round the walls, a water pot, and carpets for prayers.

The pavilion, containing apartments for the Emperor and his women, is in one

of

of thefe gardens. This is a very fpacious building, according to the ufual way of living among the Moors: for the tafte of different nations, in this refpect, always depends on their manners and cuftoms. The furniture of this palace difplays no fplendid ornaments, but is in a ftile of the greateft fimplicity. Thefe climates are unacquainted with that profufion of fantaftic novelties which are every day multiplied by the induftry, luxury, and caprice of Europe.

The prefent Emperor, who has fhewn an exclufive preference to the city of Morocco, had added to his palace a large piece of ground, on which he has caufed to be built, by Europeans, regular pavilions, in the midft of gardens. Thefe are of cut ftone, have handfome windows, are finifhed in an excellent tafte, and give an air of grandeur and magnificence to this part of the palace which we do not fee any where elfe. Between thefe pavilions and the old palace is a large vacant fpace, inclofed with walls, called Methooar, where the Emperor gives public audience four

times

times in a week. This place is entered from without the town by a large gate, which is only opened an hour before the Meshooar.

Mount Atlas, the boundary of the plain of Morocco, is situated at a small distance to the east of the city. This is the highest part of that mountain, the vallies of which, flourishing with trees and verdure, and contrasted with the snows on the summit, have a singular and picturesque effect. This chain of mountains defends the environs of Morocco from the east wind, which would be burning in summer, while the snows, that cover their tops, temper, at the same time, the heat of the climate. The nights there are constantly cool, and it is only from nine in the morning, till four or five in the afternoon, that any great heat is felt. The cold is sensibly felt in the winter, because of the snow which falls on the mountains; but the climate is extremely healthy. Foreigners, however, do not find Morocco an agreeable residence, for the houses are inconvenient and full of bugs; and, in summer, the

multi-

multitudes of scorpions, serpents, and gnats, are inexpressly troublesome.

About a league from Morocco is the river Tansif, which rises in Mount Atlas, and falls into the Atlantic Ocean, a little to the south of Saffi. This river may be forded in the fine season; it has, however, a bridge of brick, of considerable length, but not kept in repair, built about the end of the sixteenth century by the Portuguese slaves, who survived the defeat of the army of Don Sebastian.

Beside the streams which rise in Mount Atlas, and flow through the country round Morocco, some writers have described as a wonderful work, the aqueducts that bring water to the city and its environs; these, however, are only subterranean conduits, open at intervals, rudely made, and sunken in the earth about fifteen or twenty feet, according to the level of the ground. It is impossible to survey, without veneration, these first efforts of the industry of mankind, that seem to remind us of the birth of the arts; but we are not to con-

found

found or compare thefe barbarous works with other monuments of the fame kind, which are fuch noble proofs of the improvements in thofe fame arts, and the magnificence of nations.

At a little diftance from Morocco, on the weftern declivity of Mount Atlas, ftand the city of Agmet, which was for fome time the refidence of the firft Kings of Morocco, that of Amimey, and feveral wretched villages, inhabited by Jews, who have fled from the capital to avoid oppreffion and extortion. The foil of this whole country is very fertile, as are all the vallies of thefe noble mountains, which are inhabited by the Brebes, or Berebs, who are almoft independant.

After Muley Ifhmael had united the fmall kingdoms which form the empire, he determined to have two imperial cities, that he might the more eafily keep his people in fubjection, by removing alternately from one to the other. Morocco was the imperial city of the fouth; and Mequinez, which that prince greatly embellifhed

and

and enlarged, became the metropolis in the north.

The city of Mequinez is situated at the extremity of the province of Beni-Haſſen, eighty leagues north of Morocco, and twenty leagues eaſt of Sallee and the ſea. The founder of this city, named Maknaſſa, firſt built it at the bottom of a valley; but Muley Iſhmael made it conſiderably larger, by building in the plain to the weſt. The city is ſurrounded by vallies and eminences highly cultivated, ornamented with gardens and plantations of olive trees, and watered by a variety of ſtreams; the fruits and vegetables therefore are of an excellent flavour. The inhabitants themſelves, by an increaſe of civility, ſeem to prove the milder temperature of the climate. The winter, indeed, is very diſagreeable from the quantity of mud which then accumulates in this city and the environs, becauſe the ſtreets are not paved, and the ſoil is clay.

The city of Mequinez is ſurrounded with walls; the palace itſelf is fortified

with two baftions, in which there formerly
was fome fmall artillery. Muley Ifhmael
and Muley Abdallah have often defended
themfelves in this city againft the utmoft
efforts of the Brebes, when they have
confpired againft their tyranny. On the
weftern fide are ftill to be feen fome walls
of circumvallation, fix feet in height,
which probably were only intrenchments
for the infantry, as the attacks of the Brebes were merely fudden and momentary
incurfions, which did not require any long
defence.

There is in Mequinez, as in Morocco, a
quarter walled in and guarded for the Jews.
The houfes are handfomer here than in
that at Morocco; the Jews are more numerous, and make greater profit by their
induftry, becaufe the Moors of Mequinez
are richer, and, as they are nearer, have a
greater intercourfe with Europe than thofe
of the fouthern provinces.

Contiguous to the quarter of the Jews is
another, inclofed with walls, but now in
ruins, called the negro town. It was built

by

by Muley Ifhmael for the families of his black foldiers. Nothing now remains of it but the walls, as is the cafe with all the places intended for the fame purpofe throughout the empire.

At the extremity of the city, on the fouth-eaft fide, is the Emperor's palace, built by Muley Ifhmael after a plan of his own *. This is a very extenfive building, including feveral gardens, well laid out, and watered by abundant ftreams. I have vifited every part of this palace by permif-fion of the Emperor ; for, without that, it may not be entered. There is a large gar-den in the centre, furrounded by a fpacious and tolerably regular gallery, fupported by columns, which maintains a communica-tion between the apartments. Thofe of the women, which are much lefs peopled than they were in the reign of Muley Ifh-mael, are very large, and terminate in one common chamber, built on a caufeway

* This palace was greatly damaged by the earthquake, which deftroyed Lifbon, November 1, 1755.

                    that

that divides the great garden, where the women may look out at the window through an iron lattice. As we pass from one apartment to another, we meet at intervals with regular courts, paved with squares of black and white marble. In the middle of these courts is a marble bason, on which is raised a round shell; in the centre of this is a fountain that plays into the bason. There are many such fountains, in the palace, that supply water for various purposes, and those ablutions which the scruples of the Mahometans have so multiplied, especially those preceding their prayers, which, on common days, they repeat in the place where they happen to be; but on Fridays they are obliged to go to the mosque.

The palaces of the Moorish Kings are the more spacious as all the apartments are on the ground floor. These are large, long, narrow rooms, eighteen or twenty feet high. They are but little ornamented, and receive light and air from two large folding doors, that are opened, more or less, as occasion requires. The apartments
always

always receive light from a square court, the sides of which, with few exceptions, are embellished by collonades.

They make at Mequinez and Fez a kind of glazed tiles, similar to what we call Dutch tiles, of different colours; these they use to pave their rooms and face their walls, whence their houses have an air of coolness and neatness we do not meet with in other towns of the empire.

The Moors of Mequinez are much more affable and engaging than those of the southern provinces. They are very civil to strangers, inviting them to their gardens, and entertaining them with the utmost politeness. The women in this part of the empire are extremely handsome; they are very fair, have fine black eyes, and beautiful teeth. I have sometimes seen them taking the air on their terraces; they do not hide themselves from the Europeans; but if a Moor appears, they retire immediately.

There is, both at Mequinez and Morocco,

a hosa hospitium, or convent, of Spanish recollects, founded more than a hundred years ago, by the munificence of the Kings of Spain, for the benefit and spiritual comfort of the Christian captives. These two convents are much respected in the country, both for the exemplary lives of the fathers, and the service they are of to the poor, whom they supply with medicines, gratis. As their charity, however, was much abused, because the Moors, who are fond of remedies they do not pay for, made an indiscreet use of them, without observing any regimen, the friar, who acts as apothecary, composed a mixture of water, honey, and a few simples, which is refused to nobody, and called the Decoction, or Ptisan, of the Sharif. The Moors have recourse to the fathers, whenever they are indisposed, which exposes the latter to many inconveniences, when their endeavours are not successful.

Besides the cities of Morocco and Mequinez, which are two imperial cities, that of Fez is also one of the principal in the empire. It even ought to have precedence

of

of those two capitals, as it is the more ancient, and gave name to the first monarchy
in Africa, after the Moors had embraced
Mahometanism. It is, besides, the only
city in the empire distinguished by a taste
for the sciences, and the industry of its
inhabitants.

The city of Fez, the capital of the
kingdom of the same name, was built about
the end of the eighth century by Edris,
the descendant of Mahomet and Ali, whose
father, flying from Medina to avoid the pro-
scriptions of the Caliph Abdallah, retired
to the extremity of Africa, and was pre-
claimed sovereign by the Moors. Sidy
Edris, succeeding to the crown of his father, founded the city of Fez in 793, and
built the mosque in which he is buried.
From that time the city of Fez has been
considered by the Moors as a sacred asylum,
and an object of devotion. In the first mo-
ments of that zeal which every religious
novelty inspires, a still larger mosque was
built at Fez, and called Carubin, because it
was founded by the Arabs of Cairoan.
This is one of the finest edifices in the

 empire,

empire, and, perhaps, in Africa. Many other mosques were faterwards built successively at Fez ; to which were annexed, according to the custom of, the Mahometans, colleges and hospitals ; and this city was held in so high a degree of veneration that, when the pilgrimage to Mecca was interrupted, in the fourth century of the Hejira, the western Mahometans, as a substitute, repaired to Fez, while the eastern journeyed to Jerusalem.

When the Arabs had extended themselves in Asia, Africa, and Europe, they brought to Fez the knowledge they had acquired in the arts and sciences ; and, to its religious schools, this capital added academies for philosophy, physic, and astronomy. The latter insensibly degenerated ; ignorance gave credit to astrology, the constant companion of superstition, which, in its turn, gave birth to the arts of magic and divination.

Fez, resorted to from almost all Africa, and the object of the devout pilgrimages of the Mahometans, soon became the rendez-
vous

vous of the neighbouring provinces. The increase of wealth introduced the love of pleasure, and every species of luxury; licentiousness quickly followed; and as its progress in hot countries is always most rapid, Fez, the school of sciences and manners, soon became the sink of every vice. The public baths, which health, cleanliness, and custom, rendered neceffary, became the receptacles of debauchery, into which men were introduced in the dress of women; and the youth of the city ranged the streets, after sun set, in the same disguise, to prevail upon strangers to go with them to the inns, which were rather houses of prostitution than places for the convenience and repose of travellers.

The usurpers, who, after the tenth century, disputed the kingdom of Fez, connived at these abuses, and contented themselves with subjecting the masters of the inns to furnish a number of cooks for the army. To this indulgence the city of Fez owed its first splendor, and the greater part of its riches. As the inhabitants were handsome and engaging, the Africans re-

forted

forted thither in crouds; and the fubver-
fion of all morals became a pretended fource
of political advantage. The fame de-
praved inclinations ftill exift in the hearts
of all the Moors, though libertinifm is no
longer authorifed; but there, as every
where elfe, is fo far ftigmatifed with fhame
as to blufh at a difcovery.

The Mahometans of Andalufia, Grenada, and Cordova, during the revolutions
of Spain, paffed over to Fez, whither they
brought new manners, knowledge, and,
perhaps, fome fhades of civilization. They
taught the Spanifh method of dreffing
and dying red and yellow goat and fheep
fkins, then called Cordovan leather, now
Morocco, from the city of that name,
where, however, the dye is leaft in perfection. At Fez, likewife, they firft eftablifhed the manufacture of milled woollen
caps, worn by the Moors and Eaftern nations*. Gauzes, filks, ftuffs, and beautiful
fafhes,

---

* Thefe fugar-loaf caps are called Fez by the Turks,
which proves they were named from this city. The people
of

fafhes, wrought in gold and filver, are made at Fez ; and the little they do proves how much might be done, were induftry encouraged.

Some love of learning is ftill preferved at Fez, where Arabic is better fpoken than in the other parts of the empire : the rich Moors fend their children to the fchools of Fez, where they gain more inftruction than they could do elfewhere. Leo Africanus, informs us, that there was a prize in his time appointed for the beft poem written by the fcholars in praife of Mahomet, and that the prize poems were examined on the birth day of the Prophet. Clenard went to Fez in 1540 to ftudy more perfectly the Arabic tongue. He fays, that there were many men of letters there at that time, that Grammar was taught in the fchools, and that the remainder of their ftudies related to their reli-

of Tunis have brought the manufacturing of them to perfection, which has been lefs fuccefsfully attempted in France.

gion

gion and ceremonies. He adds, there were no bookfellers at Fez, but that, at certain feafons of the year, fales were held on the Friday in the Grand Mofque, and that the Moors cheapened without a defire to buy.

Leo Africanus has given a defcription of the city of Fez in the fixteenth century, which has been faithfully copied by Marmol ; and it appears, that the narratives of thofe who have written voyages and travels in their ftudies have tranfcribed thefe writers. Leo Africanus, born at Grenada, and educated at Fez, having, while very young, been taken at fea, was conveyed to Rome. The little knowledge and tafte he poffeffed, for tafte can only be acquired by habits of feeing and comparing the moft perfect models, did not fuffer him to perceive all the beauties of that capital ; and, prepoffeffed by the impreffions his memory ftill retained, he wrote a very florid defcription of Fez. I had every liberty of examining this city, which is one of the moft agreeable of the Moorifh empire ; but the minute circumftances related

by

by Leo are unworthy the attention of the
traveller. The mosque of Carubin is the
only remarkable public building, and that
cannot be freely examined. The city contains some tolerably convenient inns,
two or three stories high, with galleries
toward the court, which is always in the
centre, and admits light to the apartments.
They have no appearance of grandeur
whatever toward the ſtreets, which are ill
paved, and ſo narrow, that in many places
two horſemen cannot ride abreaſt. Their
ſhops make no ſhew, and ſhould rather be
called ſtalls, there being juſt room enough
for a ſedentary Moor, who never moves,
and the packets that are heaped round him,
to which he points as paſſengers arrive. Fez,
which, in paſt ages, attracted the attention
of travellers, is no way preferable to the
other cities of the empire, except by its
ſituation, ſchools, induſtry, and ſomewhat
more of urbanity: yet, though more poliſhed than their countrymen, the Moors
of Fez are vain, ſuperſtitious, and intolerant. The Saints, whom they pretend
have been buried in that city, ſerve them
for a pretext to forbid its entrance to Jews
and

and Chriſtians ; and an order from the Emperor is neceſſary to gain admiſſion.

The ſituation of Fez is remarkable for its ſingularity ; it is ſeated at the bottom of a valley, and ſurrounded by hills in the form of a funnel, flattened at the narrow end. The upper part of the valley is divided into gardens, planted with high trees, orange groves, and orchards. A river winds along the valley, watering it in various directions, turning by its declivity a number of mills, and ſupplying water in abundance to all the gardens and moſt of the houſes. The deſcending road impeded by, and entangled among, theſe gardens, is much lengthened. The city ſtands in the centre of a vaſt circumference, the variety of which is exceedingly agreeable.

The gardens ſeen from the city form a moſt delightful amphitheatre. Each garden formerly had its country houſe, where the inhabitants paſſed their ſummer ; but theſe have been deſtroyed by their civil wars, and thoſe revolutions in which Fez and its environs have been the ſcene of

action ;

action ; while few of them were afterward rebuilt. By order of the Prince Mulcy Ali, eldeſt ſon of the emperor, I was moſt agreeably lodged at one of theſe gardens. This Prince gave me an entertainment in another garden, through the middle of which the river paſſed, its banks ornamented by a row of trees, and under a pavilion, erected with taſte. Such ſituations are every where charming, and eſpecially ſo in hot climates, where water, though more neceſſary, is more uncommon. The ſituation of Fez, however, cannot be healthy ; the humidity of its vapours renders the air heavy in ſummer, and fevers there are rather common.

Ever ready to change their maſter, the inhabitants of Fez, at each revolution, yield to the firſt approaching conqueror : this they pretend is a privilege they enjoy from the founder of their city. It is, however very inefficacious, and only ſerves to prove either the cowardice of its inhabitants or the difficulty of defence. Fez, in reality, is ſo ſituated as to be unable to

make

make any refiftance without expofing itfelf to total deftruction.

On the height of Old Fez, in a plain capable of great cultivation, Jacob-Ben-Abdallah, of the race of Beni-Merins, built, in the thirteenth century, New Fez, contiguous to the Old, and, by its fituation, keeping the latter in awe. The high town, which is well and healthily fituated, contains fome old palaces, in which the fons of the Emperor live. The Sovereign himfelf refides here when he pleafes; but he prefers a feparate palace, built by his father, Muley Abdallah, half a league from the city. The new town is inhabited by fome Moorifh families, but by ftill more Jews, who trade with old Fez, notwithftanding the contempt with which they are treated by the inhabitants: this contempt they endeavour to find a recompence for in their gains.

Turning to the left, on the road from Fez to Mequinez, we find a valley, where the river Rafalema, which runs to Fez, takes its rife; it iffues from a rock eight

or

or ten feet above the level, in a ſtream; the contents of which is about three cubic feet, and cannot be more; ſo that, however heavy the rains may be, the river, during its ſhort courſe, is incapable of ſwell. Hence the city is never endangered by floods, although from the form of the valley it is a kind of continued water-fall. It waſhes the ramparts of new Fez, and turns a wheel twenty-four feet in diameter, by which the inhabitants, the Princes' palaces, and the appertaining gardens, are ſupplied with water. This wheel is turned by the current like that of a water mill, and has ſpaces, at intervals, which ſerve as buckets that are filled by the ſtream, and emptied, during their courſe, into a baſon on the top of the wall. The method is ſimple and cheap; but I think it can only ſucceed on rivers not liable to ſwells, and where the deſcent of the current is equal to the volume of water intended to be raiſed.

The diſtance from Fez to the ſea is about a hundred and twenty miles, and from Fez to Mequinez ſome thirty ſix; the road excellent, along a pleaſant plain, interſected by rivulets, over which are bridges, and various canals cut to water the lands. This plain is surrounded by inhabited highlands, on which abundant crops might be produced, and the most charming land-scapes formed. It is afflicting to behold climates of rich and fertile lands, the which lie waste, while men are obliged to conquer the obstacles of nature to gain sub-sistence among the mountains of Europe. The waters being abundant in this part of the empire, and the climate temperate, the vegetables produced are excellent. Rice is here cultivated, which has neither the whiteness nor taste of that coming from the Levant; and here they rear all kinds of fruit, and even cherries, which do not ripen in the other parts of the empire.

The communication between Fez and Mequinez is more easy than in many polished nations. Ready-saddled mules may be found at all hours of the day, which are returned after the journey to a place appointed. The pacing of the mules is not fatiguing, and in summer people go from Mequinez to Fez, and return in a day,

good

good mules being able to travel these six-and-thirty miles in six hours.

On the western side of the plain of Fez, in sight of Mequinez, stands the mountain Zaaron, on which is a village consecrated to Mahometan devotion. It contains the sanctuary of Sidi Edris, who came from Medina at the end of the eighth century, introduced Mahometanism, and was the first sovereign of his race in this part of Africa. This sanctuary is an asylum for malefactors, and never violated by the Emperor of Morocco.

After Morocco, Mequinez, and Fez, which are the principal inland cities of the empire, the only one remaining to be descibed is that of Alcassar-Quiber.

Alcassar-Quiber is a small city, on the western extremity of the province of Garb, three leagues to the east of Laracha, situated on the river Lucos, and separated from Arzilla by a continuance of vallies and plains, in one of which Don Sebastian, King of Portugal, lost victory and life in

1578.

1578. Alcassar is surrounded by gardens, in which are grown many very indifferent fruits. The river Lucos often overflows its banks in winter, and does great damage to the city and its neighbourhood; in the houses of which it is not uncommon for the water, at such times, to be two feet high.

This city, built in the twelfth century, owes its foundation to a singular event. The Emperor, Jacob Almonsor, who extended his domains in Africa, and even over the Mahometan provinces of Spain, was encamped in the plains of this city to enjoy the pleasures of the chace. Having lost himself one night, he was seated under a tree waiting the approach of day, when a fisherman came by, who was returning to his hut. The King pretended he was one of his own attendants who had lost his way, and wished to be conducted to the camp. The fisherman pleaded bad weather, the danger of a country abounding in marshes, and begged this pretended stray attendant would, without scruple, come and partake what his cottage

...age could afford. They set out on the morrow, and, having met the guards, who were in search of the Emperor, Almonfor made himself known, and afked his hoft what recompence he wifhed to receive. I wifh, faid the fifherman, to have a houfe inftead of a hut, in which, fhould occafion offer, I might welcome a loft fportfman. The Emperor erected a palace on the fpot where he refided when he came to hunt; the charge and ftewardfhip of which he gave to the fifherman. The grandees and courtiers eagerly built houfes around it, and a little city foon arofe. It contains at prefent near a thoufand families, and has preferved its name of Alcaffar-Quiber; that is to fay, grand palace, to diftinguifh it from Alcaffar-Seguer, or little palace, which this Prince alfo built on the fea fhore of the ftraits of Gibraltar.

Alcaffar-Quiber was befieged by the Portuguefe in 1503; but, the Moors coming to its relief, they were forced to renounce the attempt.

Exclufive of thefe four inland cities,

there

there are some other towns toward the south, which lie out of the way, and the situations of which remain undetermined.

On the far side of the kingdom of Fez, in the province of Shaus, or Chaus, near the river Mulluvia, is a walled town, called Dubudu, on a height, surrounded by fertile vallies. This town, supposed to have been built by the ancient Africans, was a considerable place in the sixteenth century, when the race of Merini reigned at Fez. At present it contains few inhabitants, though it has a garrison and a confidential Alcayde to guard the frontier,

Between Fez and the province of Rif stands the castle of Tesa, pleasantly situated, and surrounded by charming vales. This was formerly a populous town, but now, like the preceding, contains few inhabitants, with a governor, and some soldiers.

In most of the provinces are walled castles without artillery, in which the Bashaws and

and Governors live, and many more, wholly uninhabited, and falling to ruin. That of Mediona, in the province of Temfena, two days journey from Sallee, is inhabited by fome Moors and Jewifh families, where they fabricate *Haiks* and coarfe carpets. Another has been built at fome diftance to curb the mountaineers of Shayoya, who often ravage the country.

One of the moft remarkable, from its fituation, the refiftance it might be able to make, and the labour beftowed on it, is the caftle of Bulahuau, in the province of Duquella, on the banks of the Morbeya. This caftle ftands in a wild and barren fpot, on the fummit of a commanding eminence more than two hundred feet high, forming a pyramid, the angles of which are rounded, while a large river runs beneath, that, from its depth and rapidity, infpires a kind of horror.

This caftle was built at the clofe of the thirteenth century by Muley Abdulmomen, firft king of the race of the Moahedins ; but Muley Abdallah, fon of Muley

Ifhmael,

Ifhmael, made large additions ; and, during the different revolutions that difturbed his reign, he was here often befieged by the revolted Moors of the 'northern provinces. This Prince had fubterranean paffages dug, at a great expence to procure water from the river ; but as he could not fecure his water-carriers from the fire of the mufketry, he built conduits, which brought the waters from the neighbouring mountains ; and the ruins of which are ftill vifible on the road from Bulahuan to Morocco.

I lodged in this caftle, in 1781, fpite of the refiftance of fome negroes, to whom the keeping of it was entrufted.. The apartments are long and high. The profpect from the terraces lofes itfelf on the immenfe plains of Duquella, which are only feen with pleafure when covered with green herbage ; for a day's journey may be gone without fight of a fingle tree. Near the caftle is a village, and another before paffing the river ; each of which contains about two hundred houfes, or thatched huts, being piles of rough-hewn ftone without mortar. Both thefe villages, inhabited

habited by Moors, are exempt from taxes, but are obliged to give the neceſſary aſſiſtance in croſſing the river. The lonely ſituation of this caſtle, naked and expoſed to every wind that blows, and the barrenneſs of the ſandy valley in which it ſtands, inſpire a kind of gloomy horror. But, on the contrary, with equal pleaſure and aſtoniſhment, well-cultivated gardens are ſeen below, on the banks of the river, with their orchards and vineyards. Each garden contains a windlaſs and a bucket neceſſary to ſupply it with water.

Among barbarous people like theſe, who have no idea of the arts, we are taught to diſtinguiſh, with more preciſion, the diſtance there is between nations, and the power which neceſſity has in awakening the inventive faculties of man. The paſſage over the river is another proof to the ſame effect. The only ferry boat is a raft, compoſed, for the occaſion, of reeds, to which ſkins full of wind are tied with cords, made from the palm leaf. This is ſuſtained by ſeveral Moors, who, ſwimming, guide and ſupport it by their ſhoulders,

ders, though the rapidity of the current is such as to drive it down the stream a mile in an instant *.   On this crazy raft travellers and their effects are transported. The mules swim across, driven by the muleteers. In September 1781, the waters being low, because of the heats, I forded this rapid river ; a thing which had not happened before for five-and-twenty years.

The Emperor usually passes the Morbeya above Bulahuan, where the stream is less rapid, on a kind of temporary bridge. It is formed of two thick ofier cables, fastened to large piles on each bank of the river. These cables are formed into a kind of hurdle by cross stakes passed through them of about five feet long, and over which sods, six inches thick, are laid. This bridge, in consequence of its own weight, rests, and is supported by the current in the middle ; it has indeed

* We read in Livy, that, during the second Punic war, when Hannibal went from Spain to Italy, a part of his army passed the Rhone, the Ticinus, and the Po, on goat skins filled with wind.

but

but little to bear, the Emperor not passing with a numerous train.

I have still to speak of the kingdom of Tafilet, of which I can give no very accurate idea, Europeans not being suffered to pass through it. Tafilet extends along the east side of Mount Atlas; its habitations consist but of some fifteen hundred scattered houses, several of which have a tower for defence, and each standing amidst an enclosure of gardens, cultivated grounds, and palm-tree plantations ; the whole forming a variegated and pleasant country, interfected by many rivers and rivulets descending from the east of Mount Atlas, and which serve to water their lands. Their dates, which are very small, but very excellent, constitute the wealth of, and are food for, the people, who even give them to their horses. By ancient custom, perhaps, for it is contrary to the precepts of the Coran, brandy is made in Tafilet of dates, which is exceedingly strong, and drank so immoderately, by the Sharifs, that wine produces no effect on them whatever.

Tafilet

Tafilet is the abode of a race of the Sharifs, the moft of which are poor. They employ themfelves in their grounds and gardens, and, being always divided among themfelves, the fpirit of pillage inceffantly arms the ftrong againft the weak. The town of Tafilet, after which the kingdom was named under the Sharifs of the reigning houfe, is not an ancient city. The name comes from the word *Fileli*, for fo the inhabitants of thefe countries are called, as are the ftuffs and carpets which are there manufactured. In the fame territory is the town of Sugulmeffa, which appears to have been known to the Romans. Leo Africanus fays it was anciently called Meffa, that is to fay, victory ; and that a Roman general, having there followed and vanquifhed the Numidians, reftored the town, and gave it the name of Sigillummeffæ, or the feal of victory ; whence comes Sugulmeffa.

CHAP.

C H A P. V.

Of the Climate and Soil of the Empire of Morocco.

THE climate of the Empire of Morocco is in general sufficiently temperate, healthy, and not so hot as its situation might lead us to suppose. The chain of mountains which form Atlas, on the eastern side, defends it from the east winds, that would scorch up the earth, were they frequent. The summit of these mountains is always covered with snow, which falls so heavily in winter as often to bury the *Brebes*, who inhabit these vallies. Their abundant descending streams spread verdure through the neighbourhood, make the winter more cold, and temper the heats of summer. The sea on the west side, which extends along the coast from north to south, also refreshes the land with regular breezes, that seldom vary, according to their seasons. At a dis-

tance

diſtance from the ſea, within land, the heat is ſo great, that the rivulets become dry in ſummer; but, as in hot countries dews are plentiful, the nights are there always cool.

The rains are tolerably regular in winter, in the climate of Morocco, and are even abundant, though the atmoſphere is not loaded with clouds as in northern latitudes. Thoſe rains which fall by intervals are favourable to the earth, and increaſe its fecundity. In January the country is covered with verdure, and enamelled with flowers. Barley is cut in March, but the wheat harveſt is in June. All fruits are early in this climate; in forward years the vintage is over in the beginning of September, and I have eat grapes, tolerably ripe, on the thirtieth of May; but this was an extraordinary caſe.

Though in general there is more uniformity and leſs variation in hot than in northern climates, the firſt are nevertheleſs expoſed to the intemperance of weather: too heavy rains often impede the harveſt; and

and drowth has ſtill greater inconveniences, for it enſures the propagation of
locuſts. Theſe fatal inſects, which have
ſo often laid deſolate hot countries, ſometimes commit the moſt dreadful ravages
in the empire of Morocco. They come
from the ſouth, ſpread themſelves over
the lands, and increaſe to infinity, when
the rains of ſpring are not ſufficiently
heavy to deſtroy the eggs they depoſit on
the earth. The large locuſts, which are
near three inches long, are not the moſt
deſtructive; as they fly, they yield to the
current of wind, which hurries them into
the ſea, or into ſandy deſerts, where they
periſh with hunger or fatigue. The young
locuſts, that cannot fly, are the moſt
ruinous; they are about fifteen lines in
length, and the thickneſs of a gooſe-quill;
they creep over the country in ſuch multitudes, that they leave not a blade of graſs
behind; and the noiſe of their feeding an-
nounces their approach at ſome diſtance.
The devaſtations of locuſts increaſe the
price of proviſions, and often occaſion fa-
mines; but the Moors find a kind of com-
penſation in making food of theſe inſects;
proli-

prodigious quantities are brought to market
falted and dried like red herrings. They
have an oily and rancid tafte, which habit
only can render agreeable; they are eat
here, however, with pleafure.

The winters in Morocco are not fevere,
nor is there an abfolute need of fire. In
the coldeft weather the thermometer feldom finks to more than five degrees above
the freezing point; and, during a long
refidence, I never faw it lower than to
two degrees and an half. The inequality
of climate felt at Paris is not found here;
in the former there is fometimes a variation of twenty-four degrees in twenty-
four hours. This degree of variation, at
Sallee, on the weftern coaft, is the exact
difference between winter and fummer.
The longeft days in Morocco are not more
than fourteen hours, and the fhorteft con-
fequently not lefs than ten.

The foil of Morocco is exceedingly fertile; the land, light and fandy on the weftern coaft, contains in itfelf falts fufficient
to make it fruitful. To thefe falts, and to
the

the abundant dews, muſt we attribute a humidity almoſt corroſive, which, without making any ſenſible impreſſion on bodies, quickly covers with ruſt, iron, ſteel, metals, and even the keys and ſciſſors carried in the pocket; an effect never produced in northern latitudes. The ſoil is moſt fruitful in the inland provinces. On the weſtern coaſt it is in general light and ſtony, and is better adapted to the vine and olive than the culture of wheat. They annually burn, before the September rains, the ſtubble, which is left rather long; and this and the dung of cattle, every day turned to paſture, form the ſole manure the land receives. The ſoil requires but little labour, and the plowing is ſo light that the furrows are ſcarcely ſix inches deep; for which reaſon we perceive, in ſome provinces, wooden plough-ſhares are uſed for cheapneſs. It is no doubt a law of nature that, in hot climates, where men are little inclined to induſtry, there induſtry ſhould be leaſt neceſſary.

CHAP. VI.

Fruits, Productions, and Mines.

THE Empire of Morocco might supply itself with all neceſſaries, as well from the abundance and nature of its products as from the few natural or artificial wants of the Moors, occaſioned by climate or education. Its wealth conſiſts in the fruitfulneſs of its ſoil ; its corn, fruits, flocks, flax, ſalt, gums, and wax, would not only ſupply its neceſſities, but yield a ſuperflux, which might become an object of immenſe trade and barter with other nations. . Such numerous exports might return an inexhauſtible treaſure, were its government fixed and ſecure, and did ſubjects enjoy the fruits of their labour and their property in ſafety.

The increaſe of corn in Morocco is often as ſixty to one, and thirty is held to be but an indifferent harveſt. The exportation

of

of this corn is burdened by the laws, and
by the prejudices of an intolerant religion,
which permit them not to fell their fuper-
abundance to infidels. The property of
land is befide entirely precarious, fo that
each individual grows little more than fufficient for his own wants. Hence it happens, when the harveft fails, from the ravages of locufts, or the intemperance of
feafons, thefe people are expofed to mifery,
fuch as Europeans have no conception of;
who enjoy a ftable adminiftration, which
obviates and provides for all their wants.
They alfo have interefted conveniences
and motives, and that confidence which
is founded on the faith of civilized nations. They have the obligation of reciprocally aiding each other's wants on ur-
gent occafions, and rendering the moft
prompt and active fuccour; all which cannot exift under governments fo ftrangely
arbitrary as that of Morocco, where every
thing is fubordinate to the caprice of the
Sovereign, and the law of the moment.

The Moors, naturally indolent, take little care of the culture of their fruits.

 Oranges,

Oranges, lemons, and thick-skinned fruits, the trees of which require little nurture, grow in the open fields, and there are very large plantations of them found, which they take the trouble to water to increafe their product. Their vines, which yield excellent grapes, are planted as far as the thirty-third degree, as in our fouthern provinces, and are equally vigorous with ours. But at Morocco, where they yield a large and delicious grape, they are fupported by vine-poles five and fix feet above ground; and, as they are obliged to be watered, the little wine made there is feldom preferved.

Figs are very good in fome part of the empire, but toward the fouth they are fcarceley ripe before they are full of worms; the heats and night dews may, perhaps, contribute to this fpeedy decay. Melons, for the fame reafon, are rarely eatable; they have but a moment of maturity, which paffes fo rapidly that it is with difficulty feized. Water melons are every where reared, and in fome provinces are excellent. Apricots, apples, and pears, are

in tolerable plenty in the neighbourhood of
Fez and Mequinez, where water is lefs
fcarce, and the climate more temperate. .
But in the plain, which extends along the
weftern coaft, thefe delicate fruits are very
indifferent, have lefs juice or tafte, and the
peaches there do not ripen.

The tree called Raquette in France, or
the prickly pear, or the Barbary fig, is
plentifully found in the Empire of Morocco, and is planted round vineyards and
gardens, becaufe that its thick and thorny
leaves, which are wonderfully prolific,
form impenetrable hedges. From thefe
leaves a fruit is produced, covered with
a thorny fkin, that muft be taken off
with care. This fruit is mild, and full of
very hard, fmall, kernels. The Spaniards
call it Toona, which leads us to fuppofe
they received this plant from Tunis; and,
as it may well have paffed from Andalufia
among the weftern Moors, the latter call it
the Chriftian fig, while in Europe it is more
juftly called the Barbary fig. .

The olive is every where found along
                                the

the coaſt, but particularly to the ſouth. The trees are planted in rows, which form alleys the more agreeable becauſe the trees are large, round, and high in proportion. They take care to water them, the better to preſerve the fruit. Oil of olives might here be plentifully extracted, were taxation fixed and moderate; but, ſuch has been the variation it has undergone, that, the culture of olives is ſo neglected as ſarcely to produce oil ſufficient for internal conſumption. In 1768 and 1769 there were near forty thouſand quintals of oil exported from Mogodor and Santa-Cruz to Marſeilles, and ten years after it coſt fifteen pence per pound. Thus do the vices of government expoſe nations to dearth and famine, who live in the very boſom of abundance.

From the province of Duquella, to the ſouth of the empire, there are foreſts of the Arga tree, which is thorny, irregular in its form, and produces a ſpecies of almond exceedingly hard, with a ſkin as corroſive as that of wall-nuts. Its fruit conſiſts of two almonds, rough and bitter, from which an oil is produced very excellent for frying.

In

In order to ufe this oil, it muft be puriiied by fire, and fet in a flame, which muft be fuffered to die away of itfelf; the moft greafy and corrofive particles are confumed, and its acrid qualities are thus wholly deftroyed. When the Moors gather thefe fruits, they bring their goats under the trees, and, as the fruit falls, the animals carefully nibble off the fkins, and then greedily feed.

In the fame province alfo is found the tree which produces gum .Sandarac ; alfo that which yields the tranfparent gum; but the latter is-moft productive, and affords. the beft gum, the farther we proceed fouthward,•where the heat and night dews may, perhaps, render the vegetable fecretion more pure and copious.

In the province of Suz,. between the twenty-fifth and thirtieth degrees, the inhabitants have an almond harveft, which varies little, becaufe of the mildnefs of the climate ; but the fruit is fmall, for which reafon they take litttle care of the trees, and they degenerate with time.

 The

The palm tree is common in the southern provinces of Morocco; but dates ripen there with difficulty, and few are good, except in the province of Suz, and toward Tafilet, where they are still better, because of its distance from the sea.

On the coast of Sallee and Mamora there are forests of Oak, which produce acorns near two inches long. They taste like chesnuts, and are eat raw and roasted. This fruit is called Bellote, and is sent to Cadiz, where the Spanish ladies hold it in great estimation.

The empire of Morocco also produces much wax; but, since it has been subjected by the Emperor to the payment of additional duties, the country people have very much neglected the care of their hives.

Salt abounds in the empire, and in some places on the coast requires only the trouble of gathering. Independent of the salt-pits, formed by the evaporation of the soft water, there are pits and lakes in the country whence great quantities are obtained. It is

carried

carried even as far as Tombut, whence it paffes to the interior parts of Africa.

The Moors cultivate their lands only in proportion to their wants; hence two thirds of the empire, at leaft, lie wafte. Here the Doum, that is, the fan, or wild palm tree, grows in abundance, and from which thefe people, when neceffity renders them induftrious, find great advantage. The fhepherds, mule drivers, camel drivers, and travellers, gather the leaves, of which they make mats, fringes, bafkets, hats, *fhooaris*, or large wallets to carry corn, twine, ropes, girths, and covers for their pack-faddles. This plant, with which alfo they heat their ovens, produces a mild and refinous fruit, that ripens in September and October. It is in form like the raifin, contains a kernel, and is aftringent, and very proper to temper and counteract the effects of the watery and laxative fruits, of which thefe people in fummer make an immoderate ufe. That Power, which is ever provident for all, has fpread this wild plant over their deferts to fupply an infinity of wants, that would otherwise heavily burden a people so poor.

. Unacquainted with the sources of wealth of which their anceftors were poffeffed, the Moors pretend there are gold and filver mines in the empire, which the Emperors will not permit to be worked, left their fubjects fhould thus find means to fhake off their yoke. It is not improbable but that the mountains of Atlas may contain unexplored riches ; but there is no good proof that they have ever yielded gold and filver. There are known iron mines in the fouth, but the working of them has been found fo expenfive that the natives would rather ufe imported iron, notwithftanding the heavy duty it pays, by which its price is doubled. There are copper mines in the neighbourhood of Santa Cruz, which are not only fufficient for the fmall confumption of the empire, where copper is little ufed, but are alfo an object of exportation, and would become much more fo, were the duties lefs immoderate. Taxation every where impofes fhackles, de-

ftructive

structive to the industry of man, and the
prosperity of nations.

After having seen that the true riches of
the Empire of Morocco consist in the abundance of necessary products, and the ignorance the inhabitants have of artificial
wants, it will be a subject worthy curiosity
to enquire whence came the gold and silver
which the Moors accumulated in former
ages; and what was the source of those
treasures, the remainder of which the Sharifs, after the fifteenth century, dissipated,
and which insensibly dwindled to annihila-
tion.

Time has thrown this enquiry into such
obscurity as to disable us from finding positive proofs; yet suffer me to hazard a few
conjectures, that seem founded in probability.

CHAP.

CHAP. VII.

Concerning the Commerce of the Moors in former Times.

WHAT connection there anciently was between the Moors who border on Africa, and the more interior nations, we can only conjecture. It seems probable that the Carthaginians, who were the most industrious and enlightened people that have governed in Africa, as ardent in acquiring riches as in extending their power, were the first who, after having formed settlements on their borders to increase communication, must have established caravans to exchange their products for the gold, and productions, of interior Africa. This communication seems to be proved by the elephants, which were that way obtained, and with much greater ease than at present, and which formidable animals constituted in those ages the strength of armies. It may be their wildernesses were less desert,

and

and that they were watered by more ſtreams, the courſe of which have, perhaps, been turned by time, or other cauſes. If this be ſo, the tribes, that approach their borders, may now have been driven to a much greater diſtance from each other by theſe deſerts, their burning ſands, and the want of ſubſiſtence, which would no longer permit their being traverſed with their former facility.

Independent of ſuch natural effects, the conſequence of thoſe revolutions to which time daily ſubjects the earth, the changes that the minds and manners of men are likewiſe liable to muſt neceſſarily have influenced their intercourſe with each other, and the commerce of nations. The progreſs which navigation made, in the fourteenth and fifteenth centuries, muſt have affected the commerce of Africa, and have inſenſibly attracted it from the centre toward the ſea coaſt, on the weſt, which approaches the equator, and where the French, Portugueſe, Dutch, and Engliſh, each emulative of the other, have ſucceſſively formed eſtabliſhments.

The

The great rivers of Africa, which empty themſelves in theſe ſeas, united its utmoſt boundaries, and the ports of Europe then received* gold duſt, ivory, ambergreaſe, Guinea pepper, and other productions, of inland Africa; the excluſive enjoyment of which had, till then, been confined to the bordering nations, and were to them become objects of luxury. The firſt ſucceſs of this diſcovery excited the ambition of Europe, which did not then foreſee thoſe diviſions and ills that would thence reſult. The negroes, however, at the ſight of our ſhips, had a foreboding of their deſtiny; they durſt not enter, fearing the white men, whom, till then, they had utterly unknown; they imagined they beheld their maſters, and not their friends; but the inſinuating affability of the Normans, and

* We read, in La Martiniere, that the firſt expeditions were undertaken to the coaſt of Guinea in 1364 by the adventurers of Dieppe, who, at that time, had the utmoſt ſucceſs till the year 1410, when the civil wars of France brought this riſing commerce into neglect. The Portugueſe, then maſters of the Cape de Verd Iſlands, formed ſettlements on the Gold coaſt.

the

the trifling prefents they beftowed, gained
their confidence.

Wretched nations, how might you fuf-
pect, how might you dread thefe demon-
ftrations of friendſhip, and the toys with
which your ignorance was dazzled, were
the pledges of approaching flavery!
Scarcely was the new world difcovered before it was depopulated by the falfe and
ferocious politics of its conquerors. Negroes were tranfported thither in the beginning of the fixteenth century, and the enu-
meration of all thofe who, from that
time to this, have there been held in flavery, is indeed fearful. It feems poffible
that we muft one day carry back the remains of thefe nations to repeople the deferts of Africa, when the avarice of Europeans fhall have made them wholly defolate. I muft intreat pardon for thefe re-
flections; they have led me fomewhat
from my fubject.

After the deftruction of Carthage and
Rome, the Moors, having had no commercial intercourfe with Europe till to-

ward

ward the fourteenth century, muſt have confined their trade to the more central nations of Africa, with whom they reſpectively interchanged their products. There they probably vended their merchandiſe of woollen ſtuffs, ſheep ſkins *, cloth, corn, ſalt, and dried fruits.

In exchange for theſe, which were produced by labour only, and the conſumption of which was, perhaps, very great, they obtained gold duſt, ivory, Guinea pepper, and ſlaves. Such, it appears to me, muſt have been the firſt ſource of the wealth of the Empire of Morocco. The Moors on the confines of Africa might ſtill poſſeſs nearly the ſame reſources, had they the ſame facility of communication. Thoſe of Morocco, whoſe ſituation is moſt central, have, perhaps, profited the leaſt by them during the three laſt centuries, either by the fre-

---

* Sheep ſkins, unſheared, ſerve as mattreſſes, and to ſit on among theſe people ; and we may obſerve that, in the interior parts of Africa, the ſheep have hair inſtead of wool, while the men have wool inſtead of hair on their heads.

quency

quency of revolutions which their empire has undergone, or because their despotic government has so entirely shackled trade and industry. The small degree of barter which the people still maintain with Tombut, and the countries nearer to the Niger, give a colour of truth to my conjectures concerning the commerce of these nations in ancient times, and of which the modern Moors have no remembrance.

The inhabitants of Tunis and Tripoli, who have a different kind of government, gain more advantage by their intercourse with the people bordering on the Niger. They also occasionally make voyages into Egypt, to Asia, and Constantinople, whither they carry negroes, male and female; while the Moors of Morocco scarcely obtain slaves sufficient for their own service.

From these, or similar suppositions, we may obtain some ideas concerning the original source of the great wealth formerly found among the Moors. We shall see, in a future chapter, what is the present commercial intercourse between the empire of Morocco and the nations of Europe.

CHAP.

C H A P.   VIII.

Of the Inhabitants of Morocco.

THE inhabitants of the Empire of Morocco, known by the name of Moors, are a mixture of Arabian and African nations, formed into tribes; with the origin of whom we are but imperfectly acquainted. These tribes, each strangers to the other, and ever divided by traditional hatred or prejudice, seldom mingle *. It seems probable that most of the *casts*, who occupy the provinces of Morocco, have been repulsed from the eastern to the western Africa, during those different revolutions by which this part of the world has been agitated; that they have followed the standard of their chiefs, whose names they

---

* Some have imagined they perceived among these people, notwithstanding the intervention of ages, those family aversions which were remarkable among the people of Canaan, to whom the Moors appear to have owed their origin.

I 2　　　　　　　have

have preserved ; and that by these they, as well as the countries they inhabit, are distinguished. At present these tribes are called Cafiles, or Cabiles, from the Arabic word Kobeila ; and they are so numerous that it is impossible to have a knowledge of them all. In the northern provinces are enumerated *Beni-Garir, Beni-Guernid, Beni-Manfor, Beni-Oriegan, Beni-Chelid, Beni-Jufeph, Beni-Zaruol, Beni-Razin, Beni-Gebara, Beni-Bufeibet, Beni-Gualid, Beni-Yeder, Beni-Gueiaghel, Beni-Guafeval, Beni-Guamud,* &c. ; toward the east are, *Beni-Soyd, Beni-Teufin, Beni-Ieffetin, Beni-Buhalel, Beni-Telid, Beni-Soffian, Beni-Becil, Beni-Zequer,* &c.; and still farther to the south, those of *Beni-Fonfecara, Beni-Aros, Beni-Haffen, Beni-Mager, Beni-Bafil, Beni-Seba,* with an infinite number of others *. The people who depend on Algiers, Tunis, and Tripoli, are in like manner di-

* We must observe, that the word *Ben*, that is to say, Son, is usually employed to signify family descendants ; thus, *Beni-Haffen* and *Beni-Jufeph* consequently signify the children, or descendants, of Haffen and of Joseph. The Moors, as a more extensive generic term, call men *Ben-Adam* ; that is, the descendants or sons of Adam.

vided

vided into an infinite number of thefe tribes, who all are fo ancient that they themfelves have not the leaft idea of their origin.

We fhould divide the different tribes that people this empire into two principal claffes, that is to fay, the Brebes and the Moors. I fhall not dwell upon the fignification of the name Brebes, which the mountaineers have acquired and preferved; conjectures only can be formed on the fubject, the incertitude concerning the origin of thefe people, and the epocha of their firft fettlements, being confidered.

The Brebes, as well as the Moors, no doubt, adopted the Mahometan religion, analogous as it was to their manners and chief cuftoms, on the firft invafion of the Arabs; but they are ignorant, and little faithful to its precepts, except to that which infpires them with a hatred for other religions. Mahometanifm has not effaced the ancient habits and prejudices of thefe people, for they eat fwine's flefh, and, in thofe places where there are vineyards, drink wine; and

good

good reaſon why, ſay they, we make it our-
ſelves. In the ſouthern parts of Mount
Atlas they put it into earthen jars the better to preſerve it, and into barrels made
from the trunks of hollow trees, the but-
ends of which they ſpread over with pitch,
keep it in caverns, and even in water. In
the province of Rif, toward the north,
they give it a ſlight boiling, which deprives it of its fumes, and makes it leſs
intoxicating ; they, perhaps, alſo think,
that this renders it cogenial to the ſpirit of
the Koran,

Buried in their mountains, the Brebes
maintain their reſentment againſt the
Moors, whom, confounding them with the
Arabs, they regard as uſurpers. In theſe
aſylums they contract a ferocity of character, and ſtrength of body, which render
them more proper for war and labour than
the Moors of the plain in general are ; the
independence they profeſs imparts more of
character to their countenance ; but it is
neceſſary to have lived long among theſe
nations to perceive the difference. Subjected to the Emperors of Morocco by re-

. ligious

ligious prejudices, they shake off his authority whenever they think proper, and, intrenched as they are in their mountains, to attack and vanquish them are difficult.

The Brebes have a language of their own, and never marry but among each other. They have tribes or Cafiles among them who are exceedingly powerful, both by their number and courage. Such are those of *Gomera* on the borders of Rif, of *Gayroan* toward Fez, of *Timoor* extending along mount Atlas from Mequinez to Tedla, of *Shavoya* from Tedla to Duquella, and of *Mifhhoya* from Morocco to the south. The Emperor of Morocco keeps the children of the chiefs of these tribes at court as hostages for their fidelity.

The Brebes have no distinction of dress; they are always clothed in woolen like the Moors, and, though they inhabit the mountains, seldom wear caps. These mountaineers, as well as their wives, have exceedingly fine teeth, and shew signs of vigour, which distinguish them from the other tribes. It is common for them to

hunt

hunt lions and tigers, and the very mothers have a custom of decorating their children with a tiger's claw, or the remnant of a lion's hide on the head, thinking that by this means they acquire strength and courage. The same kind of superstition, no doubt, occasions young wives to give their husbands these sort of amulets. The Brebes and the Shellu having a language common to themselves, and unknown to the Moors, must both have had the same origin, notwithstanding the difference there is in their mode of life. The Shellu live on the frontiers of the empire toward the south ; their population is by no means so great as that of the Brebes, nor are they so ferocious ; they do not marry with other tribes ; and, though they practise many superstitious rites, they are faithful observers of their religion.

After the Brebes, who are considerably populous, I shall speak of the Moors, the greatest number of whom are extended over the country, and the remainder inhabit the cities.

The

The former, that is, the Moors of the country, live in tents, and have fresh encampments every year to give rest to the land, and obtain fresh pasturage; but they are not allowed to remove, without having first informed their governor. Like the ancient Arabs, they are entirely addicted to a country life. Their encampments, which they call Douhars, composed of numerous tents, form a crescent, somewhat narrowed toward the end, or else are erected in two parallel lines; and their flocks and herds returning from pasture occupy the centre. They sometimes close the entrance of the Douhars with thorn faggots, but set no other guards than a number of dogs, which bark unceasingly at the approach of a stranger. Each Douhar has its chief, who is subordinate to a still superior officer, appointed to superintend and govern a number of these encampments; and many of these lesser divisions are again reunited under the government of a Bashaw; some of whom have a thousand Douhars under their command.

The tents of the Moors are somewhat of a conic

a conic form, are feldom more than eight or ten feet high in the centre, and from twenty to five and twenty in length. Like thofe of the remoteft antiquity, their figure is that of a fhip overfet, the keel of which is only feen. Thefe tents are made of twine, compofed of goat's hair, camel's wool, and the leaves of the wild palm, fo that they keep out water; but, being black, they produce a difagreeable effect at a diftant view.

The Moors in camp live in the utmoft fimplicity, and prefent a faithful picture of the earth's inhabitants in the firft ages. Education, the temperance of the climate, and the rigour of the government, diminifh the wants of thefe people, who find in their own provinces, and the milk and wool of their flocks, every thing neceffary for their food and cloathing. It is their cuftom to have feveral wives, a luxury much lefs felt among people who have few wants than among thofe who have many; it is even advantageous to œconomy, the woman having charge of all domeftic affairs. Beneath their ill-fecured tents they are employed in milking their cows to fupply

their

their daily wants, and, when the milk is in abundance, they make butter. They sort and sift their wheat and barley, gather vegetables, and daily grind flour with a mill composed of two round stones, eighteen inches in diameter; in the upper one of which a handel is fixed while it turns on an axle, which projects from that beneath. They daily make bread, which they bake well, or ill, as it happens, between two earthern plates, and very often on the ground heated by fire.

Their common food is Cooscoofoo, a paste made of flour in the form of small grains, in the manner of Italian pastes. This Cooscoofoo they dress by the vapour of broth in a round dish, with holes like a colander, and that is fixed in the kettle in which they boil their meat. The Cooscoofoo, contained in this deep plate, or colander, is slowly softened, and prepared by the vapour of the broth, with which they take care to moisten it occasionally.

Simple as this food is, it is very nourishing, and also very agreeable, when those

habi-

habitual prejudices are overcome which each nation has for its own cuſtoms, and which cannot be eradicated but by an intercourſe with other nations. The common people eat their Cooscoofoo with milk or butter indifferently; but thoſe more at their eaſe, as the governors of provinces, or their lieutenants, who live in the centre of their encampments, have it dreſſed by a rich broth made with mutton, poultry, and pigeons, or hedge-hogs, and mix it afterward with freſh butter.

Theſe officers receive ſtrangers in their camps with like cordiality to that with which the gueſts of Jacob and Laban were received. They kill a ſheep on their arrival, which they immediately put to the ſpit, and, if they have not a ſpit ready, a wooden one is made; when roaſted by a very quick fire, and ſerved up in a wooden platter, their mutton looks and eats exceedingly well. I have often been preſent at ſimilar repaſts, the ſimplicity of which I reſpected. I imagined myſelf in a dream, and tranſported under the tents of the Patriarchs.

The

The employment of the women is also to prepare their wool, spin, and weave in looms hung lengthways in their tents*. These looms are formed by a list of an ell and a half long, to which the threads of the warp are fixed at one end, and at the other on a roller of equal length; the weight of which, being suspended, keeps them stretched. The threads of the warp are so hung as to be readily intersected. Instead of shuttles, the women pass the thread of the woof through the warp with their fingers, and with an iron comb, having a handle, press the woof to give a body to their cloth. Each piece, of about five ells long, and an ell and a half wide, is called a *haick*; it receives neither dressing milling nor dying, but is immediately fit for use; it is the constant dress of the Moors of the country, is without seam, and incapable of varying according to the caprices of fashion. When dirty, it is

* These looms are used in the country, but the looms of the town weavers are like ours. Each individual buys spun worsted at the market, and has it wove according to his own fancy.

washed;

wafhed; the Moor is wrapped up in it day and night, and this haick is the living model of the drapery of the ancients.

The country Moors wear only their woollen ftuffs, without fhirts or drawers, linen among thefe nations being an article of luxury known only to the court and city. The wardrobe of a country Moor, who is in eafy circumftances, confifts in a haick for fummer, another for winter, a cape, a red cap, and a pair of flippers. The common people, both of country and town, wear a kind of tunic of white grey, or mixed woollen cloth, which defcends half way down the leg, with large fleeves and a cape, much refembling the drefs of the Carthufian friars.

The country women likewife wear only a haick tied round their waift, the folds of which, covering the neck and fhoulders, are faftened by filver clafps. The finery of which the country women are moft defirous are large ear-rings, made in tho fhape of a crefcent, or filver rings, with bracelets and rings for the fmall of the leg.
Thefe

These they wear, amidst all their employments, lefs from vanity than becaufe they
know not the ufe of drawers, or chefts, in
which to lay them up. They alfo wear
necklaces of fmall-coloured glafs beads,
or clove grains ftrung on a filken thread.

Befide thefe embellifhments, the country women, to make themfelves more beautiful, paint the fkin of their face, neck,
bofom, and almoft of their whole body,
with the forms of flowers and ornaments.
Thefe impreffions are made with models,
in which are the points of needles that
flightly rafe the fkin, under which a blue
colour is inferted, or gunpowder pulve-
rized, which is never effaced. The cuf-
tom·is exceedingly ancient, and has been
common to numerous nations in Tartary,
Afia, the fouthern parts of Europe, and,
perhaps, over the whole earth. It is not,
however, general to all the Moorifh tribes,
the women of fome of which bear on the
forehead, or on the chin, a crofs impearled
at the four ends, or elfe the fame crofs as
if pendent from a chain, the figur: of
which, traced round the neck, defcends to
the

the bosom. These tribes are probably descendants of those who formerly were subjected to the Christians of Africa, and who, to avoid paying taxes like the Moors, thus imprinted crosses upon their skins that they might pass for Christian. This custom, which originally might serve to distinguish tribes by their religion, or from each other, afterward became a mode of decoration, that was habitually retained, after all remembrance of its origin was effaced *.

The country Moors regard their wives less as companions than as slaves, destined to labour ; tilling the ground excepted, they have the care of every thing ; and I may add, to the disgrace of humanity, that in certain poor parts women are seen with a mule, an ass, or some other animal, drawing the plough. When the Moors remove their Douhars, or encampments, the men, all seated on the ground in a circle,

* I had the curiosity to make all possible inquiries concerning the casts who follow this custom, and find they came originally from the neighbourhood of Tunis ; which circumstance seems to justify my conjectures.

with

with their elbows on their knees, converfe together, while the women take down the tents, pack up the effects, and load their camels, or oxen; the old afterward carry bundles, and the young their children upon their backs in blankets tied round the waift. In the fouthern parts the women are alfo obliged to look after the horfes, clean, faddle, and bridle them, while the hufband, always defpotic in thefe climates, commands, and feems only born to be obeyed.

The country women walk unveiled; their fkin is tanned, nor can they make abfolute pretenfions to beauty. In fome places, however, they paint their cheeks, and every where ftain their hair, their feet, and their finger-ends, with an herb called henna, which produces a deep faffron colour. This muft have been an ancient cuftom among the nations of Afia. Abu-Beker ftained his eyebrows and beard of the fame colour, and he has been imitated by many of his fucceffors. A reverence for religion might have introduced the cuftom, which the women afterwards

Vol. I.   K   made

made ornamental. It may, however, seem
more probable that the custom of paint-
ing the beard and hair, of plucking it up
by the roots, and shaving the head in warm
countries, first originated in cleanliness, for
the same reason as combs are used in those
countries where the hair is worn.

The marriage ceremonies of the Moors,
who live in tents, much resemble those of
the cities ; a description of which will be
seen in its place. The nuptials of the
Douhar are in general more gay and splendid, and they carefully invite passing strangers, that they may contribute to the expence of the festival ; and in this they are
more interested than hospitable.

The tribes dispersed over the country
usually confine their marriages each within
itself, seldom intermarrying with other
tribes. They are always embroiled by
their prejudices, which descend from generation to generation, or which, feebly slum-
bering, awake if a camel happen to be lost,
or on the least dispute concerning pasturage,
or wells of water. Intermarriages among
these

thefe tribes, far from producing harmony, have often given birth to fcenes fo tragical, as fcarcely to be believed among other nations; fuch as men murdered by their wives, or women flaughtered by their hufbands, to revenge national quarrels between their different tribes.

Their children, however numerous, are no incumbrance to the parent, for, as foon as able, they are all put to work; they keep the flocks, carry wood, affift in tilling the ground, and gathering the harveft. In the evening, when they return from their day's labour, all the children of the Douhar affemble in a common tent, where the Iman, who himfelf can fcarcely fpell, teaches them to read fome leffous in the Koran, tranfcibed on boards, and inftructs them in their religion by the light of a fire made of ftraw, under-wood, and cow-dung, dried in the fun. The heat is moft felt in the inland parts of the country, and there children, of both fexes, often run naked till they are nine or ten years old.

There

There are no inns or afylums for travellers, except in thefe Douhars, which are fcattered over the country, and always near fome rivulet or well. There is a tent for the reception of thofe travellers who do not carry any with them. Here they find poultry, milk, eggs, and forage for their horfes. Inftead of wood, they commonly burn fun-dried cow dung, which, mingled with charcoal that muft be brought with them, makes a very ardent fire. The abundance of falts found in hot countries give this cow dung a body, which it has not in northern climates*. There is a guard placed round the tents of travellers to prevent accidents, efpecially when they happen to be Europeans, becaufe that the opinion the Moors have, of their riches might tempt their avidity, they being naturally thievifh.

Their laws, for the prefervation of travellers on the road, are well adapted to the

* That of the month of May is preferred in fome places, which, on unprejudiced examination, will be found to be a decoction of herbs and flowers, when moft in feafon; and an extract of this is given to fick people as a kind of tea.

cha-

character of the Moors, and their mode of living. The Douhar is refponfible for all thefts committed in its neighbourhood, or in fight of its encampment; they are not only obliged to pay the lofs, but the Emperor takes occafion to exact from them contributions proportioned to their riches*. To foften the rigour of the law, the Douhars are accountable only for thefts committed by day, and not for thofe which happen after fun-fet; they being not able to fee or prevent them. Travellers therefore only begin their journies at fun-rife, and neceffarily reft before twilight +.

To facilitate barter, there is a public market held every day throughout the

* Hiftory informs us, that among the Egyptians, when any perfon was found murdered, drowned, or dead, by any accident whatever, the neareft city was obliged to embalm the dead, and furnifh a magnificent funeral. This law, characteriftic of the religion of the Egyptians, and their care of the dead, might alfo have a political retrofpect to the fafety of travellers.

+ This appears to be a wholefome law in any country, and is not confined to ignorant or barbarous nations, fince it is a well-known law of England. T.

country,

country, Friday excepted, which is the day of prayer, in various quarters of each province. Here the neighbouring Moors assemble to buy and sell cattle, corn, vegetables, dried fruits, carpets, haicks, and all the productions of their country. This market, called Soc in Arabic, resembles the village fairs of France; the motion of the people going and coming to market give a juster idea of the manner in which the Moors live than any to be found in their towns. The Alcaids, who command in the neighbourhood, always repair to the markets with soldiers to keep the peace, it being common enough at such places to see those seeds of rancour, which different tribes preserve against each other, burst forth. The breaking up of the Soc, as it is called in Arabic, when these quarrels happen, gives disquietude to the government, because it always betokens seditious tumults. On the outside of the market there are usually shews, buffoons, singers, dancers, and merry Andrews, who make monkies dance for the amusement of gapers. On one side is the place of the barbers, or surgeons, to whom they bring

their

their sick to be cured of strains, disloca-
tions, or other accidents. I have often,
while travelling, been amused by these
sights, and have seen men and young women, who have been troubled with swel-
lings, head aches, or other humours, arising from undue circulation, submit to
slight, regular scarifications, the men on
the head, and the women round it, very
near the hair, or sometimes on the shoulders, arms, or legs. Their regularity prevents such scars disfiguring the skin, though
they do not soon disappear. This treatment would be incompatible with the
customs and education of Europe, where
health is often sacrificed to ease and
beauty. Without giving a decided preference to this or that custom, it seems rational that rheumatic pains in the shoulders,
or other parts, might be more radically
cured by such light incisions than by per-
spiration, or means which may extend the
humours, or inclose them instead of cure.
This is mere supposition, which will be
pardoned me, as I do not pretend to be
sufficiently instructed in physic to speak
with any certainty.

K 4

The

The Moors of the country have no knowledge of the customs of other nations : at sight of them we imagine we see men as they were before, and immediately after, the flood. Confined to a rural life, they are occupied concerning their grounds and harvests, and pass the remainder of their time in rest. Habituated to fatigue, there are many of them who serve as couriers, and who, notwithstanding their avarice, are tolerably faithful and exact.

It is difficult to conceive the ignorance of these country Moors. I have seen one waiting for his dispatches in a room where there was a glass, and, his eye being caught by his own reflected figure, he imagined it was another courier waiting for dispatches in another apartment. Having asked to what place that courier was going, and being told to Mogodor, O then, said he, we will travel together. He made the proposition to his supposed comrade, who, like him, gesticulated in the glass, but gave no answer : he began to be angry till he saw another person reflected by the same glass enter the room. Astonished at his error,

ror, he could scarcely be perfuaded, in fpite of feeing and feeling, that it was pof-fible to fee one's felf, faid he, through a ftone *.

In a houfe where I lodged, at Saffi, came two mountaineers, whofe curiofity led them to examine Europeans in their own apartments. After having gone over the whole houfe, they knew not how to defcend the ftairs they had come up, which, to be fure, were rather fteep. At laft they fat themfelves down on the firft ftep, and then, fupporting themfelves by their hands and feet, fhuffled from one to the other. It is not, however, aftonifhing that a mountaineer, though accuftomed to afcend high and rugged rocks, fhould find it difficult to go up or down ftairs, when we confider that their regularily and exact meafurement require a kind of habitude, or that he is as much embarraffed, on fuch an occafion, as we fhould be at running, with agility equal to his, up and down moun-tains.

* The Moors have no words to exprefs mirrors, or glafs windows, becaufe they have not the things.

Not

[138]

Not one among thefe people are at firft
fufceptible of receiving ideas from pain-
tings or drawings ; they only perceive a
confufion of colours in a picture without
their order or defign, and in engravings
a mixture of lines : application only can
make them fenfible of what they mean.
In this they refemble a blind man reftored
to fight, who fhould be fhewn a picture
immediately after the operation of the ca-
taract *.

* The truth of this obfervation is fufficiently proved by
the flowers, with which children comprehend the pictures
in their books. T.

CHAP.

C H A P. IX.

Manners of the Inhabitants of the Cities.

THE Moors of the cities differ but little from those who live under tents, being of the same origin, except that they have somewhat more urbanity, and that their appearance bespeaks them more wealthy. The citizens, however, are vain of being thought to have no relation to the country Moors; but the revolutions and convulsions, which the empire has undergone, overthrow all such opinions, and will not admit us to suppose any distinction between the Moors of the country and those of the cities. The assertion of some writers, who call the inhabitants of the cities Arabs and those of the country Moors, appears to me totally ill founded: the former may indeed have given credit to this opinion; but it is the more ridiculous because they themselves call the Moors of the country Alarbes, which is

but

but a corruption of the word Arabs. The Brebes and the Shellu, or Chellu, of all the inhabitants of Mauritania, seem to me to be the only ones who have not mingled; but, among the inhabitants of the cities and plains, an Arab can no more be diftinguifhed from a Moor than a Frank could from a Roman, or a Gaul from a Goth, pofterior to that influx of different nations who expelled and fucceeded each other after the fall of the Roman empire.

The only probable conjecture, which could juftify fuch an affertion, is that of thofe who believe the Arabs inhabit the cities becaufe that conquerors have the right or the liberty to chufe. Moft of the cities of the empire are more ancient than the invafions of the Arabs, who themfelves were accuftomed to live in tents; and it even feems apparent that the firft cities were built by the colonies of the Carthaginians, and that the cuftom of living in and increafing them did not, till long time after, become general, in proportion as the Moors had a greater intercourfe with the Mahometans of Spain, and more

parti-

particularly after the expulfion of the latter. It may be, that, having enjoyed more
luxury and wealth, the Mahometans of
Spain might prefer to live in the cities, in
which are ftill found various families who
vaunt of being defcendants of the Mahometans of Andalufia, and who ftill preferve the family names : fuch as Bargas,
Perez *, Medina, Moreno, Marino, Tole-
dano, Probe, Marfil, Escalant, Aragon,
Lovarez, Valenciano, Meudon, Santiago-
Barciano, and others. Some even have
preferved their titles of their eftates at
Grenada, Cordova, Seville, &c. and perhaps alfo the very key of their houfe. I
do not think that the difference, which is
difcernible between the Moors of the city
and thofe of the country, can have a much

* Voltaire, in his effay on the Manners of Nations,
Chap. CLXII. has fuppofed that Perez, who was Admiral
under Muley Ifhmael, was a Spanifh renegado: but Perez
was a family name among the Moors of Andalufia. It
ought to be remarked that the Spanifh names, which the
Moors and Jews who came from Spain have preferved, are
not always family names, but the names of patrons, or of
adoption, which indicate the ftate of dependence in which
thefe Moors or Jews were to the houfe whofe name they
bear.

earlier

earlier date; nor will this any way change
or affect their origin, but will confirm my
suppositions; for whoever reads the revolution of the Mahometans of Spain,
will find that these same Mahometans
were also a mixture of Arab-Moors,
whom it was impossible to distinguish.

The houses of the Moors have in general few conveniences, their wants not
having been multiplied by whim. These
houses seldom have more than one story,
most of them are square, have a court in
the centre that is often ornamented with
pillars; which court gives light and entrance to four principal chambers that
form the four faces of the square. They
have no windows, nor is the light ever
admitted from the street. Each chamber
has a large pair of folding doors, in one of
which is a kind of wicket; and these doors
also serve to admit light into the apartments. The houses are seldom more than
sixteen feet high, are in no danger from the
wind, and are tolerably cool in summer.

The furniture of the Moors is sufficient
for

for ufe; they are unacquainted with tapef-
try, and their moveables chiefly confift in
mats, carpets, fome chairs, a cheft, a table,
and a bed, which runs lengthways the
depth of the chamber, and is concealed by
a curtain. The houfes have all terraces on
the roof, which are formed of earth and
mortar, about fifteen inches thick.

The inhabitants of the cities, from œconomy and defire of concord, have only one
wife, and very rarely increafe the number.
They have female negroes, whom they
may take as concubines; but their averfion for their colour, which the white people have every where configned to oppreffion, keep them chafte, as they do not wifh
to have mulatto children. It muft be
owned that the Moors of the cities, commonly enough, have intercourfe of gallantry with the wives of the Jews, who, in
general, are handfome; and their hufbands,
enjoying by this means a more immediate
protection, are complaifant in proportion
to the danger and percarioufnefs of their
fituation.

The

The Moors have little variety in their drefs; the rigour of government is contrary to the caprices of fafhion, and deprefles every fpecies of luxury. Unable to preferve their riches, except by concealing them, they are very careful not to bear any appearance of wealth which may awaken the avidity of government. " Thou muft needs be very rich," faid a Sharif to a Moor, who, to preferve his garden walls, had them whitewafhed.

We have already feen what is the drefs of the Moors who live in tents; the wardrobe of the inhabitants of cities is but little different; they, like the former, have a haick, and a hood more or lefs fine, and have alfo a hood of coarfe European cloth, of dark blue, for the winter. What farther diftinguifhes them from the country Moors is that they wear a fhirt and linen drawers, and an upper garment of cotton, in fummer, and of cloth in winter, which they call a caftan. The white or blue hood, the purpofe of which feems to be to guard againft bad weather, and which is called Bernus, is likewife a ceremonial

part

part of dreſs ; without which, together
with ſabre and ganger *, or canjer, worn
in a bandelier, perſons of condition never
appear before the Emperor.

The nature of the government conſi-
dered, it ſhould ſeem probable that ſubjects
preſent themſelves before their monarch in
a dreſs like this, which is that of a man
prepared to travel, only becauſe they muſt
be always ready to receive and execute
their maſter's orders. Some of the inhabitants of the capital cities, and of thoſe
who are more iinmediately about the perſon of the Emperor, wear over their dreſs
a cambric ſhirt, like thoſe which the
French ladies have lately among the ever-
laſting changes of faſhion adopted, tied
round their bodies with a ſaſh ; they alſo
put up the hood of their haick;

Obliged as they are to conceal their
riches, the Moors wear no jewels ; very

* The ganger is a dagger, ſometimes ſtraight, and ſometimes bent, about a foot in length, and two inches wide;

few have fo much as a ring, a watch, or a filver fnuff-box. Snuff has not, indeed, been introduced into Morocco till within fome fifteen or twenty years. They frequently carry a rofary in their hand, but without annexing any ideas of devotion to the practice, although they ufe it to recite the name of God a certain number of times in the day. After thefe momentary prayers they play with their rofary, much the fame as the European ladies do with their fans *. The Europeans received the ufe of the rofary from the people of Afia, or perhaps, from the Arabs. As few of thefe were fufficiently learned to read the Koran, they fupplied this defect by pronouncing the Creator's name a certain number of times in the day. A fimilar motive, probably, firft made it adopted in the prayers of Catholics.

* The Oriental Mahometans have the fame cuftom, except that they feek for a degree of elegance and fafhion unknown to the Moors.

CHAP.

CHAP. X.

Dress and Manners of the Women of the Cities in Morocco.

THE Moorish women seldom leave the house, and always veiled. The old very carefully hide their faces, but the young and handsome are somewhat more indulgent ; that is to say, toward foreigners, for they are exceedingly cautious with the Moors. Being veiled, their husbands do not know them in the street, and it is even impolite to endeavour to see the faces of the women who pass, so different are the manners and customs of nations.

There are very fine women found among the Moors, especially up the country ; those of the northern parts by no means possess the same degree of grace and beauty : it would be difficult to give any physical reason for this difference : transfmigrations

have

have continually happened among the different tribes of the empire, of whofe defcent and origin we are ignorant. Thefe tribes marry only with thofe of their own tribe, by which they are preferved without intermixture.

As females in warm countries fooner arrive at puberty, they are alfo fooner old; and this, perhaps, may be the reafon why polygamy has been generally adopted in fuch climates. Women there fooner lofe the charms of youth, while men ftill preferve their paffions, and the powers of nature.

The Moorifh women are not in general very referved. Climate has a vaft influence on the temperament of the body; and licentioufnefs is there more general and lefs reftrained, though, as in other places, its diforderly pleafures incur its attendant pains; not but that the difeafe attending illicit amours is lefs poifonous, and flower in its operations, among the Moors, than in Europe, becaufe of the heat of the climate,

mate, and the great temperance of their mode of living.

The women of the south are in general the handsomest, and are said to be so reserved, or. so guarded, that their very relations do not enter their houses, nor their tents. Yet, such is the contradictory custom of nations, that, there are tribes, in these same provinces, among whom it is held to be an act of hospitality to present a woman to a traveller. It may be, there are women who dedicate themselves to this species of devotion as to an act of benevolence, for it is impossible to describe all the varieties of opinion among men, or the whims to which the human fancy is subject.

The Moorish women who live in cities are, as in other nations, more addicted to shew and finery in dress than those of the country ; but, as they generally leave the house only one day in the week, they seldom dress themselves. Not allowed to receive male visitors, they remain in their houses employed in their families, and so totally in dishabille that they often wear only a fhift, and another coarfer fhift over the firft, tied round their waift, with their hair plaited, and fometimes with, though often without, a cap.

When dreffed they wear an ample and fine linen fhift, the bofom embroidered in gold ; a rich caftan of cloth, ftuff, or velvet, worked in gold ; and one or two folds of gauze, ftreaked with gold and filk, round the head, and tied behind fo as that the fringes, intermingled with their treffes, defcend as low as the waift ; to which fome add a ribband of about two inches broad, worked in gold or pearls, that encircles the forehead in form of a diadem: Their caftan is bound round their waift by a crimfon velvet girdle, embroidered in gold with a buckle of gold or filver, or elfe a girdle of tamboured ftuff, manufactured at Fez.

The women have yellow flippers, and a cuftom of wearing a kind of ftocking of fine cloth fomewhat large, which is tied below the knee and at the ancle, over which it falls in folds. This ftocking is

lefs

lefs calculated to fhew what we call a handfome leg, than to make it appear thick ; for to be fat is one of the rules of beauty among the Moorifh women. To obtain this quality, they take infinite pains, feed when they become nubile on a diet fomewhat like forced-meat balls, a certain quantity of which is given them daily ; and, in fine, the fame care is taken among the Moors to fatten young women, as is in Europe to fatten fowls. The reafon of a cuftom like this may be found in the nature of the climate, and the quality of the aliments, which make the people naturally meager. Our flender waifts and fine-turned ancles would be imperfections in this part of Africa, and, perhaps, over all that quarter of the globe ; fo great is the contraft of tafte, and fo various the prejudices of nations,

The Moors prefent their wives with jewels of gold, filver, or pearl, but very few wear precious ftones ; this is a luxury, of which they have little knowledge. They have rings in filver or gold, alfo ear-rings in the form of a crefcent, five inches

in

in circumference, and as thick as the end
of the little finger. They firſt pierce
their ears, and introduce a ſmall roll of
paper, which they daily increaſe in thickneſs, till at length they inſert the kernel
of the date, which is equal in ſize to the
ear-ring.

They wear bracelets in gold and ſolid
ſilver, and ſilver rings at the bottom of their
legs, ſome of which I have ſeen conſiderably
heavy. There are youths among the Sharifs, or nobility, who wear at one ear a
gold or ſilver ring from four to five inches
in circumference ; but this cuſtom is more
general among the black ſlaves belonging
to people of ſome diſtinction.

All theſe trinkets, which the women
are exceedingly deſirous to obtain, were
originally ſigns of ſlavery, which men, to
render its yoke more ſufferable, have thus
inſenſibly changed to ornaments. Europe
received ſuch tokens of dependence from
Aſia, embelliſhed them with all the riches
of nature, and the decorations of art, till at
length ear-rings and bracelets, firſt worn as
badges

badges of fervitude, are now become the paraphernalia of the empire of beauty.

The ufe of white paint is unknown among the Moorifh women, and that of red but little. It is much more common to fee them dye their eyebrows and eye-lafhes; which dye does not add to the beauty of the countenance, but confiderably to the fire of the eyes. They trace regular figures with henna, of a faffron colour, on their feet, the palm of the hand, and the tip of their fingers.

On their vifiting day they wrap them-felves in a clean fine haick, which comes over the head, and furrounds the face fo as to let them fee without being feen. When they travel they wear ftraw hats to keep off the fun, and in fome parts of the empire the women wear hats on their vifits; which is a fafhion peculiar to the tribes coming from the fouth, who have pre-ferved their cuftoms, for the Moors do not change modes they have once adopted*.

* The hat is common to men and women among the Moors who travel, and the cuftom of wearing it came from Africa

They are in no wife fufceptible of that
continual change of fafhion fo ftudied and
fo rapid in Europe, and which, particularly
in France, is become fo vaft an object,
more burdenfome, perhaps, than ufeful, of
induftry and intercourfe.

Africa to Europe. The Spaniards, becaufe of the heat of
their climate, ftill, as much as they can, wear it flapped, and
have called it Sombrero, or fhady. The French gave it the
name of Chappeau, becaufe it fupplied the ufe of the cape
or hood of their ancient drefs, which they called chapel.

CHAP.

C H A P. XI.

Of the Renegadoes and Jews.

AMONG the Moors and Jews, who together people the empire of Morocco, there is an intermediate clafs of men who, fomewhat like amphibious animals, feem to appertain to two elements. I fpeak of renegadoes, who have renounced Chriftianity to embrace Mahometanifm. Among thefe there are a great number who were originally Jews ; the Moors hold them not in the leaft refpect, and the Jews in ftill lefs, had they power freely to make their averfion known.

Thefe apoftates intermarry only among each other ; and, as in Spain, an old Chriftian carefully avoids beftowing his daughter on one newly converted, fo does a Moor of ancient race imagine his family difgraced,

graced, fhould a renegado become the hufband of his daughter. The families of
apoftate Jews are exceedingly numerous,
and are called Toornadis *. Not having
at any time married with the Moors, they
ftill preferve their ancient characteriftics,
and are known almoft at fight to be the
progeny of thofe who formerly embraced
the Mahometan religion.

The Chriftian renegadoes are but few,
and generally are fugitive peculators of
Spain, or men fallen from power, who, becaufe of their mifconduct, or in defpair,
quit one unfortunate fituation for another,
much more deplorable. Not one among
them but repents of having become a
Moor, or who does not wifh to efcape;
but this is difficult.

To conclude the accouut I have given
of the inhabitants of Morocco, I muft

* From the Spanifh word Tornadizo, which fignifies
one who has changed his religion.

  Covarrubias. *Teforo de la Lengua Caftillana.*

now fpeak of the Jews, who are very populous in the empire. After being profcribed in Spain and Portugal, multitudes of them paffed over to Morocco, and fpread themfelves through the towns and over the country. Judging by the relations they themfelves give, and by the extent of the places affigned them to dwell in, I have no doubt but there were more than thirty thoufand families, of whom at prefent there is fcarcely a refidue of one twelfth ; the remainder either have changed their religion, funk under their fufferings, or fled from the vexations they endured, and the arbitrary taxes and tolls impofed upon them.

The Jews poffefs neither lands nor gardens, nor can they enjoy their fruits in tranquillity ; they muft wear only black, and are obliged, when they pafs near mofques, or through ftreets in which there are fanctuaries, to walk barefoot.

The loweft among the Moors imagines he has a right to illtreat a Jew, nor dares the latter defend himfelf, becaufe the Koran

ran and the Judge are always in favour of the Mahometan. Notwithſtanding this ſtate of oppreſſion, the Jews have many advantages over the Moors ; they better underſtand the ſpirit of trade, they act as agents and brokers, and profit by their own cunning, and the ignorance of the Moors. In their commercial bargains many of them buy up the commodities of the country to ſell again. Some have European correſpondents, and others are mechanics ; ſuch as goldſmiths, tailors, gunſmiths, millers, and maſons. More induſtrious, artful, and better informed than the Moors, the Jews are employed by the Emperor in receiving the cuſtoms, coining the money, and in all affairs and intercourſe which the Monarch has with the European merchants, as well as in all his negotiations with the various European governments.

Thus, though but momentarily employed in the adminiſtration of affairs, they, by their active intrigues, have the power of doing ſome good, and much miſchief; and, ſuch is their cunning, they generally

nerally take care to gain both by the one and the other. Hence, though the Jews are oppressed, they find resources in their industry, and means of consoling themselves for all their indignities.

The wives of the Jews in Morocco are in general well formed, handsome, have good complexions, and exceedingly fine eyes. They are addicted to dress, and their propensity to gallantry is the greater inasmuch as the husbands of the commonality are somewhat more than indulgent. We must not, however, conclude there are not many Jewish families, whose manners are good and exemplary.

As the Jews throughout the empire live distinct and separate from the Moors, they enjoy their religious rites with considerable liberty. Those of Morocco seem even to have multiplied their superstitions by their intercourse with foreign nations, after the destruction of the Jewish empire. Their Rabbins find a remedy for all evils in prayer, and promote, instead of destroying, error. Enjoying those ecclesiastical immu-
nities

nities which are granted them by the law, these doctors live exempt from the national impositions paid by the community; and this exemption increasing, the number of the Rabbins increases, and renders more heavy the load of taxation laid on the laborious, who want sufficient capital to trade; while the Rabbins, fattening upon the public misery, employ themselves in affairs of commerce and gain.

The Jews in the empire of Morocco speak Arabic, and all know the Hebrew, because of the affinity between these two languages, the one of which is derived from the other. Every where else Hebrew is the learned language among the Jews, of which the common people are ignorant, and which is studied only by the Rabbins. The Rabbins, in some parts of Morocco, without understanding the Spanish language, have preserved the habit of translating into that language by reading the Hebrew Bible in Spanish, to which they also accustom their scholars. However extraordinary such efforts, it is ri-

diculous

diculous to fatigue the memory of children with ftudies which can be of no utility *.

The Jews, who, amid all their perfecutions and emigrations, have introduced
their religious rites and ceremonies into all
countries, obferve more fcrupuloufly in
Morocco than in any other kingdom thofe
which were anciently performed at the
death of their kinfinen.   The departure
of life is announced by them with fhrieks
and lamentations, in which hired women
join, and who fing in a kind of meafure, or
rhythmus, at the end of which they clap
their hands ; thus, in cadence, marking the
gradations of their grief. The kinfwomen of
the deceafed tear their hair, beat themfelves,
and join in this lamentable concert, which
is again repeated on the day of interment.
The Jews then obferve fix days of fevere
mourning, during which they go barefoot,

* This paffage is almoft unintelligible, and certainly can
only mean a Spanifh tranflation of the Bible is read at the
fame time with the Hebrew, and that they are both compared, perhaps tranfcribed.   T.

and muſt neither ſhave themſelves, nor
change their clothes.   On the ſeventh day
their former muſical ſhrieks are repeated, as
they likewiſe are on the firſt of the eleventh
month, which is the laſt of mourning.
The women-weepers, at theſe funeral ceremonies, ſing moral ſentences concerning
life and death ; and, when they happen to
be capable of ſinging extempore, they
rhyme and chaunt the praiſes of the de-
ceaſed.

CHAP.

C H A P. XII.

Animals found in the Empire of Morocco.

THE domestic animals found in Morocco are of the same species as those that are native in Europe. The ferocious are peculiar to these climes. I shall speak of the former first.

The Moors are a pastoral people, and their wealth consists in their flocks and herds. These are numerous throughout the empire, and would be much more so were property respected, and might commerce be enjoyed in freedom. The quality of the wool on this coast is generally good, and would even be susceptible of much perfection, were they more careful of their breed of sheep, and in their choice of pasturage. The Moors employ a part of their fleeces in their own clothing and

carpets,

carpets, and fell the refidue to foreign nations. There are few black fheep found
in the empire of Morocco. It is, perhaps,
for this reafon that the clothing of the
Moors is generally white; and, for the
contrary reafon, we fee in Spain whole
diftricts in the country, the people of
which are clothed in grey and dark colours, becaufe that their fheep are more variegated, and that black fheep there are
very numerous.

Oxen are tolerably plentiful in this part
of Africa, but the breed is fmall. The
Englifh, notwithftanding the fhackles
which the Emperor in his policy thinks
proper to lay on the exportation of oxen,
continually obtain fufficient for the maintenance of their garrifon at Gibraltar. The
Moors falt their beef for their home confumption, and thus preferve it from year
to year. Their raw hides form an object
of confiderable importance in their commerce, and are fent in prodigious quantities to Marfeilles.

The

The camel is a part of the wealth of the
Moors. It is an animal that requires little, and labours much. The Moors ufe
them as well as oxen in agriculture, but
more commonly for the carriage of their
products, and other commercial objects,
throughout the empire. The camel is a
docile animal, which is taught to kneel
down that he may be loaded with the
greater facility; he is able to carry from
fix to eight hundred weight, according as
he is more or lefs ftrong: the country
Moors alfo ufe him to travel journies; his
ftep is long and heavy, and his trot infup-
portable to thofe who are not accuftomed
to it; and he often carries a whole family,
with all its luggage. The Caliph Omar
ufed to travel upon a camel, taking with
him his provifions.

Naturalifts no longer hold the erroneous
opinion that the camel places himfelf
back to back with his female to engender.
That animal, tranquil by nature, is reftlefs
when in heat; and, after having tormented
the female, to oblige her to crouch upon
her knees, he himfelf does the fame,

 while,

while, with his frothy tongue, he makes a
very difagreeable humming. The conformation of the part of generation is fuch,
that, ftrangely difproportioned, it forms a
kind of angle, which feems to projeét and
aét by elaftic motions.

The Moors of the country eat camel's
flefh with a good appetite. The tafte of
this meat is infipid, and the broth it makes
has a white tinéture, unpleafing to the
eye. Camel's milk is wholefome, cool,
and light; it is in common ufage in the
fouth; and the fick, whofe lungs are any
way difeafed, drink it medicinally.

This animal is of the utmoft utility in
hot climates and fandy countries. The
fole of his foot is cartilaginous, and becomes
callous, but cannot long endure in thofe
countries that are humid and ftony. The
conformation of his ftomach is fuch that
he can remain feveral days without eating
or drinking. Before he begins his journey, his keeper gives him an abundant
portion of barley, and, as he chews the
cud, he ruminates on this food as he travels,

vels, which lies in his ſtomach as a depoſit, to which he has recourſe when wanted. Water is in like manner preſerved in a receptacle, which nature has prepared, of various bladders, and which is rejected or re-ſwallowed in proportion as he becomes thirſty.

Horſes abound in the empire of Morocco, and are, in general, good ; they are taught to endure fatigue, heat, cold, hunger, and thirſt.　Beautiful horſes are, notwithſtanding, uncommon here; the Moors have not taken the ſame care as the Arabs have done to preſerve and improve their breed.　The Emperor has ſtuds in various provinces, and ſome governors alſo, who are very deſirous of pleaſing him, have the ſame ; but this kind of induſtry is not generally encouraged; the exportation of horſes is prohibited, and the Emperor claims a right of ſelecting the beſt of every thing in kind, which naturally produces negligence in the inhabitants, ſince their cares could anſwer no purpoſes but thoſe of oppreſſion.　The horſes in this part of Africa are broken

while

while very young, and treated with much roughness. They teach them to gallop full speed, and inftantly to ftop fhort, by which they foon are fhook in the fhoulders and lamed, and, when feven years old, are in general no longer fit for ufe.

In the fouthern parts, where the Moors enjoy fome fmall degree of fuperior freedom, becaufe they are not infpected with equal attention, they are more careful in improving their breed of horfes, which are therefore finer in thofe countries. The Moors of thefe provinces feldom ride any but mares; they are fwifter, do not neigh*,

---

* Either the mares of Africa are very different from thofe of Europe, which latter neigh as frequently as horfes, or this is a very ftrange error, into which feveral French writers have fallen. A late very intelligent traveller, M. Volney, fpeaking of the Bedouin Arabs, fays, that the Arab mare is preferable to the horfe, becaufe, among other good qualities which he enumerates, fhe does not neigh *. Yet neither M. Volney, nor the author of the prefent work, M. Chénier, make any diftinction between the mares of Europe and Africa; and it is highly probable they have both taken this opinion upon truft. T.

* Vide *Voyage en Syrie et en Egypte*, par M. C. F. Volney, Tom. I. p. 172.

and

and are better adapted for ſudden attacks among people who are always in agitation becauſe of their diviſions. The mares and their colts are accuſtomed to enter the tents at night; they lie down among the children, and, when they turn, are very careful not to hurt them. This familiar kind of education makes theſe animals contract a vaſt affection for their maſters, by whom they are highly pleaſed to be careſſed.

Mules too are much in uſe among the Moors, who, under the preſent reign, have applied themſelves induſtriouſly to encourage their breed, the exportation of them having been for ſome time permitted *. Theſe animals are in daily uſe to perform journies and carry burdens; they are ſtronger than horſes, do not require the ſame care nor quantity of food, and are more hardy. The Mooriſh cavalry are all mounted on horſes, but private individuals

* Between the years 1765 and 1775 the Engliſh continually purchaſed and tranſported them to America; but an augmentation of the duties to be paid, and the revolution in America, has interrupted this trade.

ride

ride mules in preference; they are very careful in chusing good ones, and accustom them to an amble, which does not fatigue, and which rids much ground. Those of Fez are the finest, and go the best: many of them likewise come from the neighbourhood of Tunis.

Poultry is abundant in the empire of Morocco, but it is of a very indifferent kind. The pigeons are excellent, and some of them very large. Partridges are plentiful, but their flesh has very little taste. Woodcocks are exceedingly scarce; but, in return, snipes are numerous in the season: hares here are generally good, and of the middle size: rabbits are not found, except in the northern part of the empire from Laracha to Tetuan.

The empire of Morocco contains fallow deer, the roebuck, the antelope, with foxes, and numbers of animals, known in Europe; but these are not in general often seen, because they are hunted, or else that wild beasts destroy the breed imperceptibly. Lions and tigers are not uncommon

in some parts of the empire; they haunt
the forests or vallies in the neighbourhood
of rivers. These animals do not often de-
part far from their lairs, unless greatly pro-
voked by hunger; but they always find
prey in the destruction of young boars,
which breed in these forests, or in carrying
off the cows and sheep which come to
graze in the neighbourhood of their haunts.
What are called tigers in this part of Africa
are only leopards; the royal tiger is there
unknown.

The Moors, and more especially those
who inhabit the mountains, willingly go
in chace of lions and tigers, lying in watch
for them with their guns in the neighbourhood of their watering places. The
better to secure themselves, they climb
trees to shoot them as they pass, taking
care to provide themselves with hatchets to
attack the tiger, which runs up trees with
facility. I have known a Moor, of no extraordinary strength, who had himself
killed one-and-twenty lions.

When

When the Moors wish to take the lions alive, they dig deep ditches, where they put meat, having covered the ditch with leaves, scattered over reeds. The lion, attracted by the bait, falls into the ditch, and is caught in snares, or nooses. It is still more common to take them in wooden traps, which close upon them as the lions are stepping over. When the Moors are obliged to encamp, in places where lions make their appearance, they keep lighted fires to drive them off. It has often happened that these animals, approaching the encampments, have carried off mules from their pasture. On a certain occasion one of the negroes of a Princess, who, to avoid working, had gone to a distance from the camp, and was sleeping at his ease, was devoured by a lion.

The Moors of the country relate many tales in confirmation of what has been so often repeated concerning the generosity of this animal. I have been assured that a Brebe, who went to hunt the lion, having proceeded far into a forest, happened to meet with two lions whelps that came to caress him :

him: the hunter ſtopped with the little animals, and, waiting for the coming of the fire, or the dam, took out his breakfaſt, and gave them a part. The lioneſs arrived unperceived by the huntſman, ſo that he had not time, or, perhaps, wanted the courage to take to his gun. After having for ſome-time looked at the man that was thus feaſting her young, the lioneſs went away, and ſoon after returned, bearing with her a ſheep, which ſhe came and laid at the huntſman's feet.

The Brebe, thus become one of the family, took this occaſion of making a good meal, ſkinned the ſheep, made a fire, and roaſted a part, giving the entrails to the young. The lion, in his turn, came alſo, and, as if reſpecting the rights of hoſpitality, ſhewed no tokens whatever of ferocity. Their gueſt the next day, having finiſhed his proviſions, returned, and came to a reſolution never more to kill any of theſe animals, the noble generoſity of which he had ſo fully proved. He ſtroked and careſſed the whelps at taking leave of them, and the dam and the fire accompanied

panied him till he was safely out of the forest.

This animal, which the ancients have called the King of beasts, does not attack men who do not run from him, but look on him without fear; at least, not unless hard driven by hunger. It may be that the temperature of the climate, or the freedom in which they range, may occasion these animals to be less ferocious in Africa than they are in Europe, where they are shut up in dens. The Moors say that, in some provinces, the very women and children will drive them, by only hallooing after them, away from their habitations.

The Emperor of Morocco keeps lions and tigers in open ditches, which are exceedingly deep and vast, as well for state as to send them, by way of present, to the Sovereigns of Europe. The Jews, whose department it is to daily take them their food, ascend and descend their ditches, without the least apprehension, and govern animals so fierce and voracious with a switch. I kept a young tiger some time at

my

my houfe, which had been given me by a governor of one of their provinces. He was put in a great cage, and the fervants played with him familiarly, without ever receiving the leaft injury.

The wild boar, of all the fpecies of ferocious animals found in this empire, is the moft common. The fow has feveral litters in the year, and her young are numerous. They ferve as food for the lion. Whenever the lion difcovers in the foreft the fow and her litter of pigs, he drags himfelf, with his belly on the ground, and defcribes a large circle, leaving only a fmall opening, near which he lies in watch. The fow, wifhing to get away with her young, follows the circle which the lion has defcribed, but does not pafs it, becaufe of the fmell he has left behind, till coming, at length, to the only interval where fhe does not find the fame fetid odour, fhe rufhes precipitately forward, and the lion leaps and feizes on his prey.

There have been examples of boars that have ripped up lions with their tufks;
but

but thefe muft be regarded as particular
cafes and exceptions; and not as a rule
that fhall in any wife make the lion cede
his fuperiority to the boar.

The inhabitants of the country, and
thofe who live among the mountains, eat
the flefh of the boar without fcruple,
though it is forbidden food by the law,
as well as that of the lion. The flefh
of the latter, which appeared to me coarfe
grained and finewy, muft be very tough.
Its fcent is fo ftrong that a dog, to which
I once prefented fome, the moment he had
nofed it, fhrunk back with fear.

BOOK

BOOK II.

Religion — Government — Laws — State of Knowledge — Language — Character — Manners and
Customs.

CHAP. I.

Of the Religion of the Empire of Morocco.

THE religion of the Moors is Mahometanism; observed with the greater rigidity,
or probably increased in bigotry by superstitious practices, because these people may
have preserved ceremonies of their ancient
worship, or introduced such as they may
have received from other nations.

The Moors follow the tradition or sect
of the Iman Abdallah Melek, or Melu,
who was one of the four commentators on

VOL. I.　　　　N　　　　the

the Koran. They hold in equal refpect the works of Abu-Abdallah-Mahomet-Ben-Ifhmael-El-Boccari, who collected and reduced into a fyftematic form the oral traditions of Mahomet.

Africa has produced more reformers and enthufiafts than the other countries where the Mahometan religion has been received. Hence it has happened among the Moors, that numerous fuperftitions have been added, which the ignorance and credulity of the people have confounded with their religion. Although the weftern Mahometans and the Turks have the fame worfhip, in its general acceptation, their practice of it is, in fome refpects, different. Exclufive of the mofque, in which the Moors offer up their prayers, they have chapels, or meetings, confecrated to the devotion of individuals, who regularly meet every evening, and fing either paffages from the Koran, or prayers which they have compofed. They alfo fing when they bury the dead, and pay the moft fuperftitious devotion to their faints. As the Turks have none of thefe feparate affemblies, which

which feem foreign to the fpirit of Mahometanifm, it may be prefumed that the
Moors have adopted the frequenting of
them from the Morabethoons, who, though
no Dervifes, were more auftere In the
obfervation of their worfhip. It is poffible, alfo, that they may have brought this
practice out of Spain.

In all Mahometan ftates a kind of
Monks, or Dervifes, are found, who dedicate themfelves to religion by vows, and
who, under the veil of pretended perfection and abfurd peculiarities, multiply and
take advantage of the credulity of the un-
informed. The Turks of Europe are not
in general much addicted to monaftic infti-
tutions; yet the rich and great among
them, out of policy and refpect to the
opinions of the multitude, admit thefe
hypocrites in their houfes; but there are
few of them in whom they place any confidence.

In proportion as we enter farther into
Afia, or the interior parts of Arabia, and
in Egypt, where enthufiafm and the bi-

N 2

goted

goted spirit of superstition seem to ferment with the heat, those monkish kind of sanctuaries, in which the pretended saints, called Santons, live, are seen more frequently, and held in greater veneration. Some of these Santons mortify themselves by various means; but most of them are vagrants; the buffoneries of whom are, however, respected by the vulgar, and who there are held in the same veneration as here by the Moors of Morocco.

Saintship in this part of Africa is one of the most distinguished, and, perhaps, most lucrative professions; it is a family inheritance, descending from father to son, and sometimes from master to servant. A Saint as naturally affirms that he is a Saint as a tailor tells you he is a tailor; and the number of these self-said holy men is increased, because that fools, madmen, and ideots, are acknowledged saints. With respect, however, to their pretended miracles, those the fools never affect to perform. The house, the sanctuary, and the land of a Saint of repute, for they are not all in equal credit, form an inviolable asylum;

and

and thefe afyluins, known to the earlieft times, which originally were only places of refuge againft tyranny and oppreffion, have infenfibly extended their privileges. The Defpots of Morocco, ceding to their paffions and arbitary power, have occafionally violated them ; but, interefted as they are to maintain the prejudices of their people, they have almoft always held them in refpect *.

These

* The following extract of a narrative, written by fome French Miffionaries, who, in the year 1723, were fent to Morocco for the redemption of captives, affords a lively picture of the power, as well as avidity of thefe Saints:—" A cri-
" minal took refuge in the houfe of one of their Saints ; the
" Emperor commanded he fhould be brought to juftice, and
" punifhed for his crime : but no one durft enter and feize
" him, becaufe of the refpect they had for the houfe of the
" Saint to which he had fled : the Emperor was fo angry
" that he went himfelf, apparently with an intent to inflict
" punifhment with his own hands. The guardians of the
" houfe of the Saint remonftrated that the Imperial dignity
" was not fuperior to their law, which forbade the taking
" of any criminal out of the houfe of a reputed Saint ; but,
" they farther reprefented, there was one means of making
" him quit this houfe, which was to write a refpectful
" letter to the Saint, and with it fend him a prefent, praying
" that it might pleafe him to expel the fugitive, and the
" guardians would then drive him forth, fo that he might be
" feized. The Emperor thought proper to comply ; the

" letter

Thefe Saints, whofe fanctuaries are infinitely numerous, do not all enjoy the
fame fpecies of holy virtue ; the Moors
invoke fome of them for the cure of their
difeafes, others to obtain fertility for their
lands, or fuccefs in their undertakings,
Women fubject themfelves to a nine-day's
abftinence to obtain children, and thefe
kind of Saints are the ofteneft invoked,
and perform the moft miracles. Some of
them pretend to have charms againft
wizards, forcerers, the poifon of ferpents,
and other venomous infects, with which
they play. I have feen them eat fcor-
pions,

There is a fect in the fouth called Ben-
Haifia, defcendants of Jofhua, who, in
their wild fanatic devotion, run, leap,
dance, and, extatic in this their intoxica-

" letter was written, in his name, to the Saint, and the pre-
" fent fent ; but, as the Emperors and Bafhaws feldom think
" proper thus to condefcend, or to bear this expence, crimes
" generally remain unpunifhed." T.

*Relation du voyage pour la redemption des Captifs. Par
les peres Jean de la Faye, &c.*

tion,

tion, which becomes furious, they fall foaming upon any animal they find. A tale is related concerning a troop of thefe madmen, who once tore an afs in pieces with their teeth, and eat it up raw. The veneration of the people for fuch crazy Saints is incredible; they carefs them, fondle over, coax them, and ufe every means to quiet them during thefe fits of phrenzy.

The moft tranquil Saints, however, infpire the greateft devotion: there often come fome to the cities, who make their public entry on horfeback, preceded by a flag, and followed by foot people, who run after and attend them in multitudes, all hoping to approach the Saint, who lays his hand upon the head of the Moor, and the latter, kiffing his garments, imagines himfelf, after this ceremony, abfolved and purified from fin.

It will eafily be confidered how much the rigours of a government, which al-

N 4

ways

ways infpire agitation and terror, contribute to the increafe of fuperftition among
the Moors ; their intimidated minds habitually yield to every new fear : thus, they
are feen performing journies of five or fix
days from their places of abode, and bearing offerings to invoke fome Saint in
fafhion, that they may merit, by his hea-
venly interceflions, the favour of their Sovereign, his confidence, or fome temporal
profperity.   The Moors of the country
never fail, after harveft, to perform a vifit
of pilgrimage to the Saint whom they
have moft in reverence, carrying him their
firft fruits in homage, and as a mark of
gratitude.

Their priefts, their judges, all the
learned in the law, every well-informed
perfon, together with their Sharifs, or nobles, are, among the Moors, held to be
holy ; their veneration extends even to the
very Chriftian priefts, and more particularly to thofe friars who wear the coarfe
habits, defcribed by the Koran ; fuch as

were

were worn during the first ages of Mahometanism *.

Madmen, ideots, and dotards, are supposed by these people to be possessed by a
divine spirit. Some, cunningly profiting
by this fanatic prejudice, have acted the
madman, that they might obtain an easy
and good maintenance; but there are a
number of poor imbecile people, whom
the Moors kindly assist, and perform acts
of charity in their behalf, highly to their
honour.

Saintship thus being a trade among the
Moors, the mystery of the profession consists in the inventing of the means to take
advantage of popular credulity. Among

* The Koran having been revised in the seventh century,
under the caliphate of Omar, this Caliph recommended the
friars, who were then at Jerusalem, and whom he described
by the coarse garments in which they were clothed, to
be held in veneration. These have been supposed to be
Franciscan Friars, who have the keeping of the holy sepul-
chre; but they were Greek Monks, without a doubt, whose
habit the first Franciscans imitated, the latter order not
having been founded till the twelfth century.

the

the number of Saints whom I have known,
for it is neceſſary, in ſome degree, to have
friends of every claſs, there was one who
was exceedingly ſenſible and judicious in
private ſociety, but who in public affected
every extravagance which the wildneſs of
imagination could prompt ; and the ſallies
in which he indulged himſelf were regarded as inſpirations. He often would
paſs whole days and nights in imitating
the firing of cannon and the exploſion of
bombs, which the Moors ſuppoſed to be
preſages, ſometimes of good, ſometimes of
ill ; and the leaſt alteration in the ſeaſons,
in the weather, or the common courſe of
events, was heid a full accompliſhment of
theſe ridiculous predictions. This artful
impoſtor who, notwithſtanding, poſſeſſed
moral virtues, did ſome good ; and the
Moors of the country, who looked upon
him as one inſpired, laid aſide a portion of
their profits for him, and very ſcrupulouſly
brought him their firſt fruits. Notwithſtanding I no way aided him in performing
his miracles, he would ſometimes invite
me to partake of his offerings ; and I have
often

often rallied him on the cunning and prudence with which he played the fool.

There would be no end to this narrative, were I to recount all the tricks of a number of impostors, whom the Moors venerate, suppofing them to be holy. There certainly are fome among them, who are well-meaning people, that infpire confidence, and are themfelves ferious in their profeffions; but much the greateft part merit exemplary punifhment for the abufes they commit on ignorant credulity. There was one at Tetuan who, having in open day met women coming from the bath, after acting fome convulfive diftortions, feized on one of the moft youthful, and had commerce with her in the midft of the ftreet, Her companions, who furrounded her, uttered exclamations of joy, felicitated her on her good fortune, and the hufband himfelf received complimentary vifits on this occafion; fuch is the contrariety, fuch the caprice of opinion, and fuch the power of imagination over man.

Not

Not far from Saffi, on the high road, is
the sanctuary of a female Saint, who,
during her life, had devoted herself to the
service of passengers; and this prostitution
is the only claim to that veneration in
which her memory is preserved. Thus
do qualities, most singularly opposite, and
which every where influence the mind,
sometimes consecrate crimes, making them
holy and religious acts, and building temples even to debauchery.

The sanctuaries of the Saints throughout the empire are very numerous; there
are some to which vast possessions are annexed, and whose asylum is inviolable by
the antiquity of their titles *. Within
these lands they scarcely acknowledge the
authority of the Emperor; the Saint only
to whom the asylum is consecrated, is respected. To the southward, where men's
imaginations are most disposed to enthusiasm,

* This respect for Sanctuaries is descened from the most ancient times. Alaric, at the sacking of Rome, enjoined his
soldiers to spare the blood of those who should have taken
refuge in any sanctuary.

these

thefe fanctuaries are ftill more multiplied, the Saints are held in ftill greater venera- tion, and their religion is fuch that they will not permit Chriftians or Jews to ap- proach thefe holy places.

So great was the afcendancy of this kind of devotion that it was cuftomary, in times of civil commotion, to travel under the fafeguard of a Saint, and the traveller was then protected from all infult. The fame kind of prejudice is the caufe that a Saint is generally found travelling with the cafiles, or caravans, where he is confi- dered as a prefervative againft all unfortu- nate accidents; and he may travel from one part of the empire to the other with- out being at any expence.

The habitations of the Saints are al- ways befide the fanctuary, or tomb, of their anceftors, which they take care to adorn. Some of them poffefs clofe to their houfes, gardens, trees, or cultivated grounds, and particularly fome fpring or well of water. I was once travelling in the fouth in the beginning of October,

when

when the feafon happened to be exceedingly hot, and the wells and rivulets of the country were all dried up.   We had neither water for ourfelves nor for our horfes; and, after having taken much fruitlefs trouble to obtain fome, we went and paid homage to a Saint, who, at firft, pretended a variety of fcruples before he would fuffer infidels to approach; but on promifing to give him ten or twelve fhillings, he became exceedingly humane, and fupplied us with as much water as we wanted; ftill, however, vaunting highly of his charity, and particularly of his difintereftednefs.

On the mountain of Afkroo, at fome diftance from Fez, there formerly lived a Saint, whom the Brebes and Jews claim with equal devotion; the common opinion is, he was a Jew, who was buried in this part of Africa long before the introduction of Mahometanifm.   The wives of the Brebes and Jews who are defirous of obtaining children, devoutly go, on foot, and climb to the top of this mountain, where is the fanctuary of the Saint.   Near to

this

this sanctuary, or tomb, is a laurel tree,
that, for several ages, has revived from
its own roots, which easily persuades superstitious people that the divine property
of this Saint was that of prolific virtue.

The propensity of these people to superstition, enthusiasm, and fanaticism, not
only makes them reverence their Saints, but
inspires them with a veneration for such
Moors as have made the pilgrimage of
Mecca, and by that holy act are supposed
to have acquired an increase of perfection.
They eagerly flock to meet them when
they return, and this day is kept as a festival by the family of the *Hadgy*, for so those
Mahometans are called who go on pilgrimage to Mecca, because that this consecrated city is situated in the province of
Hagias.

When a Moor, on his return from
Mecca, re-enters the city in which he
dwells, preceded by drums and hautboys,
and followed by relations and friends, he
bestows a holy embrace on all he meets;
and though before he was held an ignorant
vaga-

vagabond, he affumes, on this day, a hy-
pocritical gravity, which impofes upon
people eager to fee and believe in wonders,
and who croud to be hugged by him and receive an infufion of his virtue. The veneration for thefe *Hadgy* is fo great among
the Moors, that it extends to the very animals ; a camel that has been on pilgrimage to Mecca is well fed, and maintained
without work, and is allowed to graze
freely wherever he fhall ftray.

CHAP.

CHAP. II.

Of the Pilgrimage to Mecca.

THE pilgrimage to Mecca is impofed by the law of Mahomet, but·is difpenfed with on the moft trivial pretext. As the Mahometans, however, attribute to this pilgrimage the remiffion of all their fins, the moft fcrupulous and devout are very defirous to undertake it, and eafe their confciences. The journey is ftill more meritorious for the weftern Mahometans than for the others, becaufe of the difficulties and dangers to which they are expofed in traverfing the whole extent of Africa. The caravan affembles at Fez with great preparations, thence takes its departure *,

* The time of this departure is not fixed; it varies as the feftivals of the Mahometans happen to vary : it is only neceffary to arrive at Cairo about the feafon in which the feftival of the Ramadan is kept; the caravan departs thirty days after, and comes to Mecca before the Corban, or the feaft of facrifices.

and croffes the leffer Atlas to come into the neighbourhood of Tunis, where it lays in a frefh ftore of provifions ; the fame is repeated at Tripoli, and it refts awhile at this laft place. It next proceeds acrofs the deferts of Barca over moving fands, which are blown and changed by every wind, and which leave no trace to guide the traveller.

When the winds of the fouth or the eaft begin to blow, the caravan is endangered, becaufe thefe winds, paffing over burning plains, bear with them a fuffocating heat. Obliged to halt, the camels are formed into a kind of fhelter, under which the travellers, extended on the ground, endeavour to guard themfelves from this dangerous wind.

Camels are the only animals which can withftand the fatigues of this painful journey, and that becaufe of the facility with which they can fupport labour, hunger, and thirft. There are always fupernumerary camels to fupply the places of thofe that fhall die on the road. The dy-

ing camels are a kind of alms for thofe poor
Moors, for fuch there are, who always follow the caravan : the poor, being defirous
to expiate their fins as well as the rich,
flock to Mecca for abfolution ; when a
camel can travel no farther, he is delivered
over to thefe hungry followers, who kill
him immediately, rip him up, drink with
avidity the water, which ftill remains in
the veficles of the ftomach, and then
drefs and eat his flefh *.

* See page 166 concerning the conformation of the ftomach of the camel

                    CHAP.

C H A P. III.

Of the Festivals of the Moors.

AS festivals are intimately connected with religion, I shall speak a few words of those of the Moors. The Oriental Mahometans by no means keep so many festivals as the Catholic Christians ; but the Mahometans of the west have multiplied them, and observed them with much greater zeal than do the Ottomans. It appears to be a general rule that the people who enjoy least wealth, and freedom, are those who, by way of compensation, are most desirous of keeping festivals. The Turks keep the passover of Biram, or Bayram, which follows their lent, only three days, and they dedicate the like space of time to that of the Corban, which happens seventy days after.

The

The Mahometans celebrate the latter feſtival, which ſignifies oblation, or the feaſt of ſacrifices, by offering up one or ſeveral ſheep each family, the fleſh of which is carefully diſtributed among the poor.

The Emperor of Morocco holds this feſtival without the city that more people may aſſemble, and thus preſerves the cuſtom the Moors had of praying in the open fields before they were converted to Mahometaniſm. He ſends a ſlain ſheep to his palace by a horſeman, and, if the heart palpitates when it arrives there, this is interpreted to be a good omen. Neither the origin nor the motive of this ſuperſtitious cuſtom are at preſent known.

The two feſtivals above mentioned are the only ones which the Mahometans of the eaſt obſerve with great ceremony, and the people do not labour during theſe three days. The Moors, either becauſe they are more devout, or leſs induſtriouſly inclined, keep each of theſe feſtirals eight days; they do the ſame on the anniverſary of Mahomet, which they

call

call Milood ; and alfo at the feftival of the
new year, which they celebrate ten days
after its commencement. It is the cuftom
at this latter feftival to beftow alms, as it
is in fome parts of Europe to fend new
years' gifts. On this occafion the Moors
are, many of them, very ready and eager
to receive ; but thofe who are capable of
giving, very œconomically, ftay at home
fhut up in their houfes.

CHAP.

CHAP. IV.

Of Alms-giving and Hospitality.

MAHOMET made alms-giving a very principal article in his religion; but it is observed with much less generosity among the Moors than among the Turks. Very few beggars are to be found in Turkey, and alms are so properly distributed to them as to prevent their increase. There, too, hospitality is so regularly observed that the house is open, at meal-time, to all who wish to enter. The same custom is also found among the Moors, who are somewhat at their ease, and persons of distinction; but it is by no means in the same general use; because, in reality, neither their wants nor their wealth are the same.

The Mahometan religion seems to enjoy an advantage over every other in teaching

a more

a more perfect refignation to the decrees of Providence. Muffulmen, of all the religious fectaries, are the leaft affected by the viciffitudes of fortune, or the lofs of riches, employments, and honours. This patience, under fufferings, feems effectually to prove a more perfect fubmiffion to the will of the Supreme Being, and a more intimate perfuafion that every accident and circumftance of life are, without exception, the invariable decrees of deftiny.

The conclufions drawn from this doctrine ought to afford prefervatives againft every kind of fuperftition; to which, notwithftanding, the Mahometans, and particularly the Moors, are utterly addicted; it is the intereft of their Priefts (as it feems to have been thought that of all other Priefts) to encourage fuch filly weakneffes that they themfelves may obtain more refpect, and give the greater credit to their amulets againft ficknefs, the malice of the evil-eyed, and the influences of fpirits and demons. Thefe amulets contain paffages of the Koran fown between two bits of morocco in a round,

fquare,

square, or triangular, form, and which the people carry about them, and make their children carry, nay, their very beasts, to prevent every kind of accident and evil augury.

The Moors invoke the Saint, whom they hold most in devotion, with the like confidence, praying him to guard them from any supposed danger. These people may have adopted such superstitions before, or after, they became Mahometans; but they are, certainly, not only foreign to, but appear to be irreconcileable with, the law of predestination. It would be a vain attempt to endeavour to explain all the various, absurd, and contradictory opinions of men.

CHAP.

CHAP. V.

Of the Government of the Empire of Morocco.

No government can be imagined more abfolute than that of Morocco : it is fubordinate to no one invariable principle which fhall reftrain the will of the Monarch, or which may ferve as a bafis of public confidence. Certain of the blind fubmiffion of his fubjects, or flaves, the Defpot here unites in himfelf every kind of power ; all is dependant on his arbitrary will ; he makes, breaks, changes, and varies, the laws, according to the caprice, the convenience, or the intereft, of the moment. Supreme power is here wholly uncontrolled, having, apparently, nothing to fear.

The fubject throughout this empire cannot

not fay, of any thing, this is mine; not
even of his opinion, or his exiftence: his
mafter deprives him of property, or of life,
whenever it fhall fo pleafe him, he holding
them merely as a depofit. The fortune,
or fate of men, in a government fo defpotic, cannot acquire the leaft ftability:
to be rich, is to be guilty of a capital
crime, which the Defpot punifhes, how
and when he pleafes, according as avarice
incites.

It may be that there are governments in
Afia equally arbitrary and defpotic; but to
be more fo than that of Morocco is impoffi-
ble. The Grand Signior, who is held to
be an abfolute Prince, cannot, in every
point of view, fo be called: he is himfelf
held in reftraint by the laws of the State,
and affumes a right over the life and property of individuals only in concurrence
with thefe laws: on them are founded the
all-fovereign power of Turkey; but this
power may alfo from them receive checks.
If the Sultan be allowed to put thofe to
death who are in the adminiftration of
affairs, it is becaufe that the minifters of
State

State are his slaves, and he therefore has
the power of life and death over them.
By punishing them for their exactions,
and confiscating their property for the benefit of the national treasury, he consoles
the oppressed people, who consider such
acts as just, and think the Despot ought
sometimes thus to take public vengeance,
and restore public tranquillity. This treasury they consider as the property of the
People, and not merely of the Prince.

Neither has the Grand Signior the power
to seize, for the use of the treasury, the
effects of a Visier, when made over in reversion to mosques. His wealth, in consequence of this title of possession, or reversion, becomes sacred and inviolable by
a law which religion sanctions; and the
Despot, who should dare to violate that
law, would no longer enjoy his rights of
sovereignty; for the People no longer
respect those rights than while they are
supposed to be according to law.

At Constantinople the men of the law,
in whom are united Jurisprudence and the
Sacer-

Sacerdotal office, form an insurmountable barrier to the despotism of the Sovereign; and this is, there, the balance of power. The legislative body influences the civil and political operations, decides on war and peace; and the destiny of the Sultan himself has sometimes depended on its resolutions and its caprices. At Morocco the will of the Monarch knows no such bounds: the Despot, according to his good pleasure, makes war and peace; his determinations are neither subordinate to a Council nor a Divan; they depend only on his convenience and his will, and he acts without restraint.

Yet the Despot of Morocco does not, by any act of authority, seize upon his neighbour's wife; he does not commit open violation on legal engagements: that would be to reverse the whole order of things, and subvert his own power. These slavish people in him behold the representative of Divinity; and, were he not to respect their received opinions and prejudices, all would be overturned, since these are the sacred ties of the public confidence, and, by tearing off this bandage, he muſt reſtore the blind to ſight.

In this barbarous government, the ſubject, who is a cypher in the State, wiſhes to remain unknown, and hide himſelf from his maſter's preſence. Princes and Kings, who ought, when raiſed over other men, to watch for their welfare, and by exerting the nobleſt qualities of man gain their love and reſpect, in Morocco inſpire only fears and terror.

The Emperor of Morocco entruſts no one with the adminiſtration of his eſtates: Such miniſters, indeed, ſeem incompatible with a government where all is ſubordinate to the arbitrary will of the Sovereign. This Monarch would ſuppoſe his power enfeebled, were he to tranſmit a portion of his authority to one of his ſlaves; he inſpects all, and employs himſelf with equal intereſt, whether it be to re-eſtabliſh order in a province, or to regulate ſome domeſtic diſpute; and as his reſolutions are always determined according to the conveniency

of

of the moment, they neceffarily vary with each varying circumftance.

All perfons in the fervice of the Defpot are no more in Morocco than the organs and inftruments of his pleafure: their offices are not fixed, or ftated; one ends what another has begun; contradictory orders are often iffued on the fame day, and he who receives them knows not which he had beft execute.

The fecretaries and agents of the Prince, who are very numerous, have neither any certain employment nor pay; their journies, and the fmall expences they are at in his fervice, are wholly gratuitous; and the Emperor leaves the means of reimburfing and rewarding themfelves for their labours to their own addrefs.

The Moorifh monarchs have not the fame ideas with European fovereigns concerning the adhering to their word; they, perhaps, regard that refpect which men and kings owe to the engagements they enter into as giving limits to fupreme power:

power: " Takeſt thou me for an infidel,"
ſaid an Emperor of Morocco to a foreigner,
" that I muſt be the ſlave of my word?
" Is it not in my power to ſay and unſay
" wh. never I ſhall pleaſe?" Such are
the ſtrange opinions they hold of their
own puiſſance, by which they ſuppoſe they
may rid themſelves of every thing moſt
ſacred *.

What is called the Court in Europe,
that is to ſay, an aſſemblage of thoſe who
moſt immediately govern the ſtate, is ex-
preſſed by the word *Magaſin*. All people
attached to the ſervice of the Sovereign are
alſo called Magaſini·†. By Magaſin is un-

* John, King of France, was taken priſoner at the bat-
tel of Poitiers, in 1356, and, afterward, preferred returning
priſoner to England to any violation of his word. " Were
" truth, ſaid he, baniſhed from the reſt of the world, it ſtill
" ought to be found in the mouths of kings."

† The word Magaſin is only a corruption of the Arabic
words *Mal-Hafac*, a place where riches are depoſited. Haſne,
ſtanding alone, ſignifies the treaſure of the Prince. It
ſhould ſeem probable that we alſo have derived our word,
Magaſin, in French, in Engliſh, Magazine, from the Arabic;
it having exactly the ſame meaning.

2   derſtood

derstood a close and respected place, and such in distinction ought a court to be among an erratic nation who live under tents.

The principal officers attached to the service of the Emperor, whom he distinguishes by the name of Sabo, that is to say, friends or companions, are employed as domestics in the palace. So, in the time of Mahomet, Abdallah, his father-in-law, took care of his pillow, his toothpick, and his shoes. Such employments at the court of Morocco are only honorary, giving those who enjoy them an opportunity of approaching the person of the Prince, and the favours he bestows are their only revenue.

In whatever part of his empire the Monarch happens to be, he grants public audiences four times a week for the distribution of justice; and this the Moors call holding the *Meshoaar*. While performing these functions, the original institution of which were equally respectable to King and People, he sits on horseback under the cover of an umbrella, carried by one of his grooms ; and this, in Morocco, is the sole distinctive mark of royalty. He is surrounded by his principal officers, who approach his person, and by a number of soldiers under arms. Here the ascendancy of opinion, and the whole power of depotism, are beheld. The Janizaries, and all soldiers at the court of the Grand Signior, are unarmed; and, were not this precaution taken, revolutions would be exceedingly frequent at Constantinople. The Janizaries, who have performed any remarkable services, are there acquainted with their power ; but the military slaves of Morocco are acquainted only with the power of their master.

All Moors, without exception, who have any complaint or remonstrance to make, have the liberty to come to the Meshooar, or public audience. Here too the couriers, who have been sent with intelligence to the Emperor, are announced, and the contents of their dispatches made known to him ; he is informed in an instant of what passes in his states, and gives necessary -

sary -

fary orders accordingly to the Alcaids, Se-
cretaries, or other officers, who are always
in his train ready to execute his commands.

The procefs of juftice is exceedingly
fwift on thefe occafions; the fentence of
the mafter is without appeal. I was at the
public audience held at Mequinez in July
1775, when the Emperor caufed a governor of the province of Rif to be killed
by clubs, after firft having had his hands
cut off, and his body was caft into the
open fields *. The Monarch, all in agitation, alighted from his horfe to kifs the
earth, and pay homage to God for this act
of juftice. Having mounted again, he
bade me approach; and I had an audience
of confiderable length.

As the Emperor of Morocco receives,
during thefe public audiences, the vifits of

* This governor was punifhed as a traitor. He had
been fufpected of a clandeftine intercourfe with the governor
of Melilla during the fiege of that place, and had afterwards
manifeftly difobeyed the orders of the Emperor.

                    Ambaffa-

Ambaſſadors, conſuls, merchants, or other
foreigners : affairs are here treated of publicly. Whatever requires ſecreſy and diſ-
cretion is either given in writing or told
to confidential perſons, if ſuch can be
found among theſe people, and in a court
where there is no other ſyſtem than that
of the intereſt and convenience of the moment.

No one is admitted to theſe public audiences without a preſent proportionate to
his wealth or ſtation, or to the nature of
the affairs concerning, and the circumſtances under, which he is obliged to treat.
Foreigners uſually make preſents to all
thoſe who are attached to the ſervice of the
Emperor ; and theſe perſons often invent
or give birth to meſſages, true or falſe,
from the Monarch, that they may multiply
the contributions. The Moors are leſs expoſed to theſe trifling vexations, which,
from cuſtom, are become law ; yet they
do not preſent themſelves without offering
ſome homage of their ſubmiſſion. The
governors of provinces give money, ſlaves,
horſes, and camels ; private perſons pre-

fent haicks, carpets, cloths, or other effects;
a poor Moor will offer an old horfe, or
camel, two fheep, a goat, nay, even three
hens, or a dozen of eggs.

This refpectable cuftom, by which the
Emperor admits all people to his audience,
and there renders public juftice, is fome
allay, fome melioration, of the rigours of the
government, and a confolation to fubjects
ever expofed to oppreffion. It reftrains
the ftill greater abufes of authority which
they elfe might fuffer from the governors
of provinces and cities, to whom alone,
becaufe of the diftance at which they live,
the fovereign is obliged to confide a confiderable degree of his power, and defpotifm paffes from the mafter to the flave.

The governors, or bafhaws, exclufively,
regulate the police of their diftricts ; they
are careful to increafe the revenue by their
authority, or by taking advantage of the
altercations which the fpirit of inquietude
raifes among the Moors. When thefe
bafhaws have amaffed riches, the Emperor
is equally careful to ftrip them ; and this

is

is a kind of retributive juſtice, which turns
to the benefit of his treaſury; money, in
this government, conſtitutes the crime, or
obtains the pardon of the accuſed.

CHAP.

CHAP. VI.

Laws and Administration of civil and cri-
minal Justice.

THERE is no code of laws in the empire of Morocco, but instead of a civil
they have a religious code; the practice of
jurisprudence is reduced to the application
of certain principles, to be found in the
Koran and its commentators, and in a prac-
tical knowledge of the precedents established in the various jurisdictions. There
are Cadis and governors in the cities and
countries for the administration of justice;
and notaries, or *Talbes,* to certify deeds,
and all which relates to the security of
property, whose pay is moderate.

All litigations concerning property, succession, and the various claims of interest,

are

are brought before the Cadi of each town, or of each diſtrict of the province; the parties ſometimes plead themſelves, but more often by attorney. Theſe ſuits are not loaded by forms; their proceedings are very ſimple, and attended with little expence. The Cadi, aſſiſted by ſome other men of the law, conſiders the pleadings and the various circumſtances, and gives ſentence according to the majority of opinions. Such ſentences are always founded on the law, the principles of which are extracted from the Koran, or on cuſtoms that, in certain diſcuſſions, ſupply the place of law.

Should the parties not be ſatisfied with the judgement given, they have the power of appeal to the Emperor; but this very rarely happens, for, in countries ſo poor, ſuits are not only very ſeldom of ſufficient conſequence to ſupport great expences, but the Moors alſo prefer the ſentence of the Cadi, or an accommodation, be it what it may, to the arbitrary judgement of the Monarch. It is policy among theſe people to hide as much as they can all knowledge

of

of what their fubſtance is from a maſter ſo abſolute, who might be liable to reconcile the parties, by ſeizing himſelf upon their property.

The governors of cities do not hear any of theſe litigated cauſes; authority with them ſupplies the place of law; their juriſdiction, unclogged by every kind of formality, extends over the police of the cities and the high roads, the regulation of markets, the price of proviſions, quarrels, thefts, aſſaults, and every thing in which the public ſafety is concerned. The judgements they give are always arbitrary, and generally conſiſt in diſtributing the baſtinado with equal liberality to the guilty and innocent *, committing them

to

---

* Mr. Boſville and three other Engliſh gentlemen of fortune, whoſe honour and veracity are undoubted, but whoſe names, not being perſonally acquainted with them, I forbear to mention, were travelling in Morocco, in the year 1767. The mule-drivers, employed by Mr. Boſville and his companions, happened to quarrel with ſome other of the low people; they were all taken before the Alcaid. The noiſy, clamorous, and iraſcible Moors, unanimouſly called for vengeance on each other, all ſpeaking together.

It

to some days imprisonment, whence they
are released by money, and in sentencing
them to pecuniary mulcts, which bear less
proportion to the delinquency than to the
wealth of the culprit, or the whim or convenience of the judge. The rich therefore rarely suffer any great punishment,
though they should have been concerned
in some criminal affair; and in this respect
the Moors, in reality, do but resemble most
other nations.

The Moors seldom come to blows; when
they quarrel, they will insult and abuse

It was a quarrel in bedlam. The ancient Alcaid, sitting
cross-legged, with his black beard to his girdle, with great
affectation of coolness and gravity, took the shortest and usual
method of quieting this uproar: he waved his hand and
ordered the Moors all out, without examination, without
any distinction, whatever, between guilty and innocent, to
receive the bastinado. This ended, they returned very
calm, and little desirous of farther hearing or *justice*.

I have the same Gentleman's testimony, and also that of
several respectable merchants, who were personally acquainted with Mr. Chenier for the authenticity of the facts
he relates, and the justness with which he depicts the manners of the Moors. They are farther confirmed, also, by
the best writers on Morocco; French and English; Travellers and Historians. T.

each

each other, but not ſtrike. It is cuſtomary among them to chaſtiſe him who gave the firſt blow, as a kind of retaliation; after which he may, if he can, prove that his cauſe was good.

Although perſonal reſpect is paid in the States of Morocco to thoſe who are well informed, the legiſlative body has neither the power nor conſiſtence which it has in Turkey; the men of the law have ho influence whatever over government, nor is there any intermediate power between the Sovereign and ſubject, the maſter and the ſlave. The Emperors of Morocco may have occaſionally conſulted people learned in the law, but it was to give an appearance of form and juſtice, and a greater degree of validity to their deciſions. Neither is this formality anywiſe neceſſary in Morocco; whereas it is indiſpenſable in Turkey, where the Mufti gives his opinion on whatever intereſts the State.

As thoſe who have ſtudied the law among the Moors are not held in the ſame degree of reſpect as among the Turks, the judges

judges are under more conftraint in the exercife of their function ; they literally follow the expreffions of the law, and dare not take upon themfelves to foften or increafe the fentence. Thus thofe remarkable and fagacious judgments, which are often pronounced in Turkey, are unknown in the courts of Morocco. The Turkifh Cadi fagely follows the rules of equity, and departs from the letter of the law, when neceffary, to increafe or mitigate punifhment.

There are numerous anecdotes among the Turks, which prove the good fenfe, juftnefs and penetration of their judges, in the decifions they pronounce ; as there likewife are of the art with which they make the office they hold profitable, and which is but a kind of annual farm. Such examples among the Moors are more uncommon and lefs marking ; but in return they poffefs governors, who are exceedingly adroit, and whofe fubtilty in watching over all that concerns their adminiftration can fcarcely be exceeded.

Several

Several anecdotes are told of a governor of Fez, which merit to be cited, because they contain traits of national character.

A young married woman had a lover, whom she met clandestinely, and who, enraged with jealousy, having some cause to suspect her fidelity, strangled her one night, and threw her into the river. Her body, washed by the current, was carried down to a mill, where her hair got entangled in the mill wheel; the miller perceiving it, went terrified to inform the governor, who commanded him to keep the secret, and bring him the head of the woman in a sack.

The governor placed this head in a chamber, and sent for the women who serve at the baths, that they might discover who she was; he then strongly recommended secresy to these women, which they are not in this country very exact in observing. He immediately went to visit the husband, and questioned him concerning his wife——" She has been at the house " of her father ever since yesterday," said

the

the Moor—" Concerning that we muſt
" enquire," ſaid the Governor. The Governor and the huſband then went to the
father, who ſaid it was true his daughter
had come to ſee him the day before, but
that ſhe had returned without making a
moment's ſtay.

The Governor then accompanied the
huſband to his own houſe, and ſhewed him
the head of his wife, recommending him
to diſſemble his affliction, and, having re-
conducted him home, aſked to ſee all his
wife's clothes. After examining them
piece by piece, he aſked the huſband whether it was he who had preſented her with
them all. All were acknowledged by the
huſband to have been his gifts, except a
rich ſaſh, worked in ſilk and gold, of the
manufacture of Fez.

The Governor took this ſaſh, and ſent
for the workmen to know by whom it had
been made, pretending he wanted one of
the ſame pattern ; the workmen, having
made but three, declared who the different perſons were by whom they had
been

been bought. Thus proceeding, ftep by ftep, he came to the knowledge of the lover who had committed the murder.

The Governor then fent for this lover, and he, confeffing his crime, prevailed on the other to keep the fecret for a gift of three thoufand ducats, or about fome eight hundred pounds; that is to fay, one thoufand for himfelf, one thoufand for the hufband, and a thoufand for the father. The Governor gave the father a portion, fuch as the law allowed, but fent nothing to the hufband, holding that he was fufficiently recompenfed in fuffering no punifhment for not having better watched the conduct of his wife. This was giving him a leffon, the value of which feems beft known among nations where the women are flaves, and where the name of hufband is fynonymous to that of tyrant.

Another adventure of gallantry had alfo occafioned the murder of another young woman. A fcavenger, being well paid, carried the body very early in the morning, cut in fmall pieces, upon his afs, among the filth

of

of the city. As he paſſed by the Governor the ſcavenger ſaluted him with an air of embarraſſment, which raiſed the ſuſpicions of the Governor, who had ſeen him paſs every day without any ſuch ceremony. The Governor, imagining there was ſome cauſe for this behaviour, called the ſcavenger, interrogated him with threats, and diſcovered the true motive of his confuſion, which he turned to his own account.

This ſame Governor having cited three young men to appear before him, who were accuſed of ſtealing pigeons of a rare ſpecies, made them a ſign to ſit down; then, addreſſing them, ſaid—"Thoſe who " would deny that they had ſtolen pigeons " ought, at leaſt, to take care not to leave " the feathers about their heads." One of the three, who was not yet old enough to have learnt diſſimulation and preſence of mind, immediately lifted up his hand to his bonnet, to ſhake off the feathers, and thus diſcovered himſelf to be the thief; after which he did not deny the fact.

Thus

Thus we find among thefe rude people, with whom inftinct feems to hold the place of reafon, men who are as intelligent and as artful as the inhabitants of civilized nations, perhaps more.fo. The art of knowing man is not indeed to be taught, nor is it the effect of education, but the fruit of experience and reflection; thofe men, therefore, whofe attention is leaft difturbed, either by diffipation, the love of pleafure, or the defire of acquiring knowledge, have, in this refpect, the moft advantage.

CHAP. VII.

Of the State of Knowledge among the Moors.

ARTS and Sciences flourish only in freedom, and find not the least encouragement under governments wholly despotic. The Moors, who derive their language and religon from the Arabs, seem not in any manner to have participated of their knowledge. United and confounded as those of Morocco have been with the Moors of Spain, the latter of whom cultivated the arts, and gave birth to Averroes, and many other great men, neighbours, dependants, or pupils, of the city of Fez, the academies of which have been vaunted, and which have produced writers. The Moors of this empire have preserved no traces of the genius of their ancestors; it is not very apparent that those revolutions,

tions, which have overthrown empires,
have altered the characterers of nations.
Subjugated by the Turks, the Greeks have
loft their liberty, but they have preferved
their genius; and, were they free, we
fhould fee the happy days of ancient
Greece revive in hiftorians, philofophers,
warriors, and poets. Men, like plants,
only degenetate when they are no longer
cultivated. I know not whether it fhould
be attributed to the influence of climate, or
to thofe effects which are the refult of a
vitiated government, but the Moors in general appear to me lefs fufceptible of
energy and virtue than other men.

The Moors have no conception of the
fpeculative fciences; in this refembling
the ancient Arabs, thofe among them
who can read, and the number is exceedingly fmall, feldom read any thing but
their books of religion. Education confifts merely in learning to read and write;
and as the revenues of the learned are derived from thefe talents, the Priefts and
Talbes among them are the fole depofito-

ries

ries of this much knowledge; the children of the Moors are taught in their
schools to read and repeat some sixty
lessons, selected from the Koran, which,
for the sake of œconomy, are written upon
small boards; these lessons being once
learned, the scholar is supposed to have
obtained sufficient knowledge to leave
school; on this occasion he rides on horseback through the city, followed by his
comrades, who sing his praises: this to him
is a day of triumph; to the scholars an in-
citement to emulation, a festival for the
master, and a day of expence for the parents; for in all countries, wherever there
are festivals and processions, there also are
eating and drinking.

At Fez, where some ideas of urbanity
are preserved, there is some small degree
more of instruction to be obtained in the
schools; and the Moors, who are a little
wealthy, send their children thither to have
them instructed in the Arabic language,
and in the religion and laws of their country. Here some of them also acquire a
little

little taste for poetry ; the Arabs not only celebrated extraordinary events in their poems, but also were accustomed to speak in verse in their assemblies, and in their ceremonial visits. It may be added that the Arabic tongue, by its copiousness, energy, and the metaphors which it is capable of, is, perhaps, better adapted to poetry than any other living language.

The Moors are also in the habit of rhyming and singing the history of any extraordinary event. Some have supposed that this custom has been introduced, among polished nations, from political motives, to amuse the people, and make them laugh, when they might otherwise become too serious ; but it is much more natural to conjecture that, orignally, the end of such rhymes was information, and the preserving of historical events in the memory of a multitude of citizens, who had not learnt to read. The Moors, who happen to be somewhat more learned than common, amuse themselves by proposing the solution of enigmas that are tolerably versified ; he who divines the

meaning,

meaning, muſt uſe the ſame rhymes as thoſe in which the enigma was compoſed, as if it were an anſwer to a queſtion.

CHAP.

C H A P.   VIII.

Of Pharmacy, Physic, and Innoculation.

THE Arabs, of all the sciences they knew, were most industrious in the study of physic and astronomy, which merited this preference, because of their utility. The art of preserving health, and of regulating agriculture conformable to the order of the seasons, must every where first have claimed the inquiries of the human mind. The Moors, who formerly inhabited Spain, gave great application to the improvement of these sciences, and they have left manuscripts behind them, which still remain so many precious monuments of their genius; nor, it is to be presumed, will these manuscripts always continue buried in oblivion, but will sometime be given to the world,

The

The modern Moors are infinitely degenerate; they have not the least inclination to the study of science; they know the properties of some simples; but, as they do not proceed upon principle, and are ignorant of the causes and effects of diseases, they generally make a wrong application of their remedies. Their most usual physicians are their Talbes, their Fakirs, and their Saints, in whom they place a superstitious confidence.

Fevers are the most common diseases of these hot countries, and are occasioned by the use of crude meats, bad food, and the daily transition from heat to humidity; and fevers are placed, by these ignorant people, among supernatural afflictions. A fiend, according to them, occasions their hot and cold fits, and the delirium which follows the body's agitation does but confirm them in their error: thus the sick die, because they do not offer them any other aids than those which depend on miracles, and because they are ignorant of the workings of nature. The history of the world every where proves men have supposed the influ-

ence

ence of evil spirits; and this influence is always the greatest in nations the least enlightened. By the force of reflection, only, and their improvements in knowledge, have Europeans at length discarded these superstitious ideas of sorcery, magic, and enchantment, and only in their most distant provinces do such absurdities still preserve some power, over the imagination of men.

The small-pox, which is said to have been brought to Europe either from Asia or Africa, some affirming it was not known before the crusades, is the only disease, perhaps, for the cure of which the Moors do not invoke their Saints; it comes when it pleases, and does little mischief, because of the temperance of the climate and the abstinence of the people. They are acquainted with inoculation in the interior parts of the country; but it is practised with less preparatory caution here than among the modern Greeks, from whom it has been learned and adopted by Europeans. The Moors, however, do not inoculate, except those who live on the moun-

mountains, the Brebes, and the Shellu of the fouth * ; and the cuftom is lefs common among the latter.   Hence it may be concluded that the fmall-pox was known in Africa before the invafion of the Arabs, and that the mode of communicating it by infertion muft have been more ancient in thefe countries than Mahometanifm ; becaufe, however powerful the afcendant of religion may be, it is very flow in rooting out the prejudices and cuftoms of nations †.

In cities, where Mahometanifm is obferved with the moft fcruple, they take no precaution whatever to avoid the effects of

* I have before faid, the Brebes and the Shellu have the fame origin, having preferved the fame language ; but the latter, by their communication with the fouthern provinces, may have varied their cuftoms.

† Some have affirmed, the fmall-pox was unknown to the Greeks or Romans ; and it is generally believed it was not introduced into Europe till after the invafion of the Arabs. Some phyficians have therefore concluded that, not being a difeafe peculiar to our climates, it might be wholly extirpated by interdicting all communication with infected places, and by purifying every fpecies of clothing which have been ufed by the difeafed.

this

this difeafe ; precaution would be incompatible with the religion of Mahomet, which leaves the care of acting and preventing to fate. Voltaire wants foundation for afferting, as he has done in his literary mifcellanies, that the Turks inoculate their children. The incertitude which the effects of inoculation have occafioned, and the inconveniences which may happen to be the confequences, have given birth in Europe to a diverfity of opinions, and doubts have arifen concerning the goodnefs of a practice fo interefting to humanity. Inoculation will, however, certainly obtain greater credit in France, fince the Sovereign has difpelled the fears of a nation which ftands diftinguifhed for an attachment to its Kings, by having had the royal children inoculated, and thus keeping this contagious poifon, which has fo often left whole families in mourning and grief, at a diftance from the throne.

Although the Moors have little knowledge of pharmacy, and little inclination for the arts, ftill neceffity, in fome inftances, has rendered them induftrious ;

fome

ſome among them have been bold enough to cut for the ſtone, a diſeaſe known in this country. I ſaw a ſtone lately extracted as large as a pigeon's egg, which had various projecting points. I ſhuddered at the ſight of the inſtruments employed by theſe ſurgeons; they conſiſted in a bad razor, and a kind of hook, rudely made, which reſembled a nail bent.

CHAP.

C H A P. IX.

Of Aſtronomy and Eclipſes.

ASTRONOMY, the firſt knowledge of which we obtained from the Arabs, (or, perhaps, the Egyptians,) and which they themſelves learnt in conſequence of their wandering lives, is entirely, or almoſt, unknown to the Moors; for, though they likewiſe wander from place to place, there are few, if any, among them who have a knowledge of the motion of the heavens, or who are capable from principle to direct their own courſe, by obſerving the courſe of the ſtars. They are therefore neceſſarily wholly unable to calculate eclipſes, which they always interpret to portend evil.

The eclipſe, which happened on the 24th of June, 1778, was central, and total

at

at Sallee. I had been careful in foretelling it would happen, that the terror of the people might thus be decreafed; and, that I might the better obferve it, I went into the country, whither I was followed by many people. In proportion as the fun was concealed, my curious, intimidated followers, difappeared one after the other to return to the city, and we remained only with two foldiers of the guard who grew pale, and whofe dread was increafed as the fun loft its brightnefs. At the moment that the eclipfe was total we heard the lamentable fhrieks of women and children, who believed the end of the world was come, and only with returning light did the minds of the people recover fome degree of confidence.

It is not extraordinary that a people, who have no theory of the circular motion of the ftars, fhould fuffer confternation at a phenomenon which feems to overthrow the order of nature. Superftitious people have every where fuppofed eclipfes were fent to prefage fome · calamity. The

Moors,

Moors, being unable to reafon on the caufes of fuch an appearance, imagine the fun or the moon are in the power of a dragon that fwallows them, and they offer up prayers that thefe luminaries may be delivered from an enemy fo cruel and voracious.

Notwithftanding the Moors have preferved the wandering manners of the ancient Arabs, they have occupied themfelves lefs in the ftudy of Aftronomy. Endarkened by ignorance and fuperftition, they have been much more eager after aftrology, an imaginary fcience proper only to feduce and deceive the weak. This chimerical doctrine, which made fo rapid a progrefs at Rome in defpite of the edicts of the Emperors, muft make ftill greater advances among a people wholly ftupid and ignorant, and ever agitated by the dread of prefent evils, or the hope of a more happy futurity. Magic, the companion of aftrology, has here alfo found its followers, and is particularly ftudied by the Talbes in the fouthern parts, who

fuccefs-successfully use it in impofing upon Moorifh credulity with ftrange dreams, and imbiguous forebodings and prophefies.

CHAP.

CHAP. X.

Of the Language of the Moors.

THE Moors, of the Empire of Morocco, as well as those to the northern limits of Africa, speak Arabic; but this language is corrupted in proportion as we retire farther from Asia, where it first took birth; the intermixture which has happened among the African nations, and the frequent transmigrations of the Moors, during a succession of ages, have occasioned them to lose the purity of the Arabic language; its pronunciation has been vitiated, the use of many words lost, and other foreign words have been introduced without thereby rendering it more copious; the pronunciation of the Africans, however, is softer to the ear and less guttural than that of the Egyptians.

Of all living languages, the Arabic is, beyond contradiction, the one moſt extenſively ſpoken : from the eaſtern to the weſtern ſhores of the ocean, which includes a ſpace of two thouſand leagues, from eaſt to weſt, the people ſpeak no other tongue; and with this a traveller may even make himſelf underſtood in the countries of the Mogul, and a part of India. The language, when written, is in effect much the ſame at Morocco as at Cairo, except that there are letters and expreſſions among the Moors which differ from thoſe of the Oriental Arabs, who, however, underſtand the Moors in converſation, notwithſtanding their vitiated manner of pronouncing. They mutually read each others writings, with ſome difficulty.

There is a very ſenſible difference among the Moors between the Arabic of the learned, and the courtiers, and that ſpoken by the people in general; and this difference is felt ſtill more in the provinces of the ſouth, or of the eaſt, and among the Moors who live in the deſerts, where

the

the Arabic is yet farther disfigured by a mixture of foreign tribes.

The Brebes and the Shellu, who, as I have said, appear to have had the same origin, for they have preserved the same dialect, speak a language which the Moors do not understand, and which seems to have no analogy with that of the latter. I dare not affirm it is the Punic, or the Numidian, but these people write their language in Arabic characters. I have thought it necessary here to collect some words of these languages, by which will be seen the intimate relation between that of the Brebes and the Shellu, and the very slight connexion these two languages have with the Arabic.

R 2. *Compa-*

Comparative list of words between the Arabic language, as spoken in Morocco, and the languages of the Brebes and Shellu.

	Arabic of Morocco.	Brebes.	Shellu.
God,	Allah, Rabbi,	Allah, Rabbi,	Allah, Rabbi.
World,	Dounia,	Dounit,	Dounit.
Heaven,	Sema,	Aguena,	Aguelna.
Sun,	Shems,	Thasokt,	Thasokt.
Moon,	Kamar,	Aiour,	Aiour.
Stars,	Nejoun,	Yzheran,	Yzheran.
Earth,	Hard,	Ashal,	Aqual.
Sea,	Baar,	Baar,	Baar.
Water,	Ma,	Aman,	Aman.
Fire,	Afia,	Tafit,	Taquat.
To drink,	Shereb,	Issou,	Issou.
To eat,	Coul,	Itch,	Itch.
To sleep,	Requot,	Guan,	Guan.
To watch,	Fcik,	Ionquir,	Oureignan.
Day,	Naar,	Souhast,	Hassal.
Night,	Leil,	Iad,	Iad.
Man,	Ragel,	Argaz,	Argaz.
Woman,	Mara,	Tamtot,	Tamgart.
Father,	Bou,	Ibbas,	Babbas.
Mother,	Imma,	Imma,	Imma.
Child,	Iûr,	Herba,	Haial.
King,	Soultan,	Aguellid,	Aguellid.
Prince,	Sharif,	Sharif,	Sharif.
Slave,	Abd,	Ismak,	Ismak.
Subject,	Raya,	Rait,	Rait.
Living,	Ait,	Idert,	Issout.
Dead,	Mout,	Imout,	Imout.

Camel,

	Arabic of Morocco.	*Brebes.*	*Shellu.*
Camel,	Gemel,	Grouns,	Haram.
Horse,	Haoud,	Hais,	Hais.
Ox,	Tor,	Ayougou,	Azguer.
Sheep,	Qbech,	Izimer,.	Izimer.
Lion,	Sba,	Izem,	Izem.
Tiger,	Nemer,	Agouerzem,	Agouerzem.

NUMBERS.

One,	Ouaed,	Ian,	Ian.
Two,	Tnein, *or* Juz,	Sin,	Sin.
Three,	Tleta,	Querad,	Querad.
Four,	Arba,	Arba,	Qoue.
Five,	Kemfa,	Kemfa,	Cemouf.
Six,	Setta,	Setta,	Sedife.
Seven,	Saba,	Saba,	Sa.
Eight,	Temenia,	Temenia,	Tem.
Nine,	Tfaeud,	Tfaeud,	Tza.
Ten,	Afhara,	Afhara,	Memon.

The Brebes count the days of the week like the Moors, and both of them employ Arabic words. The Shellu enumerate the days after the fame method, but in their own language. Both the Brebes and the Shellu denote the months of the year in the fame manner as do the Moors and Arabs, and date from the fame æra; that is to fay, from the year of the Hegira.

The

The Koran, and books of prayer, of the Brebes and Shellu, are in Arabic, as likewise are their acts and title deeds, which are written by their Talbes, or learned men.

CHAP,

CHAP. XI.

Of the Character, Manners, and Customs of the Moors.

No one can recollect the intolerable servitude in which the Moors are held without commisserating their state; and yet, on a closer inspection, the compassion which an idea of slavery inspires is considerably abated. True it is that the nature of the government, which, though it cannot totally change the character of nations, has a prodigious influence over their minds, is one of the moral causes of the ferocity, ignorance, and cowardice, of these nations. Despotism so debases the soul that it is neither susceptible of fortitude nor elevation; the slaves only know the will of their master, have not the least idea of freedom, and have even lost the re-

membrance

membrance of words which exprefs a fenfe of their own worth and honour, and which feem only to appertain to the haughty and free mind. With lefs fenfibility than other men, they are faithful neither to their relations, their friends, nor their country; their vices are the oppofite of all good faith; they love not one another, and foreigners they love ftill lefs.

It appears that the Moors, like all the other nations of hot climates, are more difpofed to fubmit to flavery than the inhabitants of the north. The fewnefs of their wants, and the fertility of their lands, render them little addicted to labour; therefore have they little vigour, little of that characteriftic energy in which noble ideas originate, which gives birth to great crimes, or great virtues. This flumber of the faculties keeps them in eternal ftupidity, and is the very prop of defpotifm; for, it feems to be a well-founded remark that, governments are more or lefs arbitrary, in proportion as the people are more or lefs informed.

From

From the difposition of the foil, or the quality of the food, the Moors are naturally meager; that licentioufnefs in which they early indulge, alfo, greatly contributes to enervate and deprive them of mufcular ftrength, rendering them timid and indolent; they have agility, but not vigour, and can longer fupport the fatigues of running than of other bodily labour; they are tolerably well formed, have regular features, good teeth, fine eyes, but countenances deprived of expreffion or mind. Perhaps thefe are rather the effect of phyfical than of moral caufes. Hence too may we trace the reafon of that melancholy, that mournful air, which is peculiar to the Moors. Their perfons, their whole appearance, bear the ftamp of flavery and oppreffion.

Avaricious by nature, thefe people are addicted to accumulate and to conceal wealth. Their belief concerning the creation of the world, however disfigured by variation of circumftances, is the fame as that of the Chriftians; and one of their authors, depicting their avarice, invented an allegory equally judicious and moral.

" Adam,

" Adam, said he, after having eaten the
" forbidden fruit, aſhamed of his naked-
" neſs, ſought to hide himſelf under the
" ſhade of the trees that form the bowers
" of Paradiſe; the gold and ſilver trees
" refuſed their ſhade to the father of the
" human race. God aſked them why
" they did ſo.; becauſe, replied the trees,
" Adam has tranſgreſſed againſt your
" commandment. Ye have done well,
" anſwered the Creator; and, that your
" fidelity may be rewarded, 'tis My decree
" that men ſhall hereafter become your
" ſlaves, and that in ſearch of you they
" ſhall dig into the very bowels of the
" earth."

That paſſion which univerſally domi-
neers over man juſtifies this ingenious allegory; but the avarice of the Moors ſeems
to juſtify it ſtill farther; with them gold
and ſilver are neither eſtimated by their
wants, nor emblematic of their paſſions,
but rather objects of adoration.

Confidence and friendſhip are generally
unknown among the Moors; they are inſen-
ſible

fible to the gentle impreffions in which the benevolent and the worthy find fuch pure delight; they are acquainted only with the fervor of the paffions, fcattering difcord in families, and infurrection in the ftate; inceffantly tormented by the impulfes of enmity, they feek to injure, and reciprocally to defpoil each other of their wealth; intereft is the fecret fource of their connections, and their hatred; obliged to hide, that they may preferve their money, their fecret often dies with them, fearing left, otherwife, their end fhould be haftened by a wife, a fon, or a brother, who are themfelves impatient to feize upon their riches.

Although the Moors do not enjoy what they poffefs, they have not the lefs avidity: in exciting the generofity of foreigners they are moft ingenious. In love with money, only, they have no perfonal predilections; he who gives is their friend *; the enmity of people who put

friendfhip

* A young Moor one day offered one of my fervants to receive as many blows with a flick as he pleafed, at the rate

of

friendfhip up to auction, and among whom intereft is the fole motive of action, is, in fact, but little to be feared.

This avaricious propenfity of the Moors renders them pliant, cunning, and more penetrating than their apparent rudenefs of manners would befpeak. Little occupied in improving themfelves, they diffemblingly ftudy the characters of others, with whom they have bufinefs, while they, with equal adroitnefs, conceal their own ; troubling themfelves little concerning delicacy, or probity, they employ all means to obtain their purpofe. A perfon in office, in this refpect, is no more to be trufted than a private individual.

I have heard of one of their governors who regularly went to drink tea with a foreigner; and who artfully ftole his fpoons. Another governor was appealed to in order to recover effects ftolen, the

of twenty four for a Blanquil, or fomething lefs than two pence. This was his firft offer ; he would, perhaps, have made a better bargain, had my fervant been fo difpofed.

theft

theft being proved. They were recovered, but the owner's lofs was not the lefs, he being obliged to make a prefent, at leaft equal in value, to obtain the intervention of the governor.

It is ufual for thefe Alcaids to divide the perquifites of their fervants and foldiers, and thofe who content themfelves with only the half are efteemed honeft. What I fay muft be generally underftood; I mean not to affirm there are no individuals whofe actions are juft or generous; yet let thofe who deal with them beware, for they will ever difcover fomething of the Moor.

CHAP.

CHAP. XII.

Thieves, Punishments, Trades, Games, and Sports.

THE lower orders, and especially the country people, thieve from each other with great address. When the nights are remarkably dark, or stormy, they creep along the Douhars, and carry off all they can seize, first undressing themselves to nudity and crawling on all fours, so that in case of surprize they are not easily held.

The Moorish thieves are not intrepid, but what they want in courage they supply in cunning : I will cite two examples.

There is an inclosure walled round in the city of Morocco called Alcaisseria, the gates of which are nightly shut, and where the merchants have their shops and

ware-

warehoufes. A thief perceiving there
was a dry-well in this enclofure, between
which and another well, without the walls,
a communication might eafily be effected,
undertook the labour of making this fubterranean communication. Having executed his project, and concealed himfelf in the Alcaifleria, he broke open the
fhop of the richeft merchant, from which
he ftole money and other effects to the value
of three or four hundred pounds. The
burglary was next day perceived and re-
ported to the Emperor, who immediately
commanded all perfons found in the
Alcaifleria, and who could not render a
proper account of themfelves, to be
brought before him; which order was
obeyed. Among the perfons feized were
many fufpicious Moors, whom the Monarch threatened all with inftant death,
if no difcovery were made of the culprit
or his accomplices.

The thief, who had been feized among
the reft, advanced, and, cafting himfelf at
the Emperor's feet, faid, " I am the
" guilty perfon, do with me whatever you
" pleafe;

" pleaſe ; the crime I have commited is
" ſufficient ; I would not load myſelf
" with the guilt of the death of ſo many
" muſſulmen."

The Emperor, aſtoniſhed at the raſcal's
generoſity, praiſed him for his confeſſion,
and commanded him to reſtore the property to ſix of his guards, to whoſe charge
he was committed. The thief led them
back into the Alcaiſſeria, told them he had
concealed the effects in a well, and that he
would deſcend and bring them up ; accordingly down he went, and, crawling
through his ſubterranean paſſage, took to
flight. The guards, at length, weary of
calling and waiting, ſent one of their comrades into the well, who ſoon perceived the
trick they had been played. They returned and gave an account of this to the
Emperor, who, when he heard it; could
not refrain laughter.

Another thief, who had been condemned
to be hanged by the arm-pits on the highway, was attended by his wife, weeping
and lamenting his ſufferings. Still deſirous
of

of exhibiting some new proof of his dexterity, he loudly and piteously called after
a muleteer, who was passing with two
loaded mules.

Have compassion, generous friend, said
he, on my wife and children ; assist them
to draw out some effects which I have hid-
den in a pit.

The muleteer refused, saying, the goods
were stolen, and that if he were caught
he should be punished. Nay, but, replied
the malefactor, if thou wilt only assist my
wife, thou shalt have the half.

On this the conscientious muleteer consented, and accompanied the wife to the
place, who fastened a cord round his body
that she might aid him as he descended into
the pit. No sooner was he at the bottom
than she threw him down the cord, and
drove off the loaded mules.

Theft in Morocco is not punished with
death ; the sentence is variable and arbitrary, depending on circumstances, which

Vol. I.   S   may

may aggravate or leſſen the crime. The hand, or foot, of a highway robber, is uſually cut off, as was practiſed among the Arabs before Mahomet. I have ſeen a thief, who, after various thefts committed, had, by the Emperor's order, loſt both his hands, yet ſtill contrived to ſteal, alledging that he had now no other means to gain his bread.

Covetouſneſs naturally induces the love of gaming ; but, as the Mahometan religion forbids betting of money, the government very carefully watches over this evil among the Moors, and they are only allowed publicly to play at cheſs, which is in itſelf a game ſufficiently intereſting without the aid of wagering. The Moors of the country are unacquainted with cards, but they play at hazard, making dice out of ſmall bones, and uſing their ſlippers as boxes.

The firſt and immediate wants of man are only felt among the Moors, as in other hot climates: the few enjoyments they taſte are all ſecret, and within their own houſes,
carefully

carefully concealed from public view. Hence their talents find small exertion; industry follows luxury and abundance, and is little seen where liberty is banished and oppression reigns. Heat, perhaps, too, may benumb the body, and with that the faculties of the mind, so necessary for the invention and perfection of the arts: those of the Moors, indeed, are few, and in a rude state; their workman have fewer tools, aids, and conveniences, than those of Europe.

A goldsmith will come and work in the corner of a court, where he presently fixes his stall; his anvil, hammer, bellows, files, and melting ladle, are all brought with him in a bag; his bellows are made of a goat's skin, into which he inserts a reed, holding it with one hand, while with the other he presses the bag, after the manner of bagpipers; and this way lights and blows up his fire.

Other trades work with the like rude simplicity; they have not sufficient employment to incite their emulation, or in-

treafe

creafe their conveniences : yet does the fight of a nation in this ftate infpire veneration ; a comparifon is neceffarily made between the various gradations of art and its progrefs toward perfection ; while the diftance between fuch its moft perfect ftate and thefe feeble attempts creates aftonifhment.

The employments and profeffions of man are fubordinate to his wants ; ufeful trades are therefore only known among the Moors ; thofe that appertain to pleafure and luxury are there wholly fuperfluous. The proceedings of government are too fimple to excite conjecture and form politicians, and the condition of men in Morocco is almoft uniform.

The governors of provinces and towns, defirous of Court favour, fend their fons to attend on the Sovereign, where they find employment, according to their talents, in his fervice, carrying his meffages, and executing his commiffions. Here are no fixed pofts or offices ; the functions are merely temporary, domeftic, and more or lefs dangerous, according to the character

of

of the reigning Monarch, or the ufe and abufe of his confidence; in governments fo cruel, courtiers ufually execute what the turbulent paffions of the tyrant command, and honour and probity there are feldom titles of recommendation.

Individuals, who have acquired fome wealth, do not willingly fend their fons into the fervice of the Emperor, left they fhould endanger their fortuue, and expofe themfelves to thofe confequences which refult from the indifcretion or inexperience of youth; they rather prefer educating them for the offices of Judges, or Talbes, if they have abilities, trufting them with money to trade, or employing them in the fuperintendance of their gardens and grounds. . Thefe are the general and prin-cipal occupations of the Moors.

They marry their children early that they may the fooner addict them to employment, and prevent diffipation. One profeffion with them is equal to another, and they indifferently teach them to trade,

S 3

make

make them tailors, weavers, tanners, or shoemakers, as it may happen : no person is ashamed of exercising a useful trade : the Cadi and the governor of a town each marry their daughter to a tradesman, without supposing they have thereby degraded themselves.

On the Friday, which is their day of prayer, or sabbath, all the inhabitants of a town, clothed in the same kind of stuff and the same colour, are nearly all equal. In absolute governments, where the despot is all, and the slave nothing, there is but little distinction of rank among men ; differences there are, but they are momentary, appear and disappear at the will of the master : the Emperor of Morocco of a soldier makes a Bashaw, and of a Bashaw a soldier*. I myself have known a governor deposed by the Monarch, and condemned to sweep the streets of the town he had governed. Such caprices of for-

---

* The Moors call a governor of a province Bashaw ; in Turkey such an one is called Pacha, or Pashaw. Perhaps the latter have changed the B to a P.

tune

rune are not uncommon in arbitrary states, where power passes rapidly from the master to the slave, and as rapidly is annihilated, making too slight an impression for the possessor to become inflated with false ideas of his own positive superiority. Few of the provincial governors but have felt the vicissitudes of this tempestuous despotism; once stripped of their effects, they may again be restored, and recover their former dignity; the sinner is absolved, having, by rendering up his riches, washed away all iniquity.

The Moors have in general but few amusements; the sedentary life they lead in cities is little variegated, except by the care they take of their gardens, which are rather kept for profit than pleasure. Most of these gardens are planted with the orange, the lemon tree, and the cedar, in rows, and in such great quantities that the appearance is rather that of a forest than that of a garden. The Moors sometimes, though rarely, have music in these retreats: a state of slavery but ill agrees with the love of pleasure: the peo-

ple

ple of Fez alone, either from a difference in education, or becaufe their organs and fenfibility are more delicate, make mufic a part of their amufements. There are not in Morocco, as in Turkey, public coffee houfes *, where people meet to enquire the news of the day ; but, inftead of thefe, the Moors go to the barbers' fhops, which, in all countries, feem to be the rendevouz of newfmongers. Thefe fhops are furrounded by benches, on which the cuftomer, the inquifitive, and the idle, feat themfelves ; and when there are no more places vacant, they crouch on the ground like monkies.

Shewmen and dancers come often into the towns, round whom the people affemble and partake of the amufement for a very trifle. There are alfo a kind of wandering hiftorians : the vulgar, who cannot read, and who every where are eager to

* Our coffee houfes, which are only an imitation of thofe in Turkey, are, however, more elegant and amufing. The police of Conftantinople, watchful of political tranquillity, will not admit coffee houfes beyond a certain dimenfion, too fmall to contain many people.

hear

hear extraordinary relations, are the more affiduous, in attending thefe narrators, as want of more extenfive information prevents the tale-teller remaining above a week in a place.

A common diverfion in the towns where there are foldiers, as well as in the country, is what the Moors call the game of Gunpowder; a kind of military exercife, that is the more pleafing to thefe people inafmuch as, by the nature of their government, they all are, or are liable to become, foldiers, therefore all have arms and horfes. By explofions of powder too they manifeft their feftivity on their holidays.

Their game of Gunpowder confifts in two bodies of horfe, each at a diftance from the other, galloping in fucceffive parties of four and four, and firing their pieces, charged with powder. Their chief art is in galloping up to the oppofite detachment, fuddenly ftopping, firing their mufkets, facing about, charging, and returning to the attack; all which manoeuvres are imitated

tated by their opponents. The Moors take great pleasure in this amusement, which is only an imitation of their military evolutions *.

Muley Yezit, one of the sons of the reigning Emperor, who passed his youth among the soldiers, and who has acquired a passionate love of war, is exceedingly expert at these exercises. I have seen him fire three times on a gallop within a hundred and fifty, or two hundred paces. He starts with one musket in his hand, another laid acrofs his saddle, and the third ballanced on his head. The first is fired at parting, and given to a soldier, who runs by his side; he then fires the second, and gives it likewife to take the third; after which he pulls up; and this is all executed in a moment.

* The Arabs appear to have introduced in Spain the exercife called *Juego de Cagnas*, which the Spaniards have adapted to their own cuftoms. The Moors, in return, renounced the exercife which the Turks call *Gaid*, the moment muskets supplied the ufe of lances.

Such

Such is the chief diverfion of the
Moors in their feftivals, marriages, and
every kind of rejoicing: the only honour
paid to ambaffadors, confuls, and all foreigners, is that of this game of gunpowder; a fport always attended with
fome danger, becaufe of the Moors want of
prudence, and fometimes with very unfortunate accidents.

The Moors, either from temperament,
or the moral and phyfical refult of their
education, are lefs fenfible of pain than
the Europeans; almoft naked, ever expofed to the effects of the air, their mufcles
acquire a numbnefs, which renders them
lefs delicate, and which at length nearly
deprives them of feeling. They feem,
like the wild plants of their deferts, to dif-
dain the inclemenices of the feafons.
Amid their military evolutions I have often
feen man and horfe overfet, and the former
rife without hurt or fprain. Their bodies,
not being encumbered by their clothing,
yield with facility to their motions, in
which, perhaps, they have an advantage
over the nations of Europe.

The

The Emperor of Morocco often orders the hands of thieves to be cut off; who, immediately set at liberty after punishment, take the diffevered hand up from the ground and run away. Such executions, being neither foreknown nor prepared, are performed with the knife of the first Moor that happens to be prefent, and who himfelf clumfily executes the fentence of his mafter.

A gallant, accufed by a hufband of being caught with his wife, was condemned by the Emperor to the baftinado, which, for fome time, made him think no more of his miftrefs. The hufband, having been abfent, was informed on his return that the lover had been as affiduous as ever; again he went with his complaint to the Emperor, who gave the gallant up to him, and commanded him to punifh him, fo as to render him incapable of ever difturbing his peace more. The hufband inftantly took his knife, and made the gallant even more wretched than Abelard. I knew the unfortunate man who fuffered this punifhment; he loft his beard by degrees,

grees, and infenfibly, but became fomewhat more flefhy.

After performing fuch barbarous ampu-
tations, the only dreffing they give the
wound is to fmear it over with tar, which,
fay they, is a remedy for all ills : it may
well be fuppofed that gallantry is not very
common among the Moors, and that in
this they have not approached European
refinement. I may venture to affirm, however, as before faid, that thefe people are
lefs alive to pain than the Europeans;
there is no doubt but that feverity of education hardens the body, and ftrengthens
the conftitution ; both of which are only
weakened by an excefs of care and effe-
minacy.

CHAP.

C H A P.   XIII.

Food, Manner of eating, Marriages of
Moors and Negroes.

THE Moors are little dainty in their
choice of food, which is simple and frugal; they breakfast in the morning before
they begin bufinefs; but their chief meal
is that which they make after fun fet.
Their moft common difh is, as I have already faid, the Coofcoofoo; they alfo have
beef, mutton, or fowls ftewed, and eat
roaft meats; but fuch delicacies are only
for extraordinary occafions, and among the
wealthy.

The Moors know not the ufe of table cloths, forks, or fpoons : their Coofcoofoo is not liquid, but, though fupplied
with broth, is left dry; and this they take

up

up in their hand in a kind of ball, which
they chuck with adroitnefs into their
mouths. Their meal ended, they lick
their fingers, and wipe them on their
clothes, which they wafh when dirty.
Thofe who keep negro flaves call them,
and rub their hands in their hair ; or, if
any Jew happens to be prefent, they make
a napkin of his garments.

Such as are tolerably at their eafe annu-
ally kill, in May, or June, an ox, or fat-
tened bull ; the flefh of which they preferve, ufing it occafionally the whole year;
they cut it into flips of about two inches
thick, and dry it in the fun for fome days;
after which they fry it in butter and oil,
and pot it ; the wealthy fill up the pot
with butter, that it may be the better preferved.

The Moors are exceedingly fond of tea,
alfo of fugar ; they buy but little, though
they are very glad to have it given them ;
they have learnt the ufe of this beverage
from the northern nations, among whom
it is not very ancient. It fhould feem they

are

are fond of tea, because it is heating; for it does not appear to me any way consonant with their frugal mode of feeding, or their dry temperament. Tea naturally is more salutary in colder climates, where the meat is fat, and where the people habituate themselves to the use of butter, cheese, milk, and beer: the Moors love coffee less than tea; however, in general, they love every thing that is given them. One of their proverbs is—" Given vinegar " is better than bought wine."

It is customary among the Moors to return home at sun set; they burn lamps in their houses, or small yellow wax candles; the use of tallow is unknown to them, and the heat would render it too expensive. According to Bochart, it should seem that we have learnt to burn wax from the people of Africa, and that the French word *Bougie*, signifying wax candles, is derived from the town of Bugia, near Algiers.

The Moors, like all other Mahometans, reckon their time by lunar months, so that their lunar year is eleven days shorter than

the

the folar year. Hence thirty-two years, two months, and fome days, of the latter, conftitute a revolution of thirty-three lunar years. In their aftronomical calculations, however, and that they may regulate the hour of prayer according to the variation of the feafons, the Moors follow the folar year, except that they ftill adhere to the old ftile ; reckoning eleven days later than the Europeans.

They count the days of the week by firft, fecond, third, &c., from Sunday to Saturday : this mode of reckoning they have received from the Hebrews, who fhould be more ancient than the Arabs, and who, according to the order of the creation of the world, faft on the feventh day ; for the word Sabbath, in Hebrew, denotes the number 7 *, a word which we have preferved with little alteration. The Mahometans feaft on the Friday, becaufe the Arabs,

---

* This is not the received etymology of the word Sabbath, which comes from שבת. He refted. The two words, however, שבת and שבע, have a near affinity. T.

before Mahomet, had confecrated that day to prayer, and had called it the day of the congregation. Mahomet did not think proper to change an eftablifhed cuftom.

The Moors marry young: the females arrive at puberty at the age of thirteen. They are permitted four wives, and as many concubines as they are able to maintain. In their cities, as I have already obferved, the Moors generally have but one wife, and that for reafons of œconomy and concord. Plurality of wifes being here a luxury, each proportions the number according to his ftate and riches.

In fome parts no portion is given with the wife; on the contrary, the hufband pays: a cuftom as ancient as the days of Laban, who made Jacob ferve fourteen years before he would give him his daughter. It is, however, moft ufual to give a portion with the bride; if fhe be repudiated, the hufband reftores it twofold: fhould the hufband die, the wife recovers her portion, and the eighth part of his effects.

The

The children of the wives all have equal claim to the effects of the father and mother; thofe of the concubines only can claim half as much. There are no baftards in thefe countries, except the children of proftitutes, who are called *Harami*; that is to fay, the children of fin. The fame expreffion is ufed to fignify a malignant perfon, or one addicted to play jocular tricks. The tone and the circumftances under which it is fpoken denote the difference.

Women not being admitted into the fociety of men, the young people here do not marry for love: they are all matches of family convenience: from the mother only can the young man, or maiden, learn what is the character, and what the accomplifhments, of the intended helpmate. The relations having firft agreed, they prepare the bridal feaft, and marriages are celebrated the moft pompoufly in the pooreft countries. A few days before the ceremony the bridegroom is accompanied on horfeback through the town, with drums, hautboys, and friends, who occafionally

fire

fire their muskets. On the nuptial day the bridegroom is again taken in procession about sun set, but with a greater train and more ceremony.

On this day he wears a red cap, his sabre in a bandelier, and his face almost covered by a veil to hide him from evil augury. Around him are several young men, one of whom fans him with a handkerchief; he behaves like the Emperor in the midst of his court, and on this occasion even bears the same title. During the procession the musketeers quicken their discharges till he re-enters his own house.

The bride then leaves the house of her father in the same order. She is seated in a kind of square or octagonal cage, about twelve feet in circumference, carried by a mule. This cage rising to a pyramid is adorned by gauzes and stuffs of various colours. The youthful bride is escorted by a number of her relations and neighbours, some with their torches, others their muskets, which they frequently discharge. Arrived at the door of her spouse, the rela-

tions

tions introduce her to her hufband, carefully obferving that, as fhe enters, fhe fhall
not touch the threfhold of the door: the
father, mother, and relations, retire ; fome
few bridemaids only remain, holding jocular difcourfe, and finging licentious
verfes *.

It is cuftomary for thefe bridemaids to receive the proofs of the confummation of
marriage, which they bear, finging, to the
parents of the bride. Virginity is fo effential a condition to the validity of marriage among thefe people, that, fhould not
the proof exift, the hufband has a right to
fend back his wife. It is common enough,
however, for them to provide a fubftitute
for thefe formal proofs, that they may

* Several of the cuftoms of the Moors are peculiar to
themfelves, and are no way connected with Mahometanifm.
Thefe it fhould feem they have adopted from the nations
that have reigned over Africa. The Romans, in their marriages, took care that the bride, at entering, fhould not touch
the threfhold of the door. When fhe was delivered over to
the bridegroom, they fung alfo at Rome licentious fongs,
which they called Fefcinnini, fo named from Fefcinia, the
place where thefe nuptial fongs were invented.

                fome-

somewhat the sooner rid themselves of the noise of the singers.

The same custom is observed in Nigritia, where these proofs must be publicly exposed on the morrow of the nuptial day. The prudence of such laws in these hot climates, where morals are more easily corrupted, will, no doubt, be perceived. Virtue suffers less temptation under a more temperate sun, where luxury only, and the prevalence of dissipation, have rendered licentiousness too general.

After the marriage, the Moors feast their relations and friends in the country * ; the two families each kill an ox, which they have taken good care to fatten ; and these, with a provision of vegetables, abundantly supply the banquet. Marriages are most usually made after harvest ; the fertility or dearth of which, especially in

* There is a proverb among the Moors, which says, The Christians spend their estates in lawsuits, the Jews in keeping their festivals, and the Moors in banqueting at their marriages,

the

the country, occasions marriages to be more or less numerous.

The marriages of the country are held with equal festivity, and even greater, when the bride and bridegroom are not of the same Douhar, because that, in this case, there is a double cavalcade, and a much greater train. Nor are the same scruples observed with respect to the proofs that should satisfy the husband, because it often happens that the marriage is consummated before the ceremony.

Independent of the families of soldiers descended from negroes, and still so called, though they have insensibly lost the colour of black, there are numerous other families of negroes, male and female, in the empire of Morocco, which have been transported from Nigritia through the southern provinces, and destined to domestic slavery. The Moors, if they please, may cohabit with their female negroes ; but the better class of people seldom indulge this licentiousness, being unwilling that their

T 4   children

children fhould be confounded with the negroes. The words negro and flave are fynonimous among the Moors, and indicate dependence and a ftate of humiliation incompatible with the ideas they have of their own freedom. Is it not aftonifhing that people, who have not the liberty of thinking, and who are only diftinguifhed from thofe they call flaves by their colour, fhould hold the idea of fervitude in fuch abhorrence ?

It is cuftomary among the Moors to marry their male and female negroes, and, after a certain period, to reftore them to freedom. Thus we fee hufbandmen are more humane toward their flaves than commercial nations, and that negroes are much more happy, among a people whom we call barbarians, than they are in the colonies of Europe. Without ill-treating them, the Moors employ them in guarding their flocks and herds, tilling their lands, and in domeftic fervices for a limited time. They depopulate one part of Africa to people another.

Europe,

Europe, on the contrary, leaves Africa desolate, and bedews her plantations with the tears and blood of men to obtain sugar and coffee. To supply imaginary wants, procure momentary pleasures, she sacrifices whole generations, forgetful of every tie, every duty of humanity ; and, if asked the reason of such cruelty, replies, These men are black.

Wherefore should prejudices, like these, exist in the mind ; wherefore should different shades of colour give rise to opinions of greater or less degrees of innocence ; yet such opinions, such prejudices, appear to be very ancient and universal. In the east sinister ideas are annexed to the colour of black ; the modern Greeks indifferently use the word Mavros, to signify a black, or an unhappy, man. An East Indian, who has committed a fault, says, with shame, he is black. The Black sea has acquired its name only because of the frequent shipwrecks on its coasts. The Turks attribute ill omens to the colour of black, and view it with repugnance. The Europeans mourn and array the mi-

nisters

nifters of religion and juftice, who are
equally fuppofed to have renounced pleafure, in black.

The negroes, who are confidered as
flaves among the Moors, even after they
are reftored to liberty, live by labour.
They have no wealth to tempt the avidity
of government ; they intermarry with
each other, are moft fingularly chearful
and gay, and delight to laugh and talk.
Their feftivals feem to bear confiderable
affinity to the feafons, and are paffed by di-
verting themfelves in finging and dancing,
which they perform with aftonifhing regularity.   They have preferved their own
particular cuftoms and fports in Morocco ;
for, in Nigritia, the youth of the village,
moft admired, is he who can invent the
moft gay and grotefque dance.

The negroes throughout this empire
conform to the religion of Mahomet, without fcarcely knowing what it means ; but
to this they daily add the adoration of the
fun, which is the firft object of their worfhip.   The marriages of negroes in Morocco

rocco greatly refemble thofe of the
Moors ; all the proceffions that relate to
them are accompanied by muficians, and
preceded by flags made of gauze handker-
chiefs, fufpended at the ends of reeds.

They marry after harveft, and when
they are certain of fubfiftence. Such, in
the firft ages of the world, muft have been
the bafis on which all fociety was formed.
The firft ceremony before a negro marriage is to carry corn to the mill, fufficient
to fupply bread for a whole year ; and this
they bear finging, accompanied by drums
and caftanets. They return two days
after with the like ceremonies to receive
the flour.

Their houfehold furniture confifts in a
mat, two fheep-fkins, unfheared, to fit
upon, a lamp, a jar of oil, fome earthen
pots, and plates ; the whole fcarcely worth
two guineas, but borne in proceffion like
their corn. The mufic at thefe feftivals is
the heavieft expence. The marriages of
the negroes are not attended by fo many
people, but there is more real mirth ; neither

ther do the women veil themselves like the Moors. Some of them paint their cheeks, which, though it does not add to their beauty, increases the vivacity of their eyes,

CHAP

CHAP. XIV.

Manner of preserving Corn — Hiding of Money — Respect for Storks. — Burial of the Dead — Feast of Saint John.

DESIROUS of preserving their corn, the Moors, on the approach of harvest, watch their fields and drive away the birds. From the same motive they do not kill birds of prey, which, by the deftruction of other birds, guard and preserve their harvefts. European luxury and plenty has occafioned the very oppofite mode to be adopted : a price is put on the deftruction of birds of prey to preferve partridges that ravage the fields. We dread the want of game, but not of corn.

The harveft over, it is the cuftom of the Moors to enclofe their corn in matamores;

that

that is to fay, in pits, where the corn is long preferved. We learn from Bochart*, that this is a very ancient cuftom, and muft have been general in hot countries inhabited by wandering tribes. To preferve the corn dry, the fides of the pit are lined with ftraw, in proportion as it is filled, and, when full, covered with the fame. On this a ftone is laid, over which a mount of earth is raifed, in a pyramidal form, to prevent the foaking of the water when the rain defcends.

Fathers, among the moft wealthy, ufually fill a matamore at the birth of a child, and empty it on the day of marriage. I have feen corn fo preferved five-and-twenty years; its whitenefs was loft, its powers of production, perhaps, injured, and, had it been fown, might have produced only ftraw.

When convenience, or the imperial command, oblige the Moors to change

* *Geographia Sacra.*

their

their place of abode, fhould they not be able to take their grain with them, they leave ftones heaped over the matamores as marks, which they afterwards with difficulty find. In this cafe they ufually obferve the ground at fun rifing, and where they perceive a denfer vapour they find a matamore : this increafe of the fun's exhalation is the confequence of the fermenting of the wheat.

Not only do the Moors depofit their fuperflux of corn in the ground to preferve it, but alfo their riches, which fufpicion and oppreffion induce them to bury, having neither furniture nor other means of hiding them from the knowledge of their relations. There is, perhaps, more money buried throughout the empire of Morocco than there is in circulation ; much of this is loft, becaufe, as I have elfewhere faid, the poffeffors, while living, fhould it be difcovered, dread the avidity of their fucceffors.

Among the frequent revolutions on the fucceffion of the feveral Sharifs, whofe family

family at prefent reigns, various fudden emigrations have taken place ; during which the Moors had neither time nor means of carrying off their money, and could only gather ftones, or make other uncertain remarks on the places where it was concealed, hoping they might re-cover it on their return. Thefe hopes muft have been often deftroyed by diftance, or death. Thofe among them who could write, who were by no means the majo-rity, defcribed with all the precifion they were able the place of depofit, to aid their defcendants in its recovery.

Such fudden removals in the encamp-ments of thefe tribes gave rife to a fpecies of impoftors, who were fuppofed to be for-cerers, but who, in reality, were knaves, that, having gained information, profited there, as elfe where, by the ignorance of others. It may be prefumed the whole art of thefe people confifted in knowing how to read, and thus difcovering the hid-ing places from the writings with which they were entrufted. Thus has an art, fo univerfal in other countries, been con-

founded

founded with magic by the Moors. The Talbes of the tribes who inhabit the south, where the imagination seems most addicted to the miraculous, study this art with assiduity.

An inferior species of superstition among the Moors is the repugnance they have to the killing of Storks; which act, they say, is sinful. It may be, that the regularity with which these birds utter their cries, and the motion they make with their bodies, which, in some sort, resembles that of the Mahometans when at prayer, have annexed ideas of piety to their preservation. It is also natural to suppose the lives of Storks are spared from a much more rational motive, since they destroy noxious insects, locusts, and serpents. In the first state of society, simple and innocent man imagined every thing which was forbidden, every thing injurious to order, decency, or the good of the whole, was sinful. The present Moors blindly obey the commands of their Prince, which they regard as the laws of religion.

It is supposed that Storks frequent Barbary, in greater numbers, because they are not killed there : it is also probable they delight in this country, on account of the many ruins, old buildings, and uninhabited lands, where they can with more facility find food and asylum. The Storks in Morocco regularly disappear at the close of summer, and return toward the end of January. That the want of subsistence is the motive of this regular and annual change there can be little doubt. The countries bordering on the Niger, inundated in June, July, and August, by the overflowing of that river, which, from similar causes, produces similar effects to those of the Nile*, must, in winter, swarm with insects, on which these birds feed. They afterward return to the north of Africa, where the regular rains of November, December, and the remainder of the winter, fill the marshes, and people them anew with insects.

* The overflowing of these two rivers, according to La Martiniere, is occasioned by the abundant rains which fall between the line and the tropic, from the month of June to September.

The

The Moors, like all other Mahometans, hold it a thing irreverent, and contrary to the fpirit of religion, to bury their dead in mofques, and to prophane the temple of the Moft High by the putrefaction of dead bodies.   In the infancy of the Church the Chriftians had the like piety, and gave example of the refpect in which they held temples, dedicated to religious worfhip. But ill-guided devotion, mingled with fuperftitious vanities, and that contagious fpirit of felf intereft which pervades all human affairs, without refpecting the altar of God, have, together, infenfibly perverted men's ideas.   The burial grounds of the Mahometans are moft of them without the city ; the Emperors have their fepulchres diftinct and diftant from the mofque, in fanctuaries, built by themfelves, or in places which they have indicated ; their tombs are exceedingly fimple : the Moors do not imitate the oftentation of Europeans, were fuperb monuments are raifed rather to gratify living pride than merit dead.

All Mahometans inter the dead at the

hour

hour set apart for prayer; the defunct is not kept in the house, except he expires after sun set; but the body is transported to the mosque, whither it is carried by those who are going to prayer; each, from a spirit of devotion, is desirous to carry in his turn.

The Moors sing at their burial service; which usage, perhaps, they have imitated after the Christians of Spain, for the oriental Mahometans do not sing. They have no particular colour appropriated to mourning; their grief for the loss of relations is a sensation of the heart they do not attempt to express by outward symbols. Women regularly go on the Friday to weep over, and pray at, the sepulchres of the dead, whose memory they hold dear.

The Moors have a custom of making bonfires at the feast of Saint John, and are less able even than the Christians to give any reason for this practice. I happened to be at Fez during this festival, which the Moors, according to the old stile, observe much in the same manner as do the Europeans.

peans. I afked a Moor, who was tolerably well informed, why they made bonfires: and he anfwered me, it was *el Anfard*, which fignifies in Arabic, pronouncing the laft *a* fhort, the companion, or defender, and fhould denote Saint John, the precurfor and companion of Chrift. He had no farther reafon to give for the fires thus publicly made.

The origin of thefe fires is of very ancient and remote date. It feems probable that, in old times, they were fignals, announcing to the people the fun's elevation, the progrefs of fummer, the maturity of their grain, or the feafon in which they might bathe without injury to their health. The cuftom, in fome of our fouthern provinces, of throwing water over the paffengers, on this bonfire day, is fome fupport to the latter conjecture. At Sallee, where the harveft is gathered before the feaft of Saint John, which among the Moors correfponds with the fifth of July, I have feen young people collect reeds and ftraw into a heap, fet them on float down the river, light them in a blaze as they fwam, and fport

U 3

round, which, apparently to me, include the two motives that I imagine gave birth to the practice; that is, to announce the summer solstice, and the proper season of bathing *. The feast of Saint John, which has been since fixed at the same season by the church, has insensibly effaced these original ideas among the Christians; and ideas of devotion, neither well founded nor consistent, have been annexed to a political regulation.

* M. Court de Gebelin says, these fires were lighted the moment the year began, and that the first of all years, that is to say, the most ancient of which men have any knowledge, began with the month of June: hence the name of this month, Junior. After a succession of years, the year no longer began with the summer solstice; the lighting of fires, however, still continued from habit.

Monde primitif. Alleg. Orien. prem. tab.

CHAP.

Military Forces of Morocco.

NO sooner had ambition, religion, and those clashing interests which disturb and desolate the earth, set nation in arms against nation, than each must be supplied with soldiers for its defence: the custom, indeed, which Kings now have of keeping standing armies, is not very ancient.

The numerous levies made by the Kings of Morocco were, at first, either to protect their religion or maintain their sovereignty over Spain; their soldiers were either actuated by the spirit of Mahometanism or the hope of pillage. These sovereigns had no troops properly their own, nor, perhaps, had they revenues sufficient for their maintenance. To this want of a concerted plan between King and People we may ap-

U 4

parently

parently attribute thofe revolutions which formerly diftracted the empire, multiplied its fovereigns, and expofed the ever-varying people to fuch continued changes in their mafters.

After the twelfth century the States conquered by Jacob Almonfor were again divided; the people more accuftomed to war, chofe their own chiefs, and, in the tumult of ftruggling independence, each province, and almoft each city, had its king. The power of fuch trifling ftates, ever in fedition, was very unable to refift the efforts of an ambitious conqueror.

At the beginning of the feventeeth century new revolutions took place, nor did the Empire of Morocco acquire its prefent form and degree of confiftency till under the government of Muley Arfhid and Muley Ifhmael. Thefe Princes chofe for their affociates, and the participators of their favours, fome determined mountaineers, and negroes brought from the South. With thefe they prefently fubjugated a multitude of thofe petty kings, without power, without

without soldiers, consequently without defence, that then existed throughout Barbary.

After Muley Ishmael had well established his authority, he obliged the provinces to supply him with troops, by whose aid he might make this authority respected. But these pastoral soldiers, who became soldiers only from fear, and whom interest or despair might occasion to revolt, inspired but little confidence in a prince so ambitious.

Desirous of acquiring a military establishment, whose interest it should be to increase his own personal glory, he transported negroe families from the South, of whom his legions might be formed, and by whom increased. Instructed in the military art during a tolerably long reign, these negroes successfully aided in establishing and confirming despotism. At the death of Muley Ishmael, near a hundred thousand negroes had served him as soldiers.

The feebleness of his successors augmented the power and arrogance of this military body,

body, that now was mafter of the throne and empire; it was become equally odious to the Sovereign and the fubject. After finding himfelf the victim of their inconftancy and avarice, Muley Abdallab felt the neceffity of humbling thefe turbulent troops. He fowed diffention between the negroes and the principal tribes of the Moors, fo that the former were at length facrificed to the hatred and vengeance of the provinces, and to the political repofe and barbarity of the defpot.

As a balance to the power of thofe negroes who furvived thefe divifions, this Prince formed bodies of troops from the mountaineers, and other diftant cafts, who became fo many hoftages for the fidelity of their tribes. Independent of the legions in actual fervice, each province, when needful, was obliged to furnifh and maintain its contingent of armed troops.

By this prudent plan the defpot always had a fufficient body of forces, at his command, to quell any provincial infurrections. In thefe national levies he alfo found a neceffary

ceffary fupport againft the enterprizes of the negroes, and his troops divided by prejudices concerning their colour, their origin, religion, for fuch prejudices exift the moft in the moft ignorant, were too much difunited among themfelves to infpire him with fear.

Such then was, and fuch ftill is, the military eftablifhment of the Empire of Morocco, and which was lefs the effect of a political and well-combined plan, than the refult of a fucceffion of accidents, that, in all kingdoms, after having deftroyed, again infenfibly reftores order; like, as in nature, we fee a calm fucceed to the fhock of elements, threatening total defolation.

Change of times and change of circumftances have given birth to new reforms. About ten years ago fifty thoufand negroes were kept in pay in Morocco. The reigning Emperor perceiving that the maintenance of thefe troops was become burdenfome, at a time when the public diftrefs required, or enforced, public œconomy,

deter-

determined, in order to prevent every difagreeable confequence, to difarm and difband the negroes, and alfo to confine them in the oppofite extremities of his empire. Of the fifty thoufand he preferved only fome five or fix as his body guard, felecting thofe in whofe commanders he had the greate't confidence. He keeps near his perfon a ftill greater number of trufty troops ; but I doubt whether the total amount to more than between fifteen and eighteen thoufand men in conftant pay ; a part of whom are always fent into the diftant provinces, to protect the tax-gatherers.

Yet muft not the military power of the Empire of Morocco be eftimated at twenty thoufand men. Although their employment is that of agriculture, moft of the Moors are foldiers, or, in cafe of need, can foon fo become ; not any of them but keep a horfe, a fabre, and a mufket, and who are not ready to march at the firft command of the Monarch.

When the Emperor is in want of troops, each province, on his requisition, supplies and maintains a number of men proportionate to its population and its wealth; but these extraordinary levies are only kept in service when the tillage of their lands does not require their presence; that is to say, between seed time and harvest, and after harvest till it is again necessary to prepare their lands. The Emperor bestows no other gratifications on these provincial troops than such as he himself pleases, and which are never of any great value.

It must be remembered that this empire, having nothing to fear from its neighbours, stands less in need of the support of numerous armies. A detachment of four or six thousand men, who march and accompany the despot, is sufficient to maintain order throughout his provinces, and to inspire the States to the west of his Empire with dread, where nature has done nothing in defence of the people, and where agriculture and the spirit of trade

have

have encouraged the love of public tranquillity.

When those tribes that inhabit the neighbourhood of the mountains give tokens of insurrection, some ten or twelve thousand additional troops, of the provincial levies, are sufficient to reduce them to obedience. These expeditions generally consist in ravaging the country, and in the destruction of those wretches who have neither money to purchase remission nor arms for self-defence. Such incursions are the more frequent in the Empire of Morocco because that fear, there, continually keeps the minds of men in fermentation; it is a smothered fire, the embers of which occasionally glow, but are unable to produce a flame. The people are too much debased; there is too little concord among the different tribes, which are always too much divided among themselves to produce any great effects.

As the military forces of states are in proportion to their population, and their progress in the arts, I presume,

these

thefe circumſtances taken into the eſtimate, there are more foldiers in the Empire
of Morocco than under the Princes of Europe, if we except thofe nations where
the people are entirely educated in the ufe
of arms, and where each man is a foldier.
The population of this empire has but little relation to its extent, fince it appears
that two thirds of it lie uncultivated and
uninhabited.   I doubt whether this population exceeds fix millions, and do not fuppofe it can be lefs than five.

Notwithſtanding that thefe people are
naturally addicted to the fhepherd's and
the farmer's life, yet, having the continual revolutions which have exifted among
their anceftors before their eyes, military ideas are kept up in their imaginations, and even give birth to the chief
of their amufements.   I fuppofe the
Emperor of Morocco might, with great
eafe, raife from two to three hundred thoufand men, did he find fo great a force neceffary.   True it is that armies thus numerous would foon experience want of fubfiftence in a country laid wafte by its own

poverty,

poverty, that they muſt preſently be diſperſed, and for this ſole reaſon annihilated.

It would likewiſe ſcarcely be poſſible to put ſo large a body in motion, and to render it actually ſerviceable in an open country, where there are no places of arms or fortreſſes to form magazines, protect a retreat, or rally a defeated army.

It may alſo reaſonably be ſuppoſed that this empire will never have need to make ſuch efforts, ſo long as it ſhall have nothing to fear from its neighbours. This time, however, will come, ſhould the regency of Algiers change its principles and conſtitution, and, buſied with projects of ambition, endeavour to extend its empire. This would apparently be difficult to execute, though ſomewhat like this is to be feared, from the diſlike theſe two States have to each other*. If the government

* The regency of Algiers is a military power, compoſed of Turks, whom the Moors regard as ſtrangers: for which reaſon there is a continual jealouſy between this regency and the court of Morocco.

of Algiers continues prudent, it will scarcely attempt to extend its domains; it is quite sufficient that it has at present a multitude of Moorish tribes under its yoke, which they support with repugnance. This regency would likewise no longer preserve its aristocracy and its strength, were it to extend itself by conquest.

Were the Moors capable of union, and susceptible of courage, it would, perhaps, be much more easy for the Sharifs of Morocco to exterminate the power of Algiers, than for the Algerines to make conquests in Morocco. According to present appearances, no change, however, can with probability be presaged; but, should the Turks receive any severe checks in Europe, it may well be feared that the regencies of Barbary would anew become the asylum of the Ottoman soldiery and marine, which might expose the shores of the Mediterranean to future revolution.

The troops kept in pay by the Emperor of Morocco, that may be looked upon as his body guard, and that at prefent do not exceed eighteen thoufand men, have various divifions; they are diftinguifhed by their tribes, the Negroes, the Ludaya, the Gayoran, and others; each have their colours, and their fignal of rallying. Thefe divifions are compofed of a number of companies, each confifting of a hundred men; every company has its chief, or captain, whom they call the chief of a hundred; under him are two officers, who command fifty each; and ten other more inferior officers, who have the command of ten men each. All that thefe troops know of military difcipline is fubmiffion to their fuperiors; they are not fubject to any precifion in their exercife or manœuvres.

The embodied troops that form the Emperor's guard are, in Morocco, known by the title of Al Boccari, or Sidi Boccari, Muley Ifhmael having put himfelf under the aufpices of this commentator of the Koran, and confecrated his firft legions in the oath he adminiftered to them.

His

His book, depofited under a tent in the centre of the army, is the fignal for rallying
the troops, and a fort of pledge for their
fidelity. Thus, likewife, had the Carthaginians a facred tabernacle, befide the tent
of the general, to which the whole army
directed its devotion.

The Emperor of Morocco has but few
infantry in his fervice; the chief force
of his armies confifts in his cavalry; but
that cavalry, always acting in diforder,
would be very little able to refift the fhock
of the European horfe. There is no kind
of uniformity either among the men or
horfes; the reigning Emperor feemed inclined to introduce fome diftinction of re-
gimental drefs, but this novelty never became prevalent.

The Moors are good horfemen; they
can endure hunger, thirft, fatigue, and
every inconvenience; they have the neceffary qualities to form good foldiers, but
they are not fo formed.

Armies

Armies among the Moors are ufually drawn up in a crefcent, the ftrength of which is in the centre: here alfo the artillery is placed; their whole art of attack confifts in acting with the detachments at the two extremities, fo as to furround the enemy, put him between two fires, and at the fame time expofe him to be cannonaded by the artillery.

When an army is in motion little care is taken of a fupply of provifions; it ufually encamps near fprings, or a river, and the provinces in the neighbourhood of the camp are commanded to fix their markets in its environs, that each, paying for what he wants, may obtain food and neceffaries; fhould there be a fcarcity in fuch provinces, the enterprize muft be abandoned; in dry feafons the Emperor has often been obliged to defift from an expedition for want of pafturage, or of water, for the horfe.

All the arms neceffary for war are not fabricated in the Empire of Morocco: the reigning Emperor, defirous of eftablifhing foundcries

founderies for artillery, about fifteen years
ago, fent for the neceffary workmen to
Conftantinople; but this project was abandoned, equally on account of the expence
and becaufe he feared left his fubjects
might turn this art to the deftruction of
his own power. He contented himfelf
with forming a manufactory for bombs at
Tetuan; that, in the fabrication of thefe,
he might melt down a number of wafte
cannon, of which he could make no other
ufe.

During the laft fifteen or twenty years
this Emperor has procured more than fixty
mortars of various dimenfions, and above
two hundred pieces of artillery, which
he has received as prefents from foreign
courts, or has purchafed by his agents.
He has likewife exercifed fome pupils in
the art of gunnery, and the firing of
bombs; but pupils never become mafters
when they do nothing but what they are
bidden, and where the mind is not fufceptible of thofe principles by which art is
brought to perfection.

X 3

The

The muſkets neceſſary for defence are forged in the Empire of Morocco, and for this purpoſe they uſe the iron of Biſcay, which is more eaſily worked and poliſhed than that of the north. Theſe muſkets are made too heavy, are about ſix feet and a half long, and are too much loaded with iron ; they fatigue the ſoldier, and the muzzles drop when they fire ; their locks are ſafe and ſolid, but ſnap hard, and are conſequently ſlow.

The ſabres uſed by the Moors are alſo manufactured in Morocco, and from the iron of Biſcay. There, as every where elſe, certain waters are found, which temper ſteel with greater perfection.

Gunpowder is likewiſe made in this empire, but the ſulpher which is uſed is brought from Europe. Not having acquired ſufficient art in purifying their powder, it is ſo glutinous that, on the fourth or fifth diſcharge, the priming will not take fire, or, at leaſt, retards the exploſion ; the bad quality of the powder

likewiſe

likewife renders it fufceptible of humidity, and prevents its being long preferved.

CHAP.

C H A P. XVI.

Maritime Strength of the Empire of Mo-
rocco.

THE world is no better informed concerning the naval than the military power
of Morocco, before and after the tenth
century. We only know that, in the time
of Jacob Almonfor, and afterward, under
fome of his fucceffors, various confiderable
armaments were formed to tranfport the
troops of Morocco into Spain, and profit
by the divifions which then diftracted that
country; but we are unacquainted with
thefe armaments in the detail. It fhould
feem that the forefts, which then remained
on the northern part of the coaft, were
exceedingly ufeful for their fhipbuilding;
but, as the marine, after the maritime efforts which had exhaufted Rome and Carthage, was only at this time reviving, we
cannot

cannot have any very high ideas of its ſtrength in thoſe countries.

Probably, after the expulſion of the Moors from Spain, and thoſe revolutions which internally diſtracted the empire of Morocco, all naval exertions, were long renounced. The coaſts of Barbary, waſhed by the Mediterranean and the Weſtern Ocean, only gave harbour to ſome pirates ; and the progreſs of theſe, it is preſumed, could not be very great, the Portugueſe having conquered Ceuta, Arzilla and Tangiers. Navigation began to be encouraged under the reign of Muley Iſhmael, when theſe towns had been abandoned, and commerce became more generally promoted throughout Europe.

The river of Sallee, which brought veſſels to the towns of Sallee and Rabat, was at that time more navigable than it is at preſent, and admitted veſſels of great burden, and heavily built. Sallee was a kind of republic, feudatory to Muley Iſhmael, the people of which addicted themſelves to trade and piracy. The Sallee rovers became

came formidable to the merchants of Europe, and their very name ſtill preſerves ſome impreſſion of the fears they at that time inſpired, but which now daily weaken.

Muley Iſhmael received ten per cent. on each prize from the Corſairs of this regency, and alſo ten ſlaves from every hundred.   The gallies that cruiſed in the ſtraits wholly appertained to the Emperor.   An old Moor, whom I knew, and who was a ſhip-boy on board theſe gallies, has aſſured me, they carried no cannon, that they were ballaſted with flints gathered on the ſea ſide, or the banks of the river, which was their whole ammunition; that, rowing along-ſide merchant veſſels, which at that time were themſelves ill armed, they ſhowered ſuch a quantity of theſe ſtones, on board, that the ſailors were obliged to run, and they took poſſeſſion of the ſhip.

Hiſtory informs us that the cuſtom of ſlinging ſtones is moſt ancient among the Moors, as it alſo was among the inhabi-

tants

tants of the Balearic iflands, now called Majorca and Minorca; for, in the wars between the Romans and the Carthaginians, the Moors were oppofed to thefe people, whom they fought at their own weapons.

Muley Ifhmael maintained flaves from oftentation, employed them in the building of his palaces, and facrificed them to his caprice and ferocity. Under the reign of Muley Abdallah, Sallee and Rabat preferved their municipal government; and piracy, fubject to fimilar taxation, had fimilar fuccefs, except that this Prince referved the flaves to himfelf, paying the pirate for them at the rate of fifty piafters per head. Equally cruel with his father, Muley Abdallah put many of them to death, in his fanguinary madnefs, but he allowed them to be ranfomed.

The reigning Emperor, who has not inherited the ferocity of his forefathers, having deprived the regency of Sallee of its riches, privileges, and independence, commanded the Corfairs to act for his profit;

profit; and, confidering the redemption of flaves as a fource of revenue, he has treated them with more humanity.

This change, in the manner of government, and in the adminiftration of the town of Sallee, has been favourable to the commercial part of Europe. The courage of the Sallee rovers, no longer excited by intereft, which is the moft powerful of motives for the undertaking of dangerous enterprizes, declines; deprived of the profits of their piracies, they are no longer eager in fearch of perils.

In the beginning of his reign the Emperor had veffels built at Sallee, which would carry fix-and-twenty, and even fix-and-thirty guns; for the earthquake, fo deftructive to Lifbon, which happened on the firft of November, 1755, increafed the depth of water at the mouth of the river to near thirty feet at flood time. The fands, however, annually accumulate, and the burden of veffels is obliged to be proportioned to the depth of water at the bar.

2

Thefe

These large vessels inspired considerable fear, but did little damage; heavily and disproportionately built, they were bad sailers, and perished, in time, through the inexperience of their captains. Piracy at this time had but little success; and the less because that France and Spain were then at war with England, and merchant ships either durst not keep the seas or were obliged to be strong enough to sustain an action. The peace of 1763 once more occasioned the people of Sallee to make new efforts; they took some Provençal ships in the Mediterranean, the crews of which, imagining they were chaced by Algerine corsairs, durst not make any defence.

They had the like success in the Western Ocean, and in two years took more than fifteen vessels, ten of which were French.

One Captain Motard is, perhaps, the only man among them who made any resistance. The memory of the action he sustained merits to be preserved to his honour;

nour; his whole ſtrength conſiſted but of four cannon, and twenty-four men, ſome of whom were paſſengers; yet did he valorouſly defend himſelf within piſtol ſhot againſt Reys Salah, a reputed deſperado, and who commanded a xebeck of twenty-four guns and a hundred-and-thirty men. Motard ſtruck juſt as his veſſel was ſinking, having loſt a part of his men, and killed or diſabled more than forty of the crew of the corſair.

When Sidy Mahomet had made peace with the principal nations of Europe, he collected all his veſſels into a ſquadron, that he might maintain his marine force, and add to its reſpectability.

Five of theſe his frigates, or xebecks, as they were returning from Tunis in September, 1773, were encountered off Cape Spartel by the Chevalier Acton *, at that

* The ſame gentleman who, ſometime afterward, entered into the ſervice of the court of Naples, to whom the King has ſince confided the adminiſtration of the marine, and alſo the war department——The Chevalier Acton is an Engliſhman, and at preſent well known in Europe.

time

time the commander of a small Tuscan frigate: After a few broadsides he disordered and dispersed four of them. Reys Laschmi Misteri, of Rabat, who led the van, had the courage singly to engage the Chevalier, as well to relieve his associates as to give them time to rally, and return to the charge; but the valorous men of Sallee were not of the same opinion; they made for the Port of Laracha, and two of the four, in their great haste, were stranded. Reys Laschmi Misteri was forced, after a short engagement, to strike, and was brought into Leghorn.

On this day the Chevalier Acton, with a small Tuscan frigate, destroyed a part of the maritime force of Morocco: the fleets of the great powers of Europe never had a similar victory. The whole naval force of Sidy Mahomet * consists in little more

* All the Emperors have the title of Muley, which, in Arabic, signifies Lord and Master: the reigning Emperor, respecting the name of the Prophet, after whom he is called, has assumed the epithet Sidy, which has the same signification as Muley, but is more respectful.

than

than fix or eight frigates of two hundred
tons burthen, with port holes for from fourteen to eighteen fix-pounders, and, perhaps,
a dozen gallies. He has a number of failors
registered, who receive a fmall pay, but
which is not fixed; fo that his fubjects
are little inclined to a feafaring life, and
become failors with reluctance.

The choice of commanders is lefs influenced by the opinion entertained of their
capacity than that of their known
wealth; the Emperor feldom will truft
his fhips to any but rich people, who are
able to anfwer for accidents: this neceffarily occafions the commanders to fail late,
and return foon, taking care to avoid all
perils which may endanger their fortune
and peace of mind.

Although the naval ftrength of the Emperor of Morocco is not very confiderable,
the fituation of his ftates will always be
an advantage: he poffeffes Tangiers and
Tetuan at the different mouths of the
ftrait, through which veffels from all parts
of the globe, failing for the Mediterranean,
muft

muſt paſs ; and his row gallies, in ſo narrow a paſſage, are always capable of cal-
culating their diſtances, and aſcertaining a
ſafe retreat.

CHAP. XVII.

Revenues of the Emperor of Morocco.

ABSOLUTE master of every thing contained within his dominions, it may seem useless, or superfluous, to form any estimate of the revenues of the Emperor of Morocco, since they depend so entirely on his will. To render his yoke more light, however, and to encourage his slaves in their labours, he nourishes among them ideas of property: the Despot contents himself with those impositions prescribed by the Koran, save and except such innovations as have been introduced by time and custom, and which are held in respect by a people so submissive.

The taxes which the Koran allows, and which the Arab Monarchs have ever ex-

acted

acted from their hufbandmen and fhepherd
fubjects, confift in tenths, on all the productions of their lands and herds. This
impoft, which is the moft ancient, the moft
natural, and the leaft deftructive of all tri-
butes paid by the cultivator, was fufficient
in thofe ages, when the Sovereign kept
no ftanding armies, and when the defence
of property, the intereft of religion, or rather the fpirit of fanaticifm, and the thirft
of plunder, made foldiers flock to his
ftandards.

Taxation remained the fame when the
various States of Morocco erected themfelves into monarchies; the wants of thefe
petty fovereigns were not fufficiently exi-
gent, nor had they fufficient ftrength, to
enforce the exaction of heavier contributions. In thefe diftant times the revenues
of the kings of Morocco could not have
been very confiderable; the burden lay
light upon the people, and they were ftill
better able to bear it, becaufe they had
few wants, and were in thofe days more
wealthy.

It

It alfo appears probable that interior commerce, which originates in barter and the exchange of the refpective products, and which moft produces intercourfe between nations, was in thefe times more active than it is at prefent, and that the communication was much greater, and more continual, between the nations who inhabit the interior parts of Africa, and thofe on the coafts of Barbary. The hiftories, the narratives, the tales which the old people of the country repeat, and traditionally tranfmit to their children, and with which they amufe their fanciful avidity, all mention the gold duft which the Moors received from Tombut, and other fouthern countries in the neighbourhood of the Niger. For this they only gave the productions of their lands, which they could obtain by labour, and which is ever a true fource of wealth. Wars, revolutions, their arbitrary government, the European fettlements on the African fhores, and other caufes, may, perhaps, have forced trade into another channel, and the provinces of Morocco may no longer have the fame refources.

It

It cannot, at first view, be doubted but that this trade in gold dust was formerly a part of the merchandize of interior Africa, before the coast had any immediate intercourse or commerce with Europe, when we consider the immense riches accumulated at Carthage, and the prodigious efforts that republic made, during wars that continued more than half a century.

After revolutions so great, the different tribes of the Moors must have kept these communications open, but with less vigour and success, the means of such communications having continued in a fluctuating state till the close of the fifteenth centuay. It is sufficiently apparent that, not before this period, as I have already observed, did the treasures of Africa find a new and swifter vent, in consequence of the progress of navigation.

Yet must we be astonished when we remember the riches that were collected and heaped together among the mountains of Morocco, at those which were seized by Muley Arshid, in the first acts of his fero-

city:

city; and afterward at the quantity of gold ducats, in the time of Muley Ifhmael, which fome wealthy families had pre-ferved, and the remains of which they have concealed from the avidity of his fuc-ceffors.

The Empire was, beyond contradic-tion, more rich in thefe ancient times, be-caufe that property was better fecured, and induftry had more freedom of exertion, whence the people were univerfally more at their eafe. Muley Ifhmael himfelf, du-ring a long reign, maintained numerous forces, was ever in motion, and erected many buildings, without augmenting the former taxes, or eftablifhing new; and, af-ter reigning fifty-four years in a ftate of continual agitation, he left behind him near a hundred millions of livres, or full four millions fterling.

The Jews, who were the collectors of taxes over the whole coaft, that the Emperor might continue them in their office, annu-ally prefented him with a faddle, the trees of which were covered with plates of
gold

gold, and the buckles, the stirrups, and the bridle furniture, were of the same metal. If we suppose the whole worth of this present to be some thirty or forty marks of gold, it still would only amount to five-and-twenty or thirty thousand livres, or from a thousand to twelve hundred pounds. The Jews, who were then ten times as numerous as they are at present, paid, as a tax upon the whole people, a hen and twelve chickens in gold, artfully wrought, the feathers in flakes, and shaded in coloured mastic.

This was less a burdensome imposition than an offering of homage from the Jewish nation to the Sovereign; and this art itself, so much vaunted, and now so utterly unknown, is a proof that the country was more wealthy, and that the industry and invention of its workmen were thereby incited. All circumstances demonstrate that gold was plentiful in Morocco a hundred years ago, while now a debtor, who is making a payment of a thousand crowns, often shall not possess, among his money, a single ducat in gold.

Y 4

A cir-

A circumſtance ſtill more fortunate, at that time, for the people was that proviſions were at a very low price. Corn was ſold for leſs than five ſhillings the *Setier* of Paris * ; the farmers who brought it into their cities, having collected money from all who wiſhed to buy, abandoned the remainder to the firſt comer. In a country where there are no wants, it cannot be affirmed there are any poor. A country Moor, already ſupplied with every neceſſary, except ſhoes, and ſope to waſh his haick, previous to ſome feſtival, took to market, perhaps, ſix quintals of wheat on his camel, and returned ſatisfied if he could only bring back two pair of ſhoes, or ſlippers, one for his wife, and another for himſelf, and two pounds of ſope to waſh their garments ; all of which would ſcarcely coſt him ſix and ſix pence, but which were quite ſufficient to make him fine enough to go to ſome wedding.

* The weight of which I eſtimate to be about two quintals and a half.

I ſhall

I shall not here enquire into all the variations to which, during a century, the revenues of the empire have been subject, nor shall I discuss the causes of these variations; suffice it in general to observe, that, in proportion as the resources of the State became insufficient, the Monarchs have taken several violent methods of supplying deficiencies; that these have insensibly drained all the channels of commerce, have relaxed every spring of industry, and have contributed to augment the poverty and oppression of the people. I shall confine myself to give a brief account of the revenues of the present Emperor of Morocco, and of the manner in which they are collected.

These revenues I shall distinguish into ancient and modern; the ancient consist in the tenths levied on the productions of the lands, flocks, and herds, the capitation tax of the Jews, the profits of coining, arbitrary taxes and impositions, and, finally, the duties laid on the importation of merchandize.

The

The tithes levied on the productions of lands, flocks, and herds, is a native right, the less burdensome among the Moors because that the husbandman pays in kind, and not according to any variable estimate. He who grows ten bushels of corn pays one, without any retrospect or enquiry concerning a more abundant harvest, which, among barbarous states, presents an example of justice well worthy the imitation of the most civilized.

The facility of collecting this tithe is increased, because that the country Moors, being all united in a body in the centre of their grounds, are tolerably exact in watching each other, and preventing any fraud being committed on the rights of the Emperor*. As this tithe is paid in kind, from every sort of product, corn, cattle, wool, and others, the Monarch has ma-

* The collecting of a like tithe would be equally and still more easy in Europe, because that it might be farmed to the communities themselves, as has been most judiciously observed by *M. de Vauban* in his *Projet de la Dixme Royale*, which is not the less precious for being old.

gazines

gazines in the great provincial towns,
wherein to ſtore theſe revenues, which he
brings to market, having firſt deducted a ſufficient quantity for the maintenance of his
palaces, and of his ſoldiers and ſailors,
among whom he often diſtributes wheat
and barley.

The profits ariſing from coining are
very moderate, for the circulation of money throughout this empire is exceedingly
ſmall.   In revenge the Emperor ſo debaſes
the coin by alloy, that the Spaniſh piaſter,
which, according to the aſſay of Paris, is
worth about five livres ſeven ſous, or four
ſhillings and ſeven-pence halfpenny, e -
changed for the money of Morocco, yields
the Emperor about ſeven livres ten ſous, or
ſix ſhillings and three pence ; whence it
reſults that, in Morocco, money muſt be
imported, and never exported.   The tax
that the Jews pay, as a tribute, or a capitation tax, is an ancient impoſt, which, as
I have already obſerved, was very moderate.   The Jews of the preſent day pay
ten fold as much as their fathers in the laſt
century, and their population, perhaps, is
alſo

alſo ten fold decreaſed, infomuch that the impoſitions upon this nation, in the courſe of a century, have increaſed in the ratio of a hundred to one.

The arbitrary taxes, or caſual impoſitions levied on provinces and wealthy individuals, form an indeterminate revenue, incapable of fixed valuation, as they depend wholly on the occaſion and temporary circumſtances. Motives for levying theſe taxes inceſſantly preſent themſelves, when the rapacious will of the Prince ſhall happen to equal his power. Let it be here remarked, that, in deſpotic States, theſe deſtructive means of raiſing wealth are like water ſprings and mines, they are exhauſted by too frequent uſe.

The duties on exports and imports of foreign merchandize form an ancient branch of the revenue, levied by all the Emperors of Morocco. However heavy theſe duties may be on importation, having once paid them, the goods and effects may be tranſported through all parts of the empire,

empire, without being liable to pay any new tax.

The duty of importation in the States of Morocco is paid in kind, which should seem to be an advantage to the merchant; but, it will easily be perceived, it is, therefore, the more advantageous to the Prince, who retails the effects he thus acquires with profit.

The custom-house duties formerly were but trifling throughout the empire, because that maritime commerce had not then extended itself as at present. The frequent revolutions, likewise, in the country rendered the condition of the merchant fluctuating and dangerous, and banished commerce from the coasts of Barbary. The revenue they produced has never been confiderable, except in the beginning of the reign of Sidy Mahomet; commerce was at that time capable of increase throughout his states; but he, since, ever forming his resolutions on momentary convenience, has successively augmented the duties. Whence it has happened here, as every

where

where elfe, in proportion as the impofts are increafed, commerce has neceffarily diminifhed. This Monarch has, perhaps, more effectually drained his country than a conqueror would an invaded kingdom, which it was his intent to abandon.

Either the defire or the neceffity of adding to the revenues of his eftates has induced the reigning Emperor to impofe new taxes, which have raifed fome commotions among his fubjects. A poor nation, tenacious of its former cuftoms, confined in its objects of induftry, and its means of barter, is impatient under new impofitions. Thefe recent taxes are laid on fnuff, which is farmed by monopolizers, to whom the Emperor has granted an exclufive privilege ; on commodities per load, as they enter and go out of towns, or pafs ferries ; on woollen ftuffs, which muft be ftamped before they are brought to market ; and, alfo, on all the trinkets made by goldfmiths. The governors of the cities are to collect thefe taxes at a fixed fum, by which they very feldom are gainers. Thefe new impofts, which would

be

be lefs burdenfome in countries where the fubjects might repay themfelves by the encouragement given to their induftry, having been confidered among the Moors as innovations, contrary to the fpirit of the Koran, almoft occafioned an infurrection at Mequinez in 1778; it was chiefly quelled through the refolution of the Chiefs, and the total want of energy among the people.

In the prefent exhaufted ftate of the Empire of Morocco, thefe taxes all united are fcarcely fufficient for its own fupport; and fo little can œconomy fet apart for the treafury of the Emperor, which formerly was very confiderable, that, drained by a concatenation of circumftances, it was reduced in 1782 to about two millions of ducats, which may amount to twelve or thirteen millions of livres, or five hundred thoufand pounds fterling *. Such is the ftate of an empire that nature has en-

---

* The ducat of Morocco, as paid in currency, is eftimated at fix livres, thirteen fous, four deniers of France.

riched

riched with her gifts, and which, after having been laid defolate by the conflicting paffions of man, is at prefent fcarcely fufficient to fupply his wants.

In the fecond volume I fhall give a brief hiftory of the fovereigns who have governed this empire, and of the revolutions which have expofed it to fo many ravages and oppreffions; the traces of which, far from being effaced, feem to revive with each reviving generation.

CHAP.

CHAP. XVIII.*

Additional miscellaneous remarks concerning the manners of the Moors, and characteristic anecdotes of the Emperors, Muley Ishmael, and his successor, Muley Daiby.

THE Moors are excellent horsemen; they ride short like the ancient Parthians and the modern hussars. Their saddles have peaks before and behind; their stirrups are placed far back. They level and fire on full speed, hold the bridle between their teeth, and turn their horses as they wish, by the pressure of their knees and

---

* This chapter is not written by M. Chenier, but added, from authentic writers, by the translator. Some account of those writers, and the reasons for inserting this chapter, are given in the preface. T.

the equipoize of their bodies. It is an opinion among them that the Christians have no horses, in which they are confirmed by the eagerness of Europeans to purchase and export the horses of Barbary. According to Braithwaite, to ride on a mare is a token of poverty and meanness *. This people seem as careful of their horses as they are negligent of themselves. Such horses as have been to Mecca are held to be Saints; they work no more, nor would the Emperor himself dare to mount them. Their necks are adorned by rosaries and relics like the tombs of their Saints. The stables of these holy horses are sanctuaries for criminals. Muley Ishmael had a quadruped Saint of this species, which he used to visit occasionally, and whose feet and tail he would in reverence kiss. After drinking himself, and giving drink to his

---

* May not this account for the mistake, if it be one, of M. Chenier, noticed at page 168? It seems probable the Moors ride mares, either, because they can sell their horses to advantage, or that, the horses are seized by their oppressive governors for their own use, and to mount the troops each governor maintains. T.

faint,

Saint, he would fometimes permit his favourites to drink out of the fame bowl.

Exclufive of their horfes, the Moors hold
various other animals in refpect. Their
dogs are numerous, almoft to incredibility,
for they think it finful to deftroy them.
Their barking is fo inceffant that a ftranger,
unaccuftomed to this noife, is incapable
of fleeping. M. Saiht Olon fays, the
ftorks at Alcaffar were more numerous
than the inhabitants; and the reafon he
gives for the averfion the Moors have to
killing of them is, that, they believe God,
at the interceffion of Mahomet, metamor-
phofed a troop of Arabs, who robbed the
pilgrims that were journeying to Mecca,
into Storks.

Muley Ifhmael had two fnow-white dro-
medaries that were daily wafhed with foap.
He likewife kept forty cats, which he diftinguifhed each by its name, and fed plentifully himfelf. One day, making a parade
of his juftice, being told that one of his
cats had eaten a rabbit, he was determined
to inflict an exemplary punifhment on this

 wicked

wicked cat. Accordingly he commanded an executioner to ſeize the cat, drag her through the ſtreets of Mequinez, with a cord round her neck, whip her ſeverely, and cry aloud—" Thus does my maſter treat ſcoundrel cats !" After this the criminal was to be beheaded ; all which was punctually executed.

One of this Emperor's pleaſures was to ſee dogs, wolves, and lions, fight ; and, when any one of them was in danger of being devoured by the other, he would command his ſlaves to ſnatch the victim from the jaws of the lions, which ſervice ſeldom was performed without the loſs of a limb. He would himſelf encounter lions, taking care firſt to ſhoot them, and afterward, entering their park with his attendants, would complete his eaſy victory with his ſpear. Chriſtian captives, by his orders, were often obliged to combat lions, for the diverſion of his wives. One of theſe captives, being commanded to fight a lion, had the preſence of mind to retire, ſabre in hand, toward a ditch full of water, into which, pretending his foot ſlipped, he

fell,

fell, knowing the lion would not follow him thither. His ftratagem, by good fortune, pleafed the tyrant, and the flave efcaped.

In their public proceffions, when attending their Bafhaws, the Moors are tumultuous, but dextrous. They fingle out each other to tilt, and will put afide the thruft of a fpear, though made at their backs; will dart their lances into the air, and catch them again, their horfes all the while on full fpeed. They are exceedingly fond of the explofion of gunpowder. To honour Mr. Ruffel, the Englifh ambaffador, the Bafhaw gave them a barrel, which they fired as faft as they could; loading, not with cartridges, but, with loofe powder. M. St. Olou, the French ambaffador, relates that Muley Ifhmael commanded him to be feated on the top of a high wall, without chair, covering, or carpet, there to be a fpectator of a review of ten thoufand horfe, and two thoufand foot. Their manœuvres were all diforderly, and their onfets began by cries and fhouts; they afterward all filed off befide the wall, and,

Z 3

that

that they might do honour to M. St. Olon, each man difcharged his firelock in his face; this being the mode in which they fhew refpect to their own chiefs. In their tilting matches they, however, are frequently unhorfed, but their tilting lances are not pointed with iron. Their military mufic confifts of drums, fifes, and hautbois, the mingled noife of which is fo difcordant that, De la Faye remarks, it flayed his ears.

Boar-hunting is one of their amufements, the fpears for which are made of a heavy and tough wood, with blades about half a yard in length, and very thick, that they may not break againft the hide of the boar. They rouze the game by hideous yells and fhouts; and, fhould a fingle Moor happen to find himfelf in the way of the boar, holding it difgraceful to recede, he ftands firm, and receives the boar upon his fpear. The animal gores himfelf to the extremity of the blade, where there is a crofs bar to prevent the farther infertion of the fpear, and the hunter from being wounded by the tufks of the enraged boar. The Moor then either quits the fpear, or, if

ftrong

ſtrong enough, keeps his prey at bay, till his companions arrive to his aid.

The Moors, if equals, ſalute by a quick motion of joining hands, and each kiſſing his own. Inferiors kiſs the hand, and often the head, of ſuperiors. The Alcaid is ſaluted by kiſſing his feet, if on horſeback; otherwiſe, his hand, cloaths, or, if ſitting, his knees.

Windus affirms, the climate of Morocco is delicious, the ſoil generous, and fertile beyond imagination; that the Moors imitate the Spaniſh mode of agriculture; that judicious people informed him not a hundredth part of the lands were tilled, and that yet, ſo bountiful was nature, the Emperor was ſuppoſed to have corn enough in his matamores to ſupply the country for five years; that the land would produce a hundred fold more than the conſumption of the empire, were the inhabitants protected in the peaceful enjoyment of the fruits of their labour; but that, ſhould the poor huſbandmen acquire a pair of oxen and plough, he would not only be liable to

be

be robbed of them by the next petty mercenary governor, but obliged to fell his corn to pay an arbitrary tribute; that therefore there were no proprietors of land beyond two or three leagues round each town, and, if by chance fome fcattered huts were feen, they certainly belonged to an Alcaid, and were inhabited by his fervants, who were treated like the beafts that aided them to plough the ground.

According to Braithwaite, the northern part of the empire will yield all the effential products of Europe, and the fouthern whatever is grown in the Weft Indies, which fufficiently fpeaks the native riches of the country.

The rains are fometimes heavy. Braithwaite, in his journal, fays, returning to Tangiers, he rode all day in the moft fevere wind and rain he ever knew, of fo long a continuance; that the ice was fometimes an inch thick at Mequinez, and that the cold was fo piercing he and his companions were one night obliged to difmount and walk. It ought, however, to be obferved

ferved that the human body feels a fmall degree of cold, after exceffive heat, much more fenfibly than a far greater, when the change is lefs fudden.

The Moors have an opinion fimilar to that of the Chriftians, that—" The king- " dom of heaven fuffereth violence, and " the violent take it by force." They think importunity will oblige God to grant their requefts. In the time of heavy rains the children all day run about the ftreets, and bawl for fair weather ; and, in the time of drought, for rain, making a hideous noife. They fometimes continue this practice for more than a week. Should God not liften to the children, they are joined by the Saints and Talbes, who proceed altogether into the fields and call for rain. If this ftill prove ineffectual, they go barefoot in a body, and meanly cloathed, to pray at the tombs of their Saints for rain, to which pious practice the Emperor himfelf occafionally conforms. Should all thefe efforts fail, they at laft drive the Jews out of the town, and forbid them to return without rain—" For, " fay
they,

they, " though God will not grant rain to
" our prayers, he will to those of the Jews,
" to rid himself of their importunity, and
" the stinking odour of their breath and
feet." This, adds Windus, was done sometime ago at Tangiers.

When the Moors happen to be caught in
the rain, on their journies, or in the fields,
they strip themselves naked, bundle up
their apparel, and seat themselves on the
packet till the shower is over; after which
they dress themselves, and proceed on their
way.

The bread of Morocco is very excellent;
the corn and flour of Fez is remarkably
sweet and white. Their cheese is little
better than curd; yet, though sour in five
or six hours, is kept and eaten when old.
They do not skim their milk to make butter, but take it from the cow, and shake it
in a skin; it is sour, and kept in plastered
holes in the ground, or buried in earthen
jars. Instead of butter, the poor use beef,
mutton, and goat suet. When eating, the
Moors place their dishes on a large piece

of

of greafy leather fpread upon the ground, which is a fubftitute for both table and cloth, and round this they feat themfelves crofs-legged. Bufnot informs us that Muley Ifhmael eat in this manner, without cloth, napkin, knife, or fork, and out of an earthen or wooden platter.

The Moors are fo temperate that a man of fixty is not thought old, but their temperance appears to be more the effect of neceffity than choice. The very brothers of the Bafhaw of Tetuan ufed to enter the kitchen, during Mr. Ruffel's embaffy, and threaten to murder the cook, if he did not give them pudding and wine. The fons of the Emperor, Muley Ifhmael, have even ftolen bread from the pockets of the flaves.

Their avidity and meannefs, like many or moft other of their peculiarities, can only be accounted for by their ignorance. A court lady, in whofe lap the drunken Emperor, Muley Daiby, ufed to fleep, accepted a moidore as a bribe. The domeftics of the palace would cut the buttons

and

and the very clothes from the back of the English ambaffador, and his attendants, if they were not careful to appear in the worſt they had; and the porters, at the various palace gates, individually refuſed to let them paſs till they were bribed. One of the guards picked the pocket of Mr. Windus as he ſtood beſide the prince, after-ward Emperor, Muley Abdallah.

When a Baſhaw travels, the Moors of his diſtrict are obliged to ſupply him and his followers with all neceſſary proviſions, gratis. The dread of ſuperior power ren-ders the inferior Alcaids exceedingly dili-gent, in not only bringing neceſſaries but preſents. This dread is the origin of the Mooriſh ſervility. Windus relates, that, when the Emperor, Muley Iſhmael, ap-peared, all preſent ſtretched out their necks, as if preſenting their heads to the ſabre, with their eyes fixed on the ground. Thus a man might (and indeed frequently did) loſe his head without knowing any thing of the matter. Some, when he ſpoke, ex-claimed——" May God lengthen thy days! " May God bleſs thy life !" Others ſwore,

by the Almighty, all he uttered was true.
Speaking of the English on a certain occafion, he faid —— " May I be called the
" greateſt of lyars if I have not always
" conceived a great eſteem for that na-
" tion." As it happened, he made a pauſe
at " the greateſt of lyars," and his eager
officious courtiers exclaimed — " By G—,
" my Lord, that is true." This, though
unintentional, was a bitter ſarcaſm ; for
Muley Iſhmael was really the greateſt of
lyars.

In the Emperor's preſence all, except
foreign miniſters and their train, are obliged
to appear barefoot. One of the firſt Engliſh ambaſſadors was obliged to ſubmit to
this ceremony before Muley Iſhmael ; and,
in revenge, the ambaſſador from Morocco
was conſtrained to appear, in the preſence
of Charles II. at the Engliſh court, without ſhoes, turban, or bonnet.

The heat of their climate, their arbitrary
government, and univerſal ignorance, render
the Moors exceedingly idle. They are but
little addiĉted to gaming : they eat, drink,

z   ſleep,

sleep, and pray, amuse themselves with their horses and their wives, and spend the rest of their time in one continued fruitless state of indolence. To walk up and down a room they hold ridiculous. "Why "should a man move, say they, without "apparent cause? Is it not more rational "for him to remain in the place where he "is, than to go to some other for no pur- "pose whatever but that of returning?" Numbers of them are seen seated on their hams, in the streets beside the walls, hold- ing large strings of beads, one of which they let fall at each prayer they repeat; and these prayers are merely repetitions of the attributes of God; such as — "God "is great! God is good! God is infinite! "God is merciful!".

The Moors, like the Turks, have no bells, but are called to prayers from the steeples of their mosques; in all of which places of worship there is either a running stream, or a well of water. Swine are ani- mals so unsanctified that a mosque at Te- tuan was pulled down, as eternally polluted, because it had been entered by one. They
have.

have a prophecy that they shall be conquered on a Friday, their fabbath; for
which reafon the gates of their walled
towns are fhut on that day, as are alfo
thofe of the Emperor's palace.

They afk their dead why they would die,
whether they wanted any thing in this
world, and if they had not coofcoofoo
enough. Their burial places are without the
town. They make their graves wide at the
bottom, that the corpfe may have fufficient
room ; and never put two bodies into one
grave, left they fhould miftake each others
bones at the day of judgement. They alfo
carry food, and put money and jewels into
the grave, that they may appear as refpectable in the other world as they had done
in this. They imagine the dead are capable of pain. A Portuguefe gentleman had
one day ignorantly ftrayed among the
tombs, and a Moor, after much wrangling,
obliged him to go before the Cadi. The
gentleman complained of violence, and
afferted he had committed no crime ; but
the judge informed him he was miftaken,
for that the poor dead fuffered when trod-

den

den on by Chriſtian feet. Muley Iſhmael
once had occaſion to bring one of his wives
through a burial-ground, and the people
removed the bones of their relations, and
murmuring ſaid he would neither ſuffer
the living nor the dead to reſt in peace.

A Jew, or Chriſtian, who ſhould enter
one of their moſques, muſt either become a
Mahometan or be burned alive. The country Moors purify the places where Chriſtians have been, by burning green branches;
and their ſuperſtition, concerning unclean
meats, is ſo great that the governors of the
ſea ports, after a naval engagement, prohibited the eating of fiſh, becauſe it was
poſſible they might be defiled by having
fed on, and partaken of, the fleſh and blood
of Chriſtians.

Their hatred of the · Chriſtians, in
ſome reſpects, exceeds their hatred of the
Jews; for they alledge that the Chriſtians
eat pork, meat ſtrangled, and blood, and do
not waſh like the Jews. When Mr. Ruſſel
and his attendants paſſed through the
ſtreets of Mequinez, three or four hundred

dred fellows would scream, all together,—
" Curfed are the unbelievers !" If a Moor
is angry with his afs, he firft calls him
Carran, that is cuckold, next, Son of a
Jew, and vents the laft effort of his malice
in the exclamation—Son of a Chriftian !
This is their term of extreme reproach,
which they never utter without the addi-
tion of " God confound him !" Or—
" May the fire of God devour his father and
" mother !" This hatred is the lefs fur-
prifing fince Braithwaite affirms he knew
not which were the worft, at the court of
Morocco, Moors, Negroes, Jews, Renegadoes, or Chriftians. A proof of the immediate
and powerful influence of evil example !

It is death for a Jew to curfe, or lift up
his hand againft a Moor. If kicked by
a boy, the Jew has no remedy but to
run away. He is obliged to approach the
meaneft Moor with the greateft fubmiffion, and every form of refpect ; whereas a
Moor difdains to addrefs a Jew in any
other terms than—Jew, do this; or, Jew, do
that ; and, fhould he think proper to beat a

.Jew, the only hope of the latter is in en-
treating for pardon for the love of the
Emperor, whom he prays God to preserve.

Muley Ishmael, ingenious at finding pre-
texts for robbing his subjects, of all religions, thought proper, one day, to assemble
the Chiefs of the Jews, on some pretended
important business.   When they came into
his presence, he, addressing them, said —
" Dogs, as you are, I have sent for you to
" oblige you to take the red cap, and turn
" Mahometans.   Above thirty years have
" I been amused with an idle tale of the
" coming of your Messiah.   For my part,
" I believe him come already ; therefore,
" if you do not now tell me the precise
" day on which he is to appear, I shall
" leave you neither property nor life.   I
" will be trifled with no longer."

Surprized at this gentle address, which they
so little expected, considering how many
obligations Ishmael was under to the Jewish
nation, and the punctuality with which
they had paid the excessive taxes with
which they had been loaded, the Jews remained

mained sometime silent. One of the most
prudent among them, at length, requested
a week to consider of the answer they
should make. The Emperor bade them
begone, but told them to beware, and not
invent any more of their fabulous tales.
They employed the interval they were allowed in collecting that answer which they
well knew he required: they amassed a
considerable sum, and, bringing this as a
pesent, said—" Sidi, our doctors have con-
" cluded the Messiah will certainly appear
" within thirty years."——" Yes, yes,"
replied Ishmael, taking the money, " I un-
" derstand you, dogs as you are, and de-
" ceivers ; you think to hush my imme-
" diate wrath in the hope that I shall not
" then be alive ; but I will deceive you,
" in my turn ; I will live, if it be but to
" shew the world that you are impostors,
" and to punish you as you shall de-
" serve."

Several Moors came to ask advice for
their wives or daughters of the doctor
who attended the embassy of Stewart, some
of whom were so infatuated they would

 rather

rather the patient should die than be seen; others consented, but not till it was too late. One man, only, less jealous and timid than the rest, took the doctor home to his wife, and treated him with kindness.

It is difficult, as Windus remarks, to give any general rule what a Saint, in this part of the world, is; or how he became so. Any extraordinary accident makes a Saint. A rascal, attending on Muley Ishmael, had committed some villany; and the Emperor, after raising his hand to kill him, declared he had not the power; for which the fellow was immediately sanctified, and continued in great favour.

All things are lawful to Saints, for they act as prompted by the spirit, consequently may steal, murder, or ravish. One of them seized a girl, in the streets of Sallee, who, not well comprehending such kind of holiness, made resistance; some of the sanctified tribe, however, soon tripped up her heels, and threw their haicks over her and the ravisher.

A Chris-

A Chriſtian entruſted a purſe of money to a Saint; and, when he afterward re-demanded it, the Saint denied all know-ledge of the tranſaction. The Chriſtian applied to an Alcaid, and deſcribed his purſe. As it happened, the Alcaid was a man of quick intellect. He told the Chriſtian, had he been a Moor, he muſt have remained ſatisfied with the affirma-tion of the Saint; but, being a Chriſtian, he would oblige the Saint to ſwear, in the great moſque, he had not the money. The complainant replied a Chriſtian could not enter the moſque; and deſired the Saint might ſwear in the porch of the houſe of the Alcaid. The Saint came; the Alcaid treated him familiarly, and amuſed him with diſcourſing on various things till he had procured his beads. He then made ſome pretence to leave the room, and ſent the beads to the Saint's wife, as a token, with a meſſage that ſhe muſt return a purſe, of ſuch a deſcription, containing ſo much money. The purſe of the Chriſtian accordingly came, and the Alcaid took this occaſion to ſeize on the effects of the Saint,

A a 3

and

and fend him to practife holinefs where he was lefs known.

From Windus we alfo learn it was cuf-tomary, under Muley Ifhmael, to purchafe men ; that is to fay, one Moor, defiring the deftruction or poffeffions of another, might buy him of the Emperor, Bafhaw, or Al-caid, for a certain fum. And this was fometimes done on fpeculation ; the buyer torturing the man bought, in the moft cruel manner, till he made him difcover what money he poffeffed. Mr. Hatfield, an Eng-lifh merchant, relates, in a letter to a friend, cited by Windus, that, paffing a prifon, in company with another Englifhman, they faw a Moor hung by the heels, with irons on his legs, pincers at his nofe, his flefh cut with fciffars, and two men employed in beating him, and demanding money. This, he fays, was a bought man, for whom they had given five hundred ducats, and by whom they expected to gain an additional five hundred.

Two rival Jews had a conteft of this kind. Memaran (or Maimoran) had been
the

the chief favourite of Muley Ifhmael, and
had obtained the fole command of the
Jews; and, fearing a rival in the enter-
prizing Ben-Hattar, he offered the Emperor
a certain number of quintals of filver for
his head. Muley Ifhmael fent for Ben-
Hattar, and told him how large a fum
had been bidden; to which the latter Jew
refolutely anfwered he would give twice as
much, for the head of the perfon who had
made the offer. The Emperor, taking the
money from both, told them they were two
fools, and bade them live friends. Ben-
Hattar, accordingly, obtained the daughter
of Memamn in marriage, and they governed the Jews between them with abfolute authority.

Indeed, fo much worfe is the government
of Morocco than that of the Turks themfelves, that the Moorifh pilgrims, who re-
fort to Mecca, frequently refufe to return.
The violence of this government was not
a little increafed, under Muley Ifhmael, by
the infolence, rapacity, and cruelty of the
Negroes. The moft powerful of the Alcaids ufed to tremble in the prefence of the

A a 4

loweft

loweſt of theſe Negroes. The collecting
of the taxes, which his neighbours, the
Algerines, could ſcarcely effect with the
aid of ten or twelve thouſand men, Muley
Iſhmael eaſily accompliſhed by ſending two
or three of theſe his negro emiſſaries : ſuch
was the terror the ſight of them inſpired.

Nor was the conduct of the imperial
Eunuchs leſs arrogant. Braithwaite thus
relates an example of their behaviour. A
negro Eunuch, lately arrived from Mequinez, came and enquired for the Engliſh
ambaſſador. Being informed the ambaſſador was not at home, he ſat himſelf down,
and called for tea, as imperiouſly as if the
houſe had been his own. The Mooriſh
admiral, Perez, paid him great reſpect, deſired he might have tea, but alſo requeſted
he might be narrowly watched, leſt he and
his attendants ſhould take what did not belong to them. He gave himſelf inſuffer-
able airs, as if he were a perſon whoſe authority was undoubted; ſerved the tea
about himſelf, gave cups to all his ſervants,
ſeven or eight in number, and filled them
with ſugar, till the Engliſh refuſed to ſupply
him

him with more. After tea he called for cyder, and drank several bottles, romancing all the while in a strange manner; affirming that the Emperor, Muley Daiby, was so handsome that spectators, having once fixed their eyes on him, were unable to look off, and that his troops were more numerous than the sands of the sea. When questioned, he gave just such answers as he thought proper, without the least regard to truth. As he went he attempted to pocket the remainder of a pound of tea.

This Eunuch was young, smooth faced, lusty, exceedingly well dressed, and well attended, with habits no way inferior to those of a Bashaw. Eunuchs were used as state messengers, from the Emperor, to the governors of towns and provinces, who caressed and made them large presents, fearful of being maliciously spoken of by them at court. The presents, likewise, of governors to the Emperor's women, and other similar correspondence, passed through their hands; so that they as often travelled on the business of the women as on that of the Emperor, which gave them great authority,

thority, and, for want of a better knowledge of the world, made them so intolerably insolent.

Among various other punishments, inflicted by the barbarian Ishmael, was that of tossing. Three or four Negroes, seizing the person, ordered to be thus punished, by the hams, would throw him up, and twirl him round, so as to make him pitch with his head foremost. Thus, by frequent practice, they became so dextrous that they could break the neck at the first toss, dislocate the shoulder, or let the body fall with less danger. Sometimes the person tossed was killed, at others, severely bruised ; and, if able, he must not move, while the Emperor was in sight, unless he would be tossed once more ; but must counterfeit death. If really dead, no one dared bury the body, until the tyrant gave orders for the burial.

Another species of torture was that of the iron ring. This was a circle of iron, the inside of which contained sharp projecting points : it opened and shut at pleasure, by means of screws, and was usually

applied

applied to the head of any perſon from whom money was meant to be extorted.

Drawing of teeth was one of the inhuman ſports of Iſhmael. He one day commanded the teeth of fourteen of his wives, or concubines, to be drawn, for no other crime than having viſited each other without his permiſſion. His ſon, the drunken, brutal, Muley Daiby, proved himſelf well worthy ſuch a father. One of his miſtreſſes having diſobliged him, he ordered all her teeth to be drawn. In leſs than a week he ſent for this woman, and was told ſhe was ill. So habitual was barbarity, and a ſtate of intoxication, to him, that he had forgotten the dreadful puniſhment he had inflicted, and enquired what was her diſeaſe. Being anſwered her teeth had all been drawn, by his command, he denied ever having given ſuch a command; ſent for the man who had been his executioner, ordered all his teeth immediately to be drawn, and returned them, incloſed in a box, to comfort the woman.

The Mooriſh houſes are not only dark

for

for want of windows, but the doors, through which light is admitted, often have curtains before them. This gloom feems neceffary to the climate; it prevents heat, and banifhes the flies. The women pay vifits over the tops of their houfes, which are more frequented by them than the ftreets; and, at Mequinez, they may walk in this manner, from houfe to houfe, over the whole town; and this is much the neareft way. The ftreets are not paved, and, therefore, are continually rendered, by the rains and heats, either infufferably dirty or dufty.

The palace, or palaces, built at this city by Muley Ifhmael, rather refemble a city than one entire building. The tower of London, fays Braithwaite, might as properly be called a palace. He eftimates the circumference of thefe buildings, including feveral gardens, meadows, and grounds, at three or four miles. De la Faye fuppofes it may be half a league, without the gardens. Windus, who gives a perfpective view of this pile of buildings, fays it is four miles in circumference, almoft

fquare,

square, and near no hill by which it can be overlooked. The walls are wholly of cast mortar, beaten in cases, and hardened like artificial stone. The outward wall is five-and-twenty feet thick. Within this vast enclosure are squares more extensive than Lincoln's inn fields, with piazzas; some of them are chequer-paved; others have gardens, sunken considerably below the surface, and planted with tall cyprefs trees, the tops of which form a beautiful variety of palace and garden. The tops of moft of thefe buildings rife in a pyramidal form, and are covered with green varnifhed tiles, which have a bright and pleafant effect. The colour of green is appropriated folely to the emperor. Thirty thoufand men, and ten thoufand mules, are faid to have been daily employed on thefe buildings, which are cumbrous and vaft, but cool and refrefhing.

Some few additional incidents, extracted from the authors cited in this chapter, will further tend to depict the manners of the Moors of thofe times; the people who, of all others, confidering their proximity to enlightened

lightened nations, feem to have made the leaft improvements, or progrefs toward refinement. Thefe anecdotes will all relate to the Emperors Muley Ifhmael, and Muley Daiby, whofe lives will be found among thofe of the hiftory of the Emperors of Morocco, in the fecond volume ; but, as they are not inferted by M. Chenier, they will fcarcely here be thought fuperfluous, or mifplaced.   They convey a melancholy picture of the dreadful errors, and caprices, of power unreftrained ; and its pernicious, its exterminating, confequences : a picture that cannot be too often, or too forcibly, prefented to the eyes of man.

So native is juftice to the human heart, and its neceffity fo evident, that Muley Ifhmael himfelf pretended to have it in the utmoft regard.   Shooting, and ftriking, at random, as he did, it fometimes happened thofe were killed at whom the ftroke was not intended ; in which cafe he would, very civilly, beg the dead perfon's pardon, but add it was not to be avoided : the fault, if there was any, was with God, for he had decreed the man muft die.   When he

killed

killed any one, without being able to assign a motive, which was frequently the cafe, he would have it underſtood that, acting wholly by the appointment of God, he could not do wrong, nor had any thing to fear from man.

His mercy was, ſometimes, as unaccountable as were his murders. A Spaniard had been bribed to ſhoot him, but, miſſing his aim, lodged the two balls with which he had loaded his gun in the pummel of his ſaddle. The Spaniard was ſeized, and it was expected he would have ſuffered a death of torture. The Emperor, however, reproaching him, aſked what he had done to deſerve this uſage; whether the people were tired of him, and if he were no more beloved: after which he took no farther notice, but ſent the man to work among his other Chriſtian ſlaves. The Spaniard ſtill had his fears, and turned Mahometan, but continued to wear his Spaniſh dreſs, perhaps becauſe he had no other. Some years had elapſed, when the Emperor, being among his workmen, aſked him why his head was not uncovered. The Spaniard
anſwered

anſwered he was a Mahometan. The Emperor made enquiries concerning him, and, being informed who he was, ordered his immediate manumiſſion, aſked him a thouſand pardons for having kept him ſo long at work, entirely new cloathed him, and made him a Baſhaw.

To ſuch kind of treatment his grandees were hourly ſubject : to-day hugged, kiſſed, and preferred ; to-morrow ſtripped, robbed, and beaten. The Negro who carried this Emperor's umbrella was remarked to be covered with ſcars. When Iſhmael had done with his lance, it was cuſtomary for him to dart it into the air, and, if it were not caught before it came to the ground, the man appointed for that office was killed. It was obſerved of him, whenever he beat a man ſeverely, that man was in the high road to preferment. The chances were greatly in his favour, that, finding him in chains, ſome few days after, in a wretched condition, the tyrant would call him his dear friend, uncle, or brother; enquire how he became ſo miſerable, as if wholly ignorant of the matter, beſtow his

own

bwn apparel upon him, which was a mark of great diftinction, make him as fine as a prince, and bid him go and govern fome great town. This, it is faid, was a part of his barbarous policy. B ing convinced he had ftripped a man of all he poffeffed, he then fent him forth again to glean.

Hypocrify was one of his greateft vices, and his example rendered it the fafhionable vice of the court, during his reign. He affected to attribute his profperity to the immediate protection of Mahomet, one of whofe decendants he is fuppofed. He called himfelf the friend of God, the exe-cutor of his councils, and it was neceffary to fay thofe whom he had maffacred, in his frenzy, had fallen by the hand of God. Thofe who fhould dare to fay otherwife would themfelves have been maffacred. The Koran was always borne before him, by his Talbe, as his guide, and the rule of his conduct. His hands were frequently raifed toward heaven, and not feldom while ftained with human blood. He would often alight to kifs the earth, and the name of

<table>
<tr><td>Vol. I.</td><td>B b</td><td>God,</td></tr>
</table>

God, and of his prophet, were continually
in his mouth, even in his fits of utmost fury.
He was vain of being himself a Talbe,
or doctor of the Mahometan law, and
preached, in his mosque, in a manner more
forcible, it is said, than any other of the
Talbes. So confirmed was the opinion
that those whom he slew went immediately
to paradise that the infatuated Moors have
come, from the farthest extremity of the
empire, to entreat the favour of being murdered by his hand. St. Olon affirms that,
while he was at Mequinez, in the space of
three weeks, he had killed forty-seven persons. It was a common mode with him,
to show his dexterity, at once to mount his
horse, draw his sabre, and sever the head
from the body of the slave who held the
stirrup.

His avarice, indeed, seems even to have
exceeded his hypocrisy. On a famous
mosque, in the city of Morocco, were three
globes, or, as they were called, apples of
gold, which were said to have been en-
chanted. They were placed on this
mosque by the wife of the renowned Almonsor,

monsor, who expended the greatest part of her jewels and wealth in their construction. Astrology had been consulted, and the magical architect had, by his conjurations, so confined certain spirits to watch over them that their removal was held to be impossible. The credulous people affirmed that various monarchs, attempting to take them down, had been prevented, by some fatal accident, and that the devil had broken the necks of all those who had been sent to execute such commands. They were, at length, undeceived by the covetous Muley Ishmael. These balls were removed, during his reign, and buried with his other invisible and useless treasures.

The education of the sons of this Emperor, if education it may be called, was such as to render them even more irrational, barbarous, and brutal, than their father. They received no instruction, nor had they any employment, except that of indulging themselves in all the malicious pranks of boys. At the sight of any of them, every man was careful to conceal whatever might attract their notice, for they seized on all

that

that came to hand, and pilfered with impunity. While Bufnot and the friars of his order were at Mequinez, one of them entered the apartment of thefe fathers. A French merchant, acquainted with their manners, rid them of his company, by giving him two or three blanquils, which he joyfully received, and ran off exceedingly happy. The Jews were peftered by their vifits. Inftead of conducting themfelves like the fons of an Emperor, their behaviour refembled that of Gipfies, who rob hedges and henroofts. M. St. Olon had a vifit from one, who paid him neither falutation nor compliment, but fell on every thing in the chamber that he thought worth his attention. His entrance and exit refembled that of a monkey, that, feeing a bafket of fruit, and having ftuffed his pouch, whifks away when he can take no more. This youth, of about twelve or thirteen, carried off a pair of piftols, and fome boxes of fome fweet meats. After ferving this noble kind of apprenticefhip, as they approached the ftate of manhood, they were fent, by the Emperor, to govern his various towns and provinces,

where

where the unhappy people soon too sensibly felt the effects of such an education. The female children of Muley Ishmael, by his concubines, were strangled at their birth.

This Emperor was an early riser. It was conjectured his rest was disturbed by the horrors of his conscience, and the exactions, cruelties, and murders of which he had been guilty. Waited on in his palace by women, young girls, boys, and eunuchs, such attendants durst not tell tales; but, according to report, in his camp, his restlessness was apparent. Starting from his reveries, he was heard to call upon those he had murdered, and, suddenly waking, he would sometimes ask for some person whom he had killed but the day before. If answered he is dead, he would reply — " Who killed him ?" Personal safety required the answer should be — " We do not " know, but we suppose God."

It was affirmed he used often to call on his favourite Hameda, when walking alone, and when he supposed he could not

be

be overheard.   This Hameda came a boy
into his army, where, being noticed, the
Emperor gave him a horse.   As he grew
up, he became a jocular, pleasant fellow,
and the Emperor indulged his familiarities
so far that he was allowed to enter the gardens, when Ishmael was with his women ;
a liberty no man, before or since, ever durst
take.   He had the title of Bashaw of Bashaws, and the Emperor used passionately
to tell him he never could be really angry
with him, and that to kill him was a thing
to him impossible.   It is indeed supposed
he did not design his death.   It was the
consequence of beating him, with the but
end of his lance, so severely that he died
the next day of his bruises.   The Emperor expressed much sorrow, confessed he
repented of what he had done, sent him
and his physicians a bag of money, and en-
treated him to live.

The common habits, and appearance,
of Ishmael, were very opposite to those
ideas Europeans entertain of imperial dignity.   On the first audience M. St Olon received, this Emperor was seated on the
threshold

threfhold of the gate of his Alcaffave, or palace, on a mat, without a carpet, with fome Alcaids, fitting upon the bare ground, round him, who were without fhoes; he had a dirty, fnuffy, handkerchief over his face, and his legs and arms were bare. As an additional mark of his character, it may be added, his punifhments were as capricious as they were cruel. He fometimes fent for the head of an Alcaid; at others, the meffenger was to fpit in his face, give him a box on the ear, or call him cuckold.

Various traits of the character of Muley Daiby have been already given. According to Braithwaite, this Emperor was in perfon fix feet fix inches high, of a fierce and bloated countenance, much pitted with the fmall pox, wanted his foreteeth, and was, altogether, very ugly. At Mr. Ruffel's firft audience, he was fo drunk he could fcarcely hold up his head. All he faid was *Buono, Buono*; except giving orders that the Chriftians fhould have plenty of wine and roafted pigs, both of which were his favourite luxuries, though both contrary to the Mahometan law. Had not his

drunk-

drunkenneſs rendered him incapable of all buſineſs, Mr. Ruſſel's embaſſy, probably, would have been ſuccefsful; for he had gained his heart by the cheſts of Florence wine he had brought, one of which, it is ſaid, this Emperor and his firſt miniſter, a fat negro, of monſtrous bulk, with two or three other drunken favourites, emptied in one night. After having drunken three or four flaſks himſelf, the Emperor took up another, and hugging it in his arms, pro‑teſted the Chriſtian, who brought it, ſhould have whatever he came to aſk.

The qualities of his heart and mind were apparent in his youth. He one day met a Jew, and ſwore he would murder him if he did not drink all the brandy in his flaſk. To preſerve his life the man drank the li‑quor; and, had the Emperor (Iſhmael) paſſed that way, he would certainly have been killed for being drunk.

Another time he obliged a Spaniard and an Engliſhman to wreſtle, and took an oath to diſpatch him who was thrown, which fell to the lot of the Spaniard. He once
made